My COUNTERFEIT Husband

CARLA PENNINGTON

Author of The Available Wife & The Available Wife Part 2

Life Changing Books in conjunction with Power Play Media
Published by Life Changing Books
P.O. Box 423 Brandywine, MD 20613

Library of Congress Cataloging-in-Publication Data;

www.lifechangingbooks.net
13 Digit: 978-1934230619
10 Digit: 1934230618

DEDICATION

Of all the things about writing that I've found to be difficult, this tops them all. On January 09, 2013, my best friend, my dear Mama, Rosa Pennington Browne departed this earth to plant roses around her new home in Heaven.

Mama, this is the hardest thing I ever had to write, but you gave birth to a strong, young lady so I will soldier through this. When Kim called and told me that you took your last breath, I froze. I didn't know what to think, how to feel or what to do. Time stood still. Eventually, I cried because I was sad, but the tears didn't last long. God gave you back to me when he could've taken you long ago. He allowed us time to repair our relationship and gave you time to see your kids live out their dreams. After learning of your passing, I was upset because I wanted to be angry but couldn't. I wanted to question God but didn't. I wanted to scream and shout but wouldn't. I knew you were in a better place. I knew you were happy and that made me happy.

Don't get me wrong, I miss you like crazy, but I'd rather have you in Heaven laughing with your mom and dad than have you on earth constantly hiding your pain. So, until we meet again, I will continue to make you proud by following my writing dream. You were always my biggest fan and hugest supporter and I'm sure you will continue to do so in Paradise. Continue your endless picnic with Grandmama Rosie and Granddaddy Ollie and save a few ribs for me.

Love always,
You little Womba,

Carla

ACKNOWLEDGEMENTS

All honors and praises to my Almighty GOD for giving me the gift of storytelling that I'm able to share with the world.

To my grandparents, Ollie and Rosie Brown, I love and miss you tremendously. Take care of my Mama, Rosa Pennington Browne, up there. Ma, I know Mama and Granddaddy are driving you crazy….in a good way. I can only imagine what's going on. LOL! I miss you all so much. RIP in Paradise!!!!!!

To my Mama, Rosa Pennington Browne, I wish you were here to experience this new novel with me. You were and will always be my biggest fan and supporter. No one will ever take your place. I love you and miss you getting on my nerves. LOL!

To my daddy, Carl Pennington, thank you for stepping up to the plate when God called Mama home. You have been wonderful and I really appreciate that as well as your continued support and love.

To the loves of my life, Kemyria, Kemberlyn and Jevon "Ju" thank you for being your individual selves and making my life worth living. Thanks for being understanding and giving Mama space when she needs to write. I love you with all my heart. Continue being the wonderful, adventurous, loving, smart and wise kids that you are. Keep following your dreams and goals. Your futures are bright.

To my big sister, Kimberly Saxton and lil' brother, Bryan, I love you dearly. Although I've thought about it several times, I wouldn't trade you for the world.

To my slew of aunts and uncles; Uncle Boo, Aunt Mary, Aunt Arby, Aunt Linda Sue, Uncle Abe, Uncle Sonny, Aunt Lela and Uncle Jimmie, thank you for always being here for me and constantly encouraging me to follow my dreams although some of you have to read my novels with your eyes closed. LOL!

To my brousin (brother + cousin), Aaron Brown, thanks for always having my back. Don't know what I would do without you.

To my girls who have been riding with me since the beginning; Rashunda, Krystal, Valencia, LaTonya, Kim T., Kim B., Tennille, Simetra, Amelia and Anna, I love you gals with all my heart. Thank you for sticking by me through thick and thin.

Dynathia "Nikki" Dunn and Andreana Nelson, thanks for showing up in my life during a difficult time and getting me out of the house to clear my head. I appreciate it!

To my homeboys; Gemini, Wesley "Chuckie," Tommie, Commie and Mike "Mouthpiece" Pendleton, thanks for being here for me.

Niyah Moore, we are still hanging strong, twin! You are more than a social network friend and literary sister. You are my friend! I love you.

Montez Rice, you are a rare jewel. Never let anyone tell you that you're not.

My Facebook husband, Scooter Meyers, I don't know what to say because I keep laughing. You know how we do. Love ya!

To my LCB crew, I thought I wasn't going to be able to finish writing this novel due to my mother's transition into Heaven, but you believed in me and gave me time until I was ready. That's very rare when deadlines need to be met. Tressa and Leslie, you ladies rock. I really love working with you. Thanks for everything.

Capone, again…thank you for being my friend. Chris Renee, girrrrrl…..that's all I'm gonna say. LOL CJ Hudson, Dannette Majette, Kendall Banks, Miss KP, Jackie D, Tonya Ridley, Jai Nicole and the rest of the LCB fam, I'm happy to be working with a group of wonderful, creative and off the wall minds. Grown Folks Fiction at its best!

Shani Green Dowdell (Nayberry Publications) and Elissa Gabrielle (Peace In The Storm Publications), you are two beautiful, wonderful, intelligent, BUSY(lol) ladies. I love working with you every chance I get. Mocha Chocolate 1 and 2, Savor and Pillow Talk Duets…..eroticism at its best!

ZANE, thank you for accepting my short story for the Chocolate Flava 4: Busy Bodies anthology. I think I am still in the twilight zone.

To my social network buddies especially Facebook, I know I will forget a lot of you, but I have to shout out to a few that I interact with a lot gives me laughs galore. DeTerrius Woods, Chrishawn Simpson, Lisa Tyrell Perry, Kisha Green, Carmen Blalock, Mary Green, Kenisha Parker, Tamasha Porter, Tashun T-Sizzle, GreatZach Tate, Kellie Hill, Steel Waters, Cicone Prince, Angie Agnew, Jereau Wilson, Jay Humble Lack, Kristine Beaman and Tyreece Patrick. I know there is more of you but I'd need a lot more pages..LOL! Just know that you were not forgotten intentionally. You guys and gals, the ones that I didn't mention included, just don't know how much you have helped me to cope with the death of my Mama as well as my writing journey. I would have never thought that people I'd never met could mean so much but a wise woman (Elissa Gabrielle) told me that I would find comfort and support from people that I don't really know. I know that I have personally met a few of you, but you get where I am coming from. I love you all and keep riding with me.

To my readers, as I stated a few lines above, it was difficult writing this novel knowing that my Mama would not be here to share this moment with me, but I fought through it and got it done. You helped me to realize that my gift is not mine. It's yours as well and it would be selfish not to continue sharing it with you.

To my '94 and '95 Mattie T. Blount High School graduates or attendees (lol) and hometown, Prichard, AL, your continued support is overwhelming. Thank you from the bottom of my heart.

To anyone that I may have forgotten, it wasn't deliberate. Your love and support are greatly appreciated.

"Follow your dreams! You're the only one who can make them a reality!"

Smooches,

Carla

Chapter One

Myles tossed his wife, Kenya's legs over his shoulders and pounded her pussy so hard it started to feel like a deflated ball. Even though sexual moans usually turned him on, this time he was happy Kenya decided to cover her face with the pillow once the erotic sounds escaped her lips. Myles could hardly stand the sight of her since she'd gained nearly eighty pounds during her pregnancy. Since giving birth to their daughter, Zoie, eight weeks ago, she hadn't tried to lose much of the weight, which pissed him off. Myles thought she'd take the hint when he bought her a gym membership and a Zumba DVD. He even went as far as to make sure their television was on an exercise channel when she hit the power button on the remote in the mornings. However, his countless efforts went unnoticed, which caused Myles to be in a terrible mood most of the time.

"Oh Myles this feels sooo good!" Kenya screamed into the pillow. "Yesss!"

This was Kenya's first time feeling her husband's thick, ten inch dick is almost nine weeks, so she was beyond ecstatic. Despite Kenya's constant advances towards him, Myles always brushed them off followed by some type of lame excuse. But this time was different. Tired of the late night or early morning masturbations, Myles was horny and needed something tight and wet. Surprisingly, the only way he could get through the sex with his wife was to think about another woman; a pretty woman with a slender waist and a curvy ass to be exact. Myles pounded Kenya even harder as he pushed her legs back as far as they would go, but quickly released them when he looked at her flabby stomach. Seeing the extra fat, wrinkled skin and numerous stretch marks instantly turned him off.

"What's wrong, baby?" Kenya asked when he suddenly

stopped.

"Just turn over," Myles frowned as he angrily flipped her onto all fours.

Little did he know, Kenya saw the look on his face before her ass was hiked up in the air. She knew that Myles had a problem with her weight, and noticed how he looked at her most of the time. She also noticed how he slept with his back turned to her when he did decide to join her in bed. Most nights he slept on the sofa and that routine actually started before the baby was born. Kenya was no fool. She was well aware that her weight gain had intensified the distance. Just like Myles, she too wanted her size eight frame back, but with the baby taking up all of her time and energy, dropping the unwanted pounds had proved to be a much difficult task.

"Oooooo! Oooooooo!" Myles moaned as he reflected on one of his past sexual encounters with an ex-girlfriend.

Myles gripped Kenya's hips and forcefully pulled her to him. "Back it up on me, baby! Give me that pussy!"

Kenya was happy for his enthusiasm and quickly complied. "Give me my dick! Is this my dick, daddy?" she added. Her words immediately angered him once she interrupted his thoughts. "Is this my dick?" Kenya asked again as she backed against him.

"Can you be quiet so I can concentrate?" Myles replied as he tried to get back into the groove of things.

He closed his eyes hoping his ex would reappear. No such luck. Then, the unthinkable happened. Zoie started crying.

"Shit!" Myles cursed as he pushed Kenya away from him. His dick went limp instantly. *How did my life get so fucked up?*

"Come on, baby. Put it back in," Kenya whined. She grabbed his shaft and attempted to pull on it, but he pushed her away.

"Zoie's crying, Kenya."

"She'll be alright for a few minutes. Come on, Myles. It's been almost three months."

"And it should've been longer. Who wants to deal with this shit?"

"C'mon, baby, don't say that. Come here."

Myles halfheartedly reentered her as he thought about getting a nut out of the deal, but Zoie's cries weren't helping. He pushed

Kenya away again. She didn't want him to be left hanging so she scurried to her knees and massaged his shaft once again. It started to soften.

"Just move, Kenya and go get the baby."

"No, let her cry. We can finish this. We need to finish this," Kenya said as she stroked faster.

When she realized that wasn't working, Kenya put his dick in her mouth. But her oral efforts didn't help either.

"Just stop. I need to get ready for my flight anyway. I don't want to get caught up in the early morning commuters going to work," Myles said coldly as he pulled away from her.

Kenya didn't know what to think as she watched Myles climb out of bed. The fact that he was no longer interested in her made Kenya uncomfortable. She hurried to the La-Z-Boy chair where her robe lay and covered her body with it. After watching him disappear inside his walk-in closet, she lowered her head in shame and went to tend to their daughter.

Myles peeped outside the closet when he heard their bedroom door open. He then shook his head as he watched Kenya walk out in her ratty, red robe.

"And she wonders why I'm no longer attracted to her ass," Myles mumbled as he fumbled through the closet for his Prada shoe box. Although he had multiple Prada boxes, he searched for the one with a small dot beside his shoe size.

Once he located it, Myles removed the box top and smiled when he saw four missed calls and two text messages on his black iPhone 5; a phone that Kenya knew nothing about and one where the volume constantly stayed on mute; a phone he referred to as his private bat line. Myles checked to see if Kenya was coming before he looked back at the screen. The sneakiness aroused him. As soon as he read the texts, Myles snapped a picture of his dick then typed the words: *You did this so you need to do something about it.*

A smile dashed across his face as he hit the send button, eagerly waiting for a reply. However, the joy didn't last long. Thinking he heard Kenya walking across their hardwood floors and back toward their bedroom, Myles quickly shoved the phone inside one of his Ferragamo loafers. Trying to control his excitement, Myles eagerly pulled out his black Damier Louis Vuitton duffle bag and placed a few items of clothing inside. Before heading for the shower, he went to the back of his closet and kneeled down in front of the safe where he kept emergency funds. After keying in the code, Myles took out three grand, and shoved it inside the front zipper pouch of his luggage. Making sure the safe was secure again, Myles then dashed to the bathroom to shower. Still erect from the text, he decided to relieve himself of the pressure. Five minutes later, his babies were swimming down the drain.

After showering, Myles walked back into the bedroom with a towel wrapped around his waist. He couldn't help but wonder what was on Kenya's mind as she sat on the bed with a suspicious look on her face while breastfeeding Zoie at the same time. The sight turned Myles' stomach. He hated when Kenya breastfed their daughter in his presence. When she did, he visualized a piglet feeding from her mom and that was not something he cared to see.

"Couldn't you have done that shit in the nursery?" he asked after pulling a pair of green boxer briefs from his drawer. "And you really need to focus on getting your sexy back. You lost it, babe."

"Who is she, Myles?" Kenya questioned.

Myles froze. He quickly thought about his private cell phone in the closet. He wondered if Kenya had decided to snoop around and found it in his shoe.

He played dumb. "What are you talking about?"

"You know what I'm talking about, Myles. You look at me like I disgust you. You don't kiss me like you used to. You don't make love to me like you used to. There has to be someone else. So, who is she?"

At that point, Myles figured that his wife was just pulling at straws for information. "Don't be silly, Kenya," Myles assured as he walked over then sat next to her on the bed.

"Then what is it? Is it because of the weight? We used to have sex three times a week, sometimes more. In these past three months, I've tried to have sex with you countless time, but all you ever allow me to do is give you a blow job." Kenya kept her tears at bay as she poured her heart out.

"Don't even start with that crying shit. You've cried enough to fill the Mississippi River by now. That doesn't work for me anymore," Myles replied as he pecked her on the cheek before standing back up. "Just fix yourself up."

"Wow," Kenya replied in awe.

It was at that moment when she thought back to him sweeping her off of her feet a year and a half ago. She couldn't help but wonder where that man was; the man that she'd fallen in love with; the man who used to be so sincere and caring. Kenya laid Zoie on their bed after realizing she'd fallen back asleep. She walked up to Myles.

"Let's finish what we started, then," Kenya suggested as Myles pulled his crisp white Polo shirt over his head. She tugged on his boxers, but once again he moved away.

"I'm good, actually. I took care of me in the shower," he responded after moving her hands. "Besides, I need to get going. My flight leaves soon."

"Do you still love me?" Kenya tried to hug him. Myles continued to get dressed without acknowledging her hug.

"Look, I'm tired of your little pity party, Kenya. I already told you that I loved you, and you're still asking me dumb questions. Now, let me get dressed. Besides, begging makes you look bad. It's degrading actually."

Tears immediately welled up in Kenya's eyes. She was tired of being dismissed. She stepped away from him with a hurt look on her face. She couldn't believe the way he treated her. There was once upon a time in their marriage where Myles couldn't keep his hands off of her. However, all that started to change; when she told him that they were going to have a baby.

Myles looked at his wife. "Listen, calm down before you have an asthma attack. You know that's happened before when you got upset."

"When will you be back this time?" Kenya asked him.

"Look, I told you about questioning me. I'm the man of the house."

"Myles, I just asked a simple question."

"Hopefully, I'll only be in Chicago for one day. My flight comes in tomorrow morning at ten."

"What do you mean by *hopefully*?" Kenya stressed.

"You know how these recruitment sessions can be. One minute everything can be going well then *boom*, it rolls over into another day. Let's just pray that it doesn't."

As a former high school basketball coach and now a top freelancing scout, Myles' job required constant travel.

Kenya rolled her eyes. "I'm getting tired of this."

"Look, Kenya please let's not go there again. You already know that my job consists of more than just watching a player run up and down the damn basketball court. I'm responsible for finding the right player for the right program. This shit is serious. I get paid top dollar to do this."

"Yeah, I know all of that but…"

"But nothing. I'm under a lot of pressure right now, so I don't need you catching an attitude every time I walk out the door. The kid I found in Chicago is supposed to head to Duke next year if everything works out. Besides, you knew I traveled a lot for my job when you first met me."

"You're right. But I thought once the baby came you would slow down. Hell you left to go out of town two days after she was born, so yeah you travel a lot. A little too much actually!"

Myles gave her an evil glare. "And."

Seeing the nonchalant look on Myles' face, Kenya knew the conversation would end up in another one of their shouting matches, so she decided to change the subject. "Just remember I have that meeting at the office tomorrow at one."

"What kind of meeting?" Myles asked with little concern in his voice.

"So, it was your idea that I sell the company, and now you don't even remember what kind of meeting it is?"

Myles' face finally lit up. "Oh, the meeting with the potential buyers," he replied. "Yeah, it slipped my mind, but I'll definitely be back in time for that."

"You know I've been thinking. If I do decide to sell the company, I think I wanna be a stay-at-home mom."

Myles chuckled. "A stay-at-home mom? Are you kidding me? Umm I can tell you now, my answer is no to that dumb idea," Myles answered sternly.

Kenya jerked her neck at his words. "Excuse me? Last I checked, my father was dead. Both my parents died in a car accident two years ago," she reminded.

"And last I checked, you put me in charge of our finances, so my answer is final. Why would you wanna be a stay-at–home mom anyway, so you can sit around and get even bigger? Hell no! And you need to stop saying *if* you decide to sell the company. We've already talked about you selling that marketing company since it's not doing well. Besides, that company was your father's dream...not yours. Once you sell, maybe you can become a chef like you're always talking about." Myles looked at her. "I mean it doesn't look like you've been missing any meals lately, so you must be doing a lot of damn cooking when I'm gone."

Again, Kenya was appalled. "I can't believe you just said that shit."

"Whatever, Kenya. I don't have time to go back and forth with you anymore."

Myles walked into the closet. After slipping on a pair of jeans and some sneakers, he retrieved the private iPhone, slipped it inside his pocket then walked out with his duffle bag. He then walked over to the dresser and grabbed his wallet before sliding on his wedding band.

"I'm tired of replacing wedding bands, Myles. That's your third one, so don't lose it. As a matter of fact, maybe you shouldn't even take it off until you get back."

Myles walked over to his wife and pulled her into his arms.

"I promise not to lose this one, especially with all these women vultures wanting to attack me when they think I'm single."

"Well, you know women these days don't care if you're single or married. Besides, all they want is a nice, tall, handsome man," Kenya said as she admired his 6'4, two hundred and twenty pound frame.

He had broad shoulders and a light scar on his cheek that could easily be mistaken as a dimple on his cocoa brown skin. No matter how Myles currently felt about her, she was still in love with everything about him.

"You look very handsome by the way," she added.

"Thank you, baby. I really appreciate that."

"You're welcome," Kenya replied as she used her hand to press out a wrinkle in his shirt. "Oh before I forget, can you leave me a few hundred dollars. I want to go shopping later."

"For what?"

"A few items for Zoie's room, a few things for the house and maybe a few things for me."

"Are these *things* needed?" he questioned.

"You're the one to talk. You shop more than I do," Kenya reminded with a hint of resentment in her voice.

Myles glanced inside the closet and couldn't help but agree. All the sales reps at Saks in Southpark Mall knew him by name. Knowing she had a point, Myles went into his wallet.

"Is five hundred okay?" he asked after counting the crisp bills. Myles needed to keep her spending under control so that she wouldn't interfere with his.

"It'll do," Kenya replied casually.

It actually wasn't enough, but Kenya didn't complain. She even convinced herself that it was a good idea that Myles was so strict when it came to how much money they spent. Since Myles proved to be good with numbers and budgeting, she allowed him to handle all their finances.

"See you when I get back tomorrow," Myles said as he kissed her on the forehead. He then walked over to the bed and kissed their daughter.

"Myles, can you please think about what I said about me being a stay-at-home mom."

"There's nothing to think about. It's not happening, Kenya," he responded before exiting the room, then the house.

As soon as Myles stepped outside, he put on his Tom Ford sunglasses to hide from the bright June sun. It was only ten a.m. and already humid, so it was probably going to be a scorcher by noon. Just before Myles backed his jet black, Mercedes CLS coupe out of the driveway, he pulled the private phone from his pocket to send a text.

On my way to the airport. Can't wait to see you, baby.

8

Chapter Two

An hour later, Myles raced through the Charlotte airport like he was trying out for the Olympics. The *now boarding* reminder that flashed across the monitors as he ran through and around other passengers infuriated him.

"*Last boarding call for flight 1204 to New York,*" the speaker announced.

Shit…I should've never decided to fuck Kenya this morning, Myles thought. *The pussy wasn't even that good anyway.*

"Watch where the hell you're going!" a thin, Asian man with glasses shouted at him.

Myles only had one thing in mind and one thing only…to catch his flight. If he had to run over a few feet and bump into a few bodies to get there, so be it.

I could've calmly walked through this damn airport if it wasn't for Kenya and Zoie's ass. That's okay though because I know what's awaiting me in the Big Apple, he thought.

A sinister smile formed as he thought about Kenya thinking he was on his way to Chicago.

"Dumb ass," he mumbled.

"Right on time," the attendant spoke. She flashed a smile at Myles when he finally reached his gate.

"Better late than never," Myles replied as he slyly removed his wedding ring and placed it inside his pocket.

Myles smiled back trying to conceal the fact that he was nearly out of breath. After handing her his boarding pass, the attendant scanned the crumbled up paper and allowed him entry.

"You're not coming?" he flirted after pausing at the entrance.

He winked at her. The attendant blushed then turned back to her computer. "I hope you'll be here when I return."

"Y-Y-You'd better hurry before you get left behind," she stammered.

Myles winked at her again then hurried through the corridor. "Women," he chuckled.

Once he boarded the plane, Myles didn't have to walk far as he always flew first class. After locating his seat, Myles placed his lap top bag in the overhead compartment. As he was about to place his carry on suitcase in the compartment, he caught a Spanish woman staring and smiling at him. Myles formed a corner smile with his lips when he realized that she was seducing him with her lustful eyes. She had every right to. His body was lean and toned. His skin was like a smooth glaze of caramel. He was also no stranger to the gym and wasn't embarrassed to frequent the nail salon for a manicure and pedicure. He made sure that his fade was tapered and lined once a week. One thing he knew about women, they loved a man who took care of himself.

"Do you play football?" the busty, Latina asked. She was seated next to the window.

Myles gave her an inquisitive look before realizing he was carrying a copy of *Sports Illustrated* magazine.

"No, I'm more of a basketball man. I like to take it to the hole," Myles flirted.

She shifted in her seat. "Nothing but net, huh?" she flirted back.

"From time to time, I like to hit the rim, but the ultimate goal is to get it in the hole."

She bit her bottom lip. As Myles placed his suitcase in the overhead, he knew the Latina was still watching him. He couldn't help but smile when he flipped his eyes at her, and saw that she was nearly drooling.

This is going to be a long flight, he thought after looking down at his boarding pass and realizing he'd be sitting next to her.

Several minutes after takeoff, Myles pulled out his *New York Times* newspaper from between the magazines. His heart began to flutter when his eyes landed on the article about the grand opening of a new hotel in Manhattan. There was one line that he read to himself over and over again:

Millionaire hotel owner, Camilla Ellington, is sure to deepen her pockets with the newly upscale hotel called, The Bella Grand.

I'll be right beside you when you do, baby, Myles thought before blowing a kiss at the photo.

"Friend of yours?" the Latina asked as she crossed her leg revealing a toned thigh.

Myles instantly took notice.

"No, she's not," he lied hoping that she didn't see him blow the kiss. "I just love to see people making money. Money is everything…power and respect."

He could've sworn that he saw a twinkle in her eye when he spoke those words.

"I can appreciate that. I love money, too," she said before playfully scratching his arm with her light pink fingernails. "I noticed you're not wearing a wedding ring," the Latina spoke.

Myles smiled revealing the small, discreet gap between his teeth. "That doesn't mean that I'm not married," he replied evasively as he rubbed the imprint of his wedding band in his side pocket.

"I guess you have a point there," she giggled before finishing off her glass of champagne.

"I really love your raspberry colored hair. It compliments your beautiful green eyes," he charmed. "You are a very attractive woman."

She blushed and twirled a lock of her hair around her finger. "Thank you."

"No need to thank me for the truth."

"So, what do you do for a living?"

"I'm a stock broker," he lied.

"That's interesting. As tall as you are, I figured you were some type of athlete."

Not wanting to engage in that particular conversation, Myles quickly changed it. "I'd rather know more about you," he suggested.

"It's not much to tell actually." She motioned toward him, then spoke in a low tone. "How about we get to know each other instead of this unnecessary conversation?" she proposed.

Myles knew what those words meant.

"What do you have in mind?"

"How about you meet me in the bathroom and find out."

She stood up and crossed over him making sure that her breasts were fully in his face. Myles quickly placed the paper in his lap when he realized an erection had formed. He laughed internally as he thought about the lengths women would go to in order to snag a man with status and money.

"Women," he mumbled before standing up. *May as well finish what Kenya started*, he thought.

Myles dropped the paper in his seat and glanced around nervously as he made his way toward the restroom. Luckily for them, there were only three other passengers in first class and they each were buried in their laptops. No one seemed to be paying attention.

When Myles finally made it to the restroom, the stewardess gave him an awkward look when he reached for the door handle. He assumed that she must've seen the Latina go in just a minute ago. He smiled at her then stepped inside the cramped space. There was barely enough room for one person inside airplane lavatories, much less two.

"I think the flight attendant is on to us," Myles informed. He looked at the sexy woman who sat on top of the tiny toliet.

"Don't worry about her, that's my friend, Valerie. She's not gonna say anything."

"Oh, so you do this type of thing all the time, huh?" Myles questioned.

She placed her finger against his lips, then stood up. "Sssshhh. Just be quiet and enjoy." She breathed seductively into his ear after pushing him against the narrow door. "So, basketball is your favorite sport, huh? Well, I like to play with balls, too." She lowered to her knees never taking her dreamy, doe eyes off of him. "We're at the two point line now," she said as she stared at his erectness. "I hope I don't miss."

"Sweetie, I shoot nothing but threes," he informed.

As she swallowed his rock hard ten inches, Myles couldn't help but roll his eyes into the back of his head. Her dick sucking skills was definitely porn star status.

12

Ten minutes later,
they both returned to their seats like nothing happened.

"I really appreciate you allowing me a free throw," Myles whispered into her ear.

"The game doesn't have to be over, darling," she responded while massaging his crotch. "We can hook up once we get to New York."

Myles nodded his head. "I don't mind the game going into overtime."

They both smiled at all the basketball analogies.

After talking for at least twenty minutes, Myles knew he needed to refocus. The flight from Charlotte to New York was only an hour and forty minutes, and he'd already let the sexy Latina occupy most of his time. He reopened the newspaper. Again, he smiled as he read his favorite line again:

Millionaire hotel owner, Camilla Ellington, is sure to deepen her pockets with the newly upscale hotel called, The Bella Grand.

Myles' smile slowly faded as he thought about not having to cheat on Kenya if only she had the kind of money that Camilla Ellington possessed. Born and raised in a crime riddened housing projects in East St. Louis, Myles grew up extremely poor with his mother, Marian, his abusive, alcoholic father, Dennis and older brother. When Myles' brother was killed in a shootout when he was only fifteen, his father took the death extremely hard and started staying out all times of the night, and using Marian and Myles as a punching bag whenever he saw fit.

One night after coming home reeking of alcohol and sex, Marian and Dennis engaged in a brutal, physical confrontation. Myles tried to defend his mother but was thrown into the wall by his father. The demonic look on Dennis' face was more than enough to keep Myles from interfering. He was tired of the bruises him and his mother sustained from his father's fists.

When Dennis' guard was down, Marian clobbered him over the head with a vase, but the blow didn't seem to faze him. Instead,

Dennis turned to Marian, punched her as hard as he could then caught her by the neck before she hit the floor.

The vicious words that Dennis spewed at Myles' mother were embedded in his head as he remembered his father choking the life out of his mother. Myles was mute and stunned as he watched his mother fight for her life. Myles couldn't move out of fear that he'd be next. A few minutes later, Marian stopped flailing her arms and Dennis dropped her limp body to the floor. Myles would never forget his father's words as he glared at him: "*get your ass up and help me get rid of this bitch's body.*"

Marian's death was eventually deemed an unsolved murder and Myles knew that he'd join his mother if the truth was ever told. He kept quiet and cried endlessly in the wee hours of the night when his father wasn't home or was asleep. Months after his mother's death, Dennis' drinking spiraled even more out of control. Myles could remember the countless times when he hadn't eaten in days. At one point, he became so skinny his clothes became extremely big; causing him to be the topic of everybody's joke at school. Instead of stepping up to the plate and being a good father since he was ultimately responsible for Marian's death, Dennis took what little money he had and spent it on alcohol and the slew of women he paraded around the house. Instead of providing, Dennis even had the audacity to tell Myles to go out and make his own money. When Myles asked him how he was supposed to do that since he had school, he didn't expect his father's next words, "*just like men pay for pussy, women pay for dick. You can fuck some of my girlfriends that I bring up in here. A few of 'em have had their eyes on you anyway.*"

Myles thought his father had lost his mind, but he also knew that if he wanted to get even the most basic necessities, he had to give it a try. In his eye it wasn't about having sex for money, it was about survival. It worked like magic.

Even at a young age, Myles had good looks. Not to mention, his height instantly made him look older, and he had a pimp-like tongue game that could charm the panties out of any young girl. But younger girls who could only afford a pair of sneakers from time to time didn't have what he needed. Instead, he focused on older women, especially ones with good jobs. On any given day Myles could be seen hanging out in hospital cafeterias preying on nurses who didn't have wedding bands on or sitting in fancy coffee shops looking for women who carried briefcases and appeared lonely. Myles was self-centered, and believed he was entitled to lie to get what he wanted. He was also good at what he did.

By the age of twenty-one, Myles was living rent free in a nice St. Louis suburb apartment, and had just purchased a brand new Nissan Maxima; all courtesy of a pharmacist fifteen years his senior. Myles never slowed down or thought about quitting. Instead, his deception became a full time occupation. He even made sure every fake name he used, started with an 'M' in honor of his mother.

On his twenty-third birthday, Myles received a call that his dad had died of liver failure. Although Myles knew about his father's illness, they hadn't spoken in years. Dennis would often try to reach out to Myles, but Myles would ignore his father's efforts. As far as Myles was concerned, his father died as soon as Myles moved out. Thinking back to his mother's death, Myles allowed the state to bury Dennis. He neither claimed the body nor did he foot the bill for a funeral.

As he aged, Myles realized that women were eager to give him whatever he wanted as long as he gave them what they needed: attention, time and great sex. He was a man who said all the things women wanted to hear and someone who was totally devoted to them. But once he got them wrapped up into his web of lies and deceit, the party was over.

Myles closed the paper and began to reflect on the beginnings of him and Kenya's relationship. After leaving Connecticut two years prior, he decided to make Charlotte, North Carolina his next home. Two months into his new move, he met Kenya at Panera Bread in Uptown where he frequented since arriving. She was sitting in his favorite spot in the corner with one of the saddest looks he'd ever seen. He hadn't been with a woman in the two months he'd been in Charlotte, so his intentions were merely to play on whatever vulnerability that had caused her such sadness in order to get laid.

Surprisingly, Kenya allowed him to join her at the table after he displayed his charismatic ways. It took a while, but he soon learned that she was upset due to a personal matter regarding her best friend. Kenya mentioned not being there for her because of an investors' meeting she desperately had to attend. The mention of the investors meeting made Myles want to console her even more. He took a seat close to her and allowed Kenya to pour her heart out. Myles was also intrigued when he learned that Kenya was the CEO of Creative Minds Marketing Group, the only black owed marketing company on the East Coast. Once that information was divulged, his eyes flickered with dollar signs. She even shared the story about her parents' deaths nine months prior where he learned that was how she ended up with the company. He could see it in her eyes that she was still grieving, so Myles went in for the ultimate kill. He told her that his mother had recently passed as well, which was a slight lie, since she'd died several years ago. However, their similar stores worked because it suddenly allowed Kenya to drop her guards even further. The conversation went so well that they decided to see each other again.

It didn't take long for Kenya to cling to him like fabric softener to a cotton shirt. Myles knew she wouldn't be able to resist his charm and he poured it on as thick as molasses. In his world, chivalry was not dead especially if he hoped to gain something from it. Opening doors, cooking, complimenting the way she looked, taking her shopping, whisking her away spontaneously, listening attentively, asking questions, ignoring his phone, and socializing with her employees got him the gold medal. He'd stolen her heart.

Myles' number one rule used to be to never get serious enough to marry a woman. However, as time progressed, that rule slowly disappeared. Myles figured if he was married then he'd have better access to the money instead of having to sneak and steal it. Four months into their relationship, Kenya informed him that she was pregnant. A baby was never part of his plan, but he figured it could only help. If he married Kenya then he would have *trustworthy* access to everything she owned. She was overjoyed when he proposed to her with a nice, three carat princess cut ring.

Everything about their fairytale romance seemed to be going well, until a few months after marrying her, Myles learned about a secret that sent his world spiraling. As it turned out, Kenya's marketing company was going under and she was in desperate need of keeping it afloat. He wanted to cut his losses and divorce her because there was

,,.

no way he could continue to live his life without her kind of money. Myles needed another scapegoat and he was on his way to see the one that he had found.

"By the way, I'm Gabrielle," the Latina addressed Myles breaking his chain of thoughts.

"Oh, nice to formally meet you, Gabrielle. I'm Mitchell," he lied. "By the way, you know what my profession is so might I ask what is it that you do?"

Gabrielle flipped her hair then leaned in to his ear.

"I'd like to be doing you."

"Oh really?" Myles smiled wickedly.

"I'd like to finish what we started in the bathroom once we get to New York?" She opened her purse to reveal a wad of cash. "Everything's on me. Are you down?"

Gabrielle's dominating words and actions turned him on and he couldn't help but toss her into his *new money* category. The lavish hotels, country clubs, sky boxes at football games, flights to anywhere his heart desired were just the tip of the iceberg for him and he wasn't prepared to give any of them up. Kenya's diminishing net worth was no longer doing it for him. He had to follow the money.

Myles rubbed his chin while in deep thought. "The ball is in your court," he finally answered.

Carla PENNINGTON

Chapter Three

Kenya stood over the kitchen sink and took out her sexual frustrations on Zoie's bottle as she scrubbed the inside with a brush. Her body craved to have Myles inside of her. She missed him breathing on her nipples causing them to quickly harden. She also missed him talking dirty in her ear causing her lower half to react wildly to his words and thrusts. The thought of it all caused her clit to throb. Kenya wished he'd just ignored Zoie's cries and continued making love to her. Part of her felt like a horrible mother for wanting to have sex while her baby girl wailed in the other room, but desperate times called for desperate measures.

"I gotta lose some fucking weight," she said after placing the bottle on the dryer rack.

When Kenya placed her hands back into the soapy water, suddenly her doorbell chimed. It was a much needed distraction. The fire that had started between her legs needed to be doused. She grabbed a hand towel and dried her hands before walking towards the front door.

Kenya smiled as soon as she looked through the peep hole. "Who is it?" she joked.

"Who the hell do you think it is? I just called your ass and told you that I was coming over," Kenya's best friend, Jada, replied.

As soon as Kenya opened the door, she was caught off guard with a huge bear hug. "Put some clothes on. I'm taking you out to lunch."

Kenya smiled again at her petite, feisty friend. "Well, hello to you, too."

"Later for all that. Just go put some clothes on. I'm tired of you being cooped up in this damn house," Jada said after walking inside.

Kenya closed the door. "Girl, you do remember that I have a child now, right?"

"Yep I sure do. Now, go get my Goddaughter because she needs to get out just like you do. I know you're over here moping about Myles going out of town *as usual*."

Kenya stared at her friend. It bothered her slightly that Jada didn't really care for her husband.

"I'm not moping about him going out of town. I'm actually used to that. I'm just frustrated that Zoie interrupted our sex session earlier."

"I don't blame Zoie for cock-blocking. I wouldn't want a brother or sister either." Jada laughed.

Kenya playfully slugged Jada in the right shoulder. "Besides, I think my weight gain is playing a big part in our lack of sex nowadays."

Jada examined Kenya from head to toe. "Well, I can see why he might have an issue with it. You are fat!"

"Jada!" Kenya exclaimed.

"Well, it's the truth. I know men like *love* handles but damn. You're starting to look like that big bitch from the show *Dance Moms*. I mean you used to have a bad ass Beyonce shape, but now you…"

"Alright! I get it!"

Jada chuckled. She then ran her fingers through Kenya's wavy, ebony-colored hair that cascaded like a waterfall down her back. Two small moles rested on both of Kenya's high cheekbones and her eyes were a piercingly sharp shade of grey.

"You're still beautiful though, bestie. You know y'all mixed Halle Berry bitches get all the dudes," Jada said. She would often tease Kenya from time to time about her white mother and black father having such a gorgeous child.

"Oh, thanks for the compliment after calling me fat," Kenya responded.

"You know I don't sugarcoat shit," Jada replied with a huge grin. "Now, come on and get out of this house. Forget about that sorry ass husband of yours."

Kenya stabbed Jada with her eyes. "Look, today is not a good day. I'm not in the mood for one of your bash Myles segments."

"And how do you think my day is going? Need I remind you that I have cancer? I'm the one who should be moping around and shit," Jada said while adjusting the purple and silver scarf on her head.

Kenya instantly felt bad. While she was complaining about something so minor, her friend was dealing with a much bigger issue. "I'm sorry that I couldn't make it to your radiation treatment yesterday."

"Girl please, don't worry about that. My mother went with me. Like you said, you have a baby," Jada responded. "But the best way to make it up is to go have lunch with me. Especially since it's not very often that I get hungry with the treatments and all."

"Can I get a rain check?"

Jada shook her head. "Not this time."

"Jada, do you even care about what's going in my life?" Kenya asked with a hint of irritation in her voice.

"How dare you?" Jada blasted. "Yes, I do give a damn what's going on in your life, but I'm thirty-two-years-old and there's a possible expiration date on my life. So, actually I'm not gonna apologize for caring more about that than your silly issues."

After hearing those words, Kenya felt like the scum of the earth once again. She tortured herself for being so inconsiderate and selfish.

"Jada, I'm sorry for being so insensitive. Please forgive me."

"You're forgiven. Now, I know you're going through some crazy shit, but you can fix your problems. I can't fix mine."

Kenya hugged Jada after seeing a tear escape her eye. After being in remission for almost three years, Jada's cervical cancer had recently come back; this time with a vengeance and much more aggressive. The first time she'd received the devastating news luckily the cancer was only in stage one, so the doctors were able to remove it all with only a cone biopsy. However, this time around Jada's treatments had been much more intense. Radiation, chemotherapy, and countless amounts of prescription pills were starting to deteriorate her body. Not only did Kenya cry like a baby when she first found out about her friend's condition, but she cried the first time she saw Jada with a bald head. It was one of the reasons why she always skipped out on her treatments. It killed her to see Jada that way.

"Now, look what you've made me do. Now, I need this damn scarf to wipe my eyes." They both laughed when Jada pulled the scarf off. "So, how about that lunch?"

Kenya tried not to stare at her friend's frail body, but Jada's weight loss was very noticeable. Standing at 5'2, Jada once had a voluptuous figure that poured into a nice hourglass shape. Now, instead of thirty-two, she looked more like a twelve-year-old. The only thing she'd managed to maintain was her feisty, personality.

"I can't say no after this," Kenya finally replied.

"Great!" Jada cheered while pulling a curly wig from her purse. "While you're getting Zoie together, I'll put this ugly ass thing on." They both laughed again as Jada adjusted the fake hair on her head. "I hate synthetic wigs, but they didn't have any cute human hair ones in the beauty supply store. I had to get it though because I can do without the 'she must be a cancer patient' stares today."

"Girl, you're too much. Well, I was going shopping for window panels so I can finish Zoie's nursery," Kenya responded. "I hate the ones the interior decorator bought, but that can wait. Actually, let me take you to lunch. With the money that Myles left me we can have a nice lunch at Ruth's Chris. I know how you love that place. Or better yet I can cook you something. How about some seared peppercorn tuna with julienne vegetables."

Jada raised an eyebrow. "Don't try to distract me with your cooking skills. What in the hell do you mean by *the money that Myles left you*? You own a business. Why is he giving you money like you're a child getting a weekly allowance?"

"Jada, please don't start. You know Myles takes care of all our finances. He just wants to make sure that we're okay...financially."

"I still don't understand why you gave him complete control over your finances and what really pissed me off was you fired Lance. I know that was Myles' idea. Lance was with Creative Minds for years. I mean the new guy, Julius you hired is fine as hell, but that still wasn't right. I loved Lance. You and him were so close at one point."

"Lance had been talking about opening his own CPA firm for a while now so it all worked out."

Jada wasn't convinced. "I just think you should be more involved with your money, Kenya. After all, it is *yours*."

"I appreciate your concerns, but I've got this. Besides, we all know that I'm not that great with money anyway so it made sense to put him in control."

"That's the right word...control. He's very controlling...the money, the bills, your wardrobe. You're the damn lady of the house. Shouldn't you take care of the bills?"

"Jada, you're not married. When you're married, you have to make compromises."

"I understand what you're saying, but what are you getting out of it?"

Kenya folded her arms in anger.

"Look, I'm not trying to piss you off, but I just wished you would've waited before you married Myles. You really didn't know him. I get it that he was there in your time of grief, but you all got married way too soon in my opinion."

Kenya sighed. "You don't care what comes out of your mouth, do you?"

She studied Jada's features. Although she'd lost tons of weight, Jada was still striking. With a Hennessey colored complexion, deep chocolate-colored eyes, and perfect, icy white teeth, she reminded Kenya of a babydoll most times. Before losing her hair, Jada wore bangs with her thick, shoulder length tresses that stayed neatly done.

"No, actually I don't. Oh, and before I forget to ask you. Are you still serious about selling your father's company?"

"First of all, my father died, so the company belongs to me now and yes, I'm still gonna sell it. It's not doing that great financially anyway, so why try to keep it afloat. I want to stay home with Zoie anyway. I also want to get back into cooking like I used to. Besides, you know I'm only doing this marketing thing because it was dropped in my lap unexpectedly."

"Yeah I know."

"When my parents died so did my dream of opening a restaurant. Besides, Myles said it's a good idea to sell the company, but I'd need to find something else to do."

Jada frowned. "Find something else to do? What kind of shit is that? You will have something to do…take care of your damn baby."

"Look, I know that you don't care much for Myles, but I love him."

Kenya desperately wanted her best friend to be happy for her especially since Jada was all she had besides Myles and Zoie.

"It's not that. It just bothers me that you jumped right into the marriage without getting to know him," Jada informed. "I mean even the fact that he refused to take pictures on your wedding day still doesn't sit well with me. Not to mention, it's bad enough that you went to the Justice of the Peace. You always talked about having a big wedding."

"I know," Kenya agreed. "He hates taking pictures."

"Umph…the shit is weird. Does he know anything about the life insurance policy that your parents left you?"

"No."

"Well, that's good. Keep it that way because he shops like he's a damn Kardashian and you should've been pissed when he bought that Benz without your permission."

"He needed a car, Jada."

"Girl, stop it! He'd just gotten rid of that Audi Q7 truck. How did he *need* a new damn car that quickly?"

"Does it really matter at this point?"

"Yes! It's your fucking money and he's running wild with it."

"He has his own money, Jada. Besides, did it ever occur to you that we got married so soon simply because we loved each other? True love does exist you know. My parents got married after only knowing each other for two months and they were married for thirty-six years," Kenya stated with a hint of bitterness in her voice.

"I didn't mean to upset you," Jada apologized after realizing that she'd insulted her friend.

Kenya was happy when the phone rang and interrupted them.

"Hello?" she answered after retrieving the receiver from the coffee table. "Yes, this is Mrs. Whitaker. What do you mean my mortgage is behind? Four months…that's impossible! We pay our mortgage on time every month." She paused for a few moments. "Let me check my records and get back to you." Kenya hung up the phone then turned to Jada who gave her an inquisitive look.

"Kenya, this house is paid for, right? Your father bought this for you, years ago. Why is the mortgage company calling you?"

As much as she wasn't in the mood to discuss it, Kenya knew Jada wouldn't let go of the issue until she gave her an answer. "Myles thought it would be a good idea to take out a second mortgage and earn a little equity in the house."

"Kenya, no!" Jada sighed disappointedly. "That's crazy! Why would you do that?"

Kenya didn't respond.

"Plus it doesn't make sense. If you own your company and he makes good money as a recruiter, then why would the mortgage company call? Why are you just receiving a call from them about this?"

"The rep said they normally call Myles on another number, which I'm sure is his cell, but he hasn't been answering lately." She paused for a moment. "This is probably just a misunderstanding. Let me go in the office and check this out. I'm sure Myles has proof of our payments."

When they retreated into the office, Jada shook her head as she watched her friend tug at the locked file cabinet. "Maybe the key is in the desk," Jada suggested. She hoped that it was for Kenya's sake.

Kenya walked to the desk, but couldn't find a key inside any of the drawers. "Why would the file cabinet be locked?" she mumbled.

"Yeah, my thoughts exactly. Haven't you ever noticed that before?"

"I honestly haven't been in here for a while."

"I mean why the fuck is he so secretive?"

Actually, he's not the only one, Kenya thought as she flipped through several papers on the desk. She paused when she came across a Delta Airlines receipt.

"What is it?" Jada asked when she noticed Kenya's demeanor change.

"A plane ticket receipt to Aspen."

"So, what's wrong with that? I thought you said he travels a lot, right?"

"What's wrong with it is that this ticket is dated two days after

25

Zoie was born. Myles told me that he was going to fucking Cleveland."

Kenya began to wonder if a lot of his frequent, work related, out of town trips were actually leisure trips.

"That mutherfucker. If you want me to break into that file cabinet and drawer, you know I can," Jada said before picking up a letter opener.

"No, I don't want you to get caught up in any of me and Myles' mess."

"You're like my sister, Kenya. I'm already caught up." Jada stepped over to the file cabinet.

"No, Jada! He probably has personal things in there."

Jada stared at Kenya in complete disbelief. It angered her that Kenya was so naïve and blind to the fact of what was really going on.

"Personal and private went out the damn door when the two of you said *I do*."

"Like I said before, when you get married…"

"I don't want to hear that *when I get married* shit, Kenya. I'll be dead in about a year or two so my chances of getting married have been shot to hell anyway. You need to open your eyes. This isn't you. You used to be sharp as a blade. You've never been this gullible before when it came to a man. If anything, you made them worry and wonder."

Kenya had heard enough from Jada and realized that her friend was right. She really needed to find out what was going on with her husband.

Chapter Four

At exactly 6:15 that evening, and after a much needed nap, Myles stepped inside the ballroom of the Bella Grand Hotel with his head held high and nose wide open. The scent of money flowed through his nostrils. He'd almost missed the after work social event due to Gabrielle's insatiable appetite during their sexual escapades at her apartment in Chelsea. As good as the sex was, he didn't want to leave her, but money was calling him.

Myles was on the brink of a money orgasm as he walked through the ballroom. Diamonds, Rolexes and platinum money clips caught his eye. Myles was in the right place and he fit right in. Camilla had gone far and beyond with the black, Dolce & Gabbana suit that she'd left for him in her penthouse suite. His plan seemed to be falling into place.

After scouring the crowd, Myles spotted Camilla in a small circle of older, gray-haired men. They were talking and laughing. This sparked Myles' interest and he was ready to stir the pot. He walked toward her. Although she was in her mid fifties, Camilla looked amazing and could keep up with the agility of Myles' thirty-three year-old body. She worked out just as much as Myles did to keep her size six frame intact. Her thick, honey colored, curly locks bounced each time she laughed. Her butterscotch skinned glowed in the midst of the men and when one of them tried to get a little touchy feely with her, she playfully popped his hand. Myles chuckled as he drew closer. He couldn't blame the man because Camilla was a knock out and the way she unknowingly flirted was enticing. Of all the women he defrauded, she was the richest and he wanted a huge chunk of her action.

"Oh my, God!" Camilla exclaimed then jumped when Myles

crept behind her and wrapped his arms around her waist.

Her face gleamed when she saw that the culprit was Myles. He laid a passionate kiss on her neck and stared at the other men while doing so. The four of them shifted a little or sipped from their champagne flutes as Myles' actions had obviously made them uncomfortable.

"You're late sir," Camilla said with a huge smile.

"I know I'm sorry. I took a later flight out."

"Why didn't you let me know that you were here?" Camilla asked. She seemed so happy to see him.

"I wanted to surprise you," he answered before turning Camilla around and kissing her nude glossed lips.

"I'm happy that you did," she cooed. "You look great."

"I must say the same about you," Myles replied as he twirled Camilla around to admire her stunning body in the knee length embellished Alexander McQueen dress.

"The things that I could do to you right now could get us arrested," she whispered in his ear before planting another kiss on his lips. She didn't care who watched.

"Mmmmmmmm. You may want to save that for later," Myles answered as he welcomed her tongue in his mouth again.

At that point, the four men drizzled away.

"Or we can disappear upstairs for about thirty minutes," Camilla suggested. "I haven't seen you almost two weeks. I'm overdue for some of you."

"Baby, you're the face of this party. You have to be here. Besides, you know I need more than thirty minutes." Camilla giggled and blushed. "You've run your friends off," Myles spoke of the four men.

"To hell with them. I got what I needed and wanted out of them."

"Spoken like a real business woman." Myles kissed Camilla again and was seriously contemplating taking her up on her offer to ditch the party for a while. Her last statement turned him on. He pressed his body closer to hers so that she could feel his bulge. "You see what you've started?"

"There's only one way to finish it." Camilla slid her French manicured fingers between his.

As soon as she was about to step away with him, they were interrupted by a male, business associate along with Camilla's niece, Brooklyn.

"Camilla, this grand opening is turning heads. You've outdone yourself again," the associate spoke excitedly before hugging Camilla.

Camilla sighed knowing that her spontaneous moment with Myles would have to wait.

"Kenneth, I just want to thank you for your contribution. You had a huge hand in making all of this happen," Camilla poured on her charm. She hugged the associate again then pecked both of his cheeks. "Let me introduce you to my fiancé, Maverick. I don't think the two of you have ever met."

Myles smiled deviously at the mention of the false name he'd given Camilla. When he met her, Myles knew he had to come strong; name and all. Maverick was a great choice: an independent individual who did not go along with a group or party. That fit him perfectly.

"Maverick, I don't know what you've done to snag this one," Kenneth joked while shaking Myles' hand. "Congratulations to you both. When is the big day?"

"August 3rd. It's gonna be in Anguilla," Camilla boasted.

Brooklyn stood on the sideline and eyed her aunt's new man. Myles caught the look then dusted imaginary dust from his shoulder.

"Kenneth, I've definitely snagged a great one. I'm a very lucky man. I don't know what I'd do without her, so I made sure that I'd have her forever. This rock is proof of how bad I want her," Myles bragged while showing off the engagement ring to Kenneth.

"Maverick, tell Kenneth how you proposed to me," Camilla gushed.

"Well, it wasn't that big of a deal," Maverick downplayed although he wanted to share.

"It was to me," Camilla whined.

"Okay well we were in Aspen and I had a tray of carrots delivered to our room. She loves carrots by the way. I waited all day for her to finish them before she found the main karat. She eventually did."

29

"Oh, I get it. Carrots and *karats*," Kenneth chuckled. "That's creative…I guess."

Myles could tell that Kenneth had a thing for Camilla. He felt that it was only fair that he made him even more jealous. Myles gently grabbed Camilla's face, and planted a huge kiss on her full lips.

"Again, congratulations to you both." Kenneth skipped away.

"Men are so typical," Brooklyn huffed.

"What is that supposed to mean?" Myles asked.

"It was like a *who has the bigger dick* contest between you two."

"Brooklyn, watch your language," Camilla barked then quickly smiled when a few party goers turned in her direction.

"It's okay, Camilla," Myles soothed. "She's just jealous."

Myles winked at Brooklyn and smiled maliciously. Myles knew Brooklyn didn't care much for him so, in his eyes, it was only fair to make her miserable.

Brooklyn ignored him. "Aunt Camilla, we haven't had our picture taken together yet," she addressed while waving for the photographer to come over. "This would be a perfect opportunity for the company's public relations department."

"Good idea," Camilla agreed. "You always know what to do."

"Well, that is why you hired me. You know that my marketing and public relations skills are the bomb," Brooklyn replied.

The two ladies smiled.

"Maverick, you stand in the middle of us," Camilla addressed Myles.

Myles turned his head when the photographer reached them and positioned his camera to snap a photo. "No pictures."

"Baby, this will be a wonderful photo op for us," Camilla propositioned.

And have Kenya or another one of my past women see that shit somewhere…no thanks, he thought. "No pictures, Camilla!" Myles growled.

Camilla and Brooklyn stared at each other. When Myles never turned back around, Camilla waved the photographer away.

"What kind of model doesn't like to have his picture taken?" Brooklyn asked while tooting her nose at him.

"One who gets paid for every shot," Myles replied nastily then thought back to when he told Camilla he was a high fashion model signed with the infamous IMG agency. He had to keep his lives separate in every aspect; name and occupation.

Brooklyn crinkled her perfectly arched eyebrows. "That's stupid! If she is about to be your wife, you'll be in the limelight at all times. She's Camilla Ellington, remember…famous female hotel owner."

"If they don't pay, they don't shoot. I don't give a damn what it's for," Myles defended.

Camilla emptied her glass of champagne and grabbed another from a tray when a waitress walked by. "Maverick, what kind of wedding pictures will we have if you're not in any of them?" she asked. "You can't expect to be paid for every picture that's taken of you, especially by the paparazzi. They like to bother me from time to time."

"Then I'll sue," Myles responded arrogantly.

"So, tell me again, why is it that you don't model in the states?" Brooklyn tossed in her two cents.

Myles scowled at Brooklyn's question. He resented the fact that she was always in their business, constantly questioning him and trying to convince Camilla that she shouldn't get married. He also resented the fact that he was immensely attracted to her snappy attitude and vivacious body.

"Be careful where you get your information from because I never said that I didn't model in the states," Myles fired back.

"Well, you must be modeling for mom and pop stores because I've never seen you. I thought you were supposed to be this big deal," Brooklyn added.

"Enough!" Camilla seethed. "This is neither the time nor the place for this. We're supposed to be celebrating," she reminded. "We'll deal with this later." When her phone rang from inside her clutch, she pulled it out then stepped away from them.

"That was a corny ass proposal by the way. It sickens me every time Aunt Camilla talks about it," Brooklyn said as she rolled her eyes.

"And where's your ring?" Myles hoped she caught the sarcasm and insult.

"I don't need a ring. I'm..."

"Please don't give ne that independent woman bullshit. Every woman needs a man and that's a damn fact."

"Well, my aunt doesn't need you. I think you're lying about being a model. I haven't found any photos of you anywhere."

"That just means you need to keep your nose out of grown folks business."

"I am grown, asshole. I'm twenty-six."

"Then act like it and stay out of me and Camilla's lives."

"You must think you've hit the jackpot, huh since you're about to marry my aunt after three months of dating? She's twenty-three years older than you. Doesn't it bother you that she's old enough to be your mom? And she's too old to have kids, so I hope you're not looking forward to having any."

Each word Brooklyn spoke went in one of Myles' ear then quickly out the other. He was too busy admiring her beauty and sexy body as he'd done so on several other occasions. Myles hated himself for experiencing wet dreams of lying inside of her while squeezing her apple bottom ass. She wasn't his type...not financially anyway, and he hated the long Brazilian weave she wore. But he couldn't deny his physical attraction toward her. Her long neck begged for him to taste it whenever she was around. He wanted to taste her milk chocolate skin. Myles imagined ripping off her Versace dress and squeezing her 38D's. He felt an erection forming.

"Brooklyn, that was your mom. She says she's on her way," Camilla joked, interrupting his thoughts.

Myles was happy for the interruption because he wasn't prepared to explain the rise in his pants.

"Ha-ha-ha...very funny. She's not my mother," Brooklyn pouted.

"Well, your dad's new fling is on her way," Camilla corrected.

"Whatever."

Camilla knew that would upset Brooklyn to the brink of leaving. She didn't want Brooklyn to upset her man any more that she already had with her bickering. Brooklyn kissed Camilla on the cheek. But before walking off to mingle with other guests, she rolled her eyes at Myles. He chuckled, then snuck in one last glance of her plump ass before directing his attention back to Camilla.

After twenty minutes of mingling, Myles was bored. He couldn't engage in too many conversations. He was illiterate to what most of them were about, but if need be, he could bullshit and charm his way through anything.

"Camilla, I need to get some rest. I'm pretty tired." Myles said when he managed to pull her away from a group of heckling hens.

Camilla poked out her bottom lip. "So, you're not going to have any energy for me later tonight?"

"I'll always have energy for you, sweetie."

"Actually I have a better idea. Instead of you going upstairs to the penthouse and being bored, why don't you go shopping or something," Camilla suggested before opening her clutch and pulling out her Amex black card. "I can't leave yet, but I don't want you to be cooped up in the penthouse doing nothing. Hell, there's no need for *both* of us to be bored." Camilla laughed as she cased the room to see if anyone heard her remark.

"Oh, it's okay. As nice as that place is, I can find something to do."

"I know, isn't it gorgeous," Camilla responded. She was proud of the 2,900 square foot room that was the true definition of luxury. The penthouse featured everything you would expect in a world-class suite including floor to ceiling windows, marble-floor bathrooms, a master bedroom with a king-sized bed and down-filled duvets, multiple HD TVs, a kitchen with state of the art appliances, and a second bedroom.

"I'm not gonna let guests book it for a while. I'm gonna stay in it until my apartment in Tribeca is finished being remodeled.

"But I feel silly going to shop in a suit. Besides, it's after seven o'clock. I thought most stores in Manhattan closed early."

"The Saks on 5th Avenue closes at eight and Bloomingdales on Broadway closes at nine. You can buy something to wear before you start shopping." She handed him the card. "This was an early party, and should be over by nine." She then motioned for her driver to come over. "Issac, take Maverick wherever he wants to go."

Myles smiled widely.

"Yes, Ms. Ellington," Issac agreed then left to retrieve her car.

"Maverick, if you'd like, Brooklyn can keep you company. I'm sure she wants to get out of here as much as you do, too. She hates her dad's new toy."

Myles knew being in close proximity to Brooklyn would be a bad idea.

"That's okay, sweetie. I'd rather be alone. From the way she was acting earlier, she needs to be tortured."

They both laughed.

"You're bad, but I like it," Camilla whispered.

Myles leaned into her ear. "Make sure that pussy is extra wet for me later so that I can show you just how bad I can be." He pecked her on the cheek and playfully swiped his hand over the front of her dress. Remember, baby…the wetter the better."

He kissed her lips then walked off with a conniving smile on his face. He had Camilla in the palm of his hands.

Chapter Five

At ten p.m., Myles walked into Camilla's penthouse suite with a handful of shopping bags. Camilla didn't hear him come in as she twirled in front of the full mirror admiring her wedding dress that she was anxious to show off. This was a dream come true for her. After one failed attempt at jumping the broom, she'd given up on the likelihood of being happily married. She'd lost all hope and trust in men until Myles entered her life and showed her that true love was still possible.

"Isn't it bad luck for me to be seeing you in the dress now?" Myles startled her as he watched Camilla dance around like a blissful child.

"I'm too old for silly traditions. I wanted you to see it. Do you like it?"

Her cheeks were flushed red with excitement. Myles dropped the bags on the floor and walked up to her. He gazed into her eyes and she returned the look.

"I love it, but it would look much better once it's...off," he responded.

Seconds later, he ripped the dress from her body, then disappeared under her neck.

"Maverick, have you lost your damn mind?" Camilla shrieked as she stepped out of the ruined dress and backed away from him. "This is a custom-made Reem Acra wedding gown! I spent fifty thousand dollars for this!" Camilla snatched the dress up from the floor and proceeded to inspect the damage.

At that moment, Myles yanked it from her hands, tossed it

across the room then backed Camilla into the mirror.

"Maverick what the hell is wrong with you? There's a huge rip in the back and all the beading fell off!" she yelled.

"So what. You're loaded. Just buy another one." He removed her strapless bra, then tossed it with the dress. He then kissed Camilla from her neck to her belly button. "That's the beauty of being a successful business woman. You can easily replace things."

"B-B-But…" Camilla stammered, but quickly lost her voice when Myles spread her legs apart and blew his warm breath into her wet spot.

Camilla's thighs trembled. When Myles noticed, he stood up and turned her around. Her face was plastered against the mirror. Camilla watched Myles step back and maul her with his eyes. When she tried to turn around, he ordered her not to. She watched him as he slowly undressed. Her eyes stayed glued on the silver tie that he slowly pulled from around his neck. Camilla's body shivered with excitement because she knew what was coming next. After approaching her, he grabbed her hair and forcefully yanked it. Moments later, he wrapped the tie around her neck, then gently pulled when he saw her eyes give him the go ahead. Her life was in his hands, but that was a chance she was willing to take…again.

Myles reached his left hand around Camilla's waist then between her thighs. She moaned when his fingers entered her. He squeezed the tie tighter. Myles watched as she seductively begged for her life in the mirror. Once he turned her around to face him, Myles allowed her a quick breath then lifted her off of the floor. Camilla wrapped her legs around his waist. She screamed when he unleashed his weapon inside of her. He loved the fact that she could hardly handle him.

Myles grabbed her hands and placed them above her head. He then locked his hands around her wrists so that she couldn't move. Her mouth wanted his so she pushed her head toward him, but Myles wouldn't allow it. He yanked at the tie.

"Obey," he ordered.

She nodded as Myles circled the tie around his hand as far as it would go. Camilla could barely breathe. At that moment, he parted her lips with his tongue, and kissed her. Myles felt Camilla wiggle her fingers, but didn't release his hold. She didn't want him to either, but her body was reacting naturally to the fact that she wasn't getting any air. She moaned helplessly inside his mouth as Myles pounded her pussy as fast and as hard as he could. He had to make sure they both had an orgasm before giving back her freedom. He stared at Camilla to see if she was okay. She was at the brink of passing out, but he was too turned on and far too caught up in the moment to stop. When her left leg unhinged from around his waist, Myles finally had to release the tie in order to keep her in the position.

"Maverick! Maverick! Slow down!" Camilla cried out to him once she caught her breath and the color returned in her face.

Myles ignored her. Instead of slowing down, he actually increased his speed. He then wrapped his hands around her throat. Camilla's eyes bucked but she didn't say a word as Myles pounded her like a jack hammer against concrete. Seconds later, Myles quickly pulled out. Both of them collapsed to the floor. Camilla watched as he jerked his dick back and forth.

"Oh shitttttttt," Myles said as the thick white cum exploded from his manhood.

It took several minutes for Myles to get himself together. Once he did, he noticed Camilla rubbing her neck in a circular motion. Ever since they'd met, Myles often had rough, fetish type sex with Camilla. However, this time Myles wondered if he'd gone too far. When he approached her, she quickly hopped to her feet.

"I'm going to take a shower," she spoke.

"I'll join you."

"Not this time."

Camilla retreated to the bathroom. Her actions were proof that he'd definitely gone too far. When he heard the shower start, Myles went to join Camilla against her wishes, but the door was locked. He tapped on it, but she didn't respond. He'd have to wait until she came out.

In the meantime, Myles slipped back into his boxers, walked up to the bar and pulled the bottle of Perrier-Jouet champagne from the wine cooler. Once he opened it, instead of pouring the champagne in a glass, Myles drank the expensive liquid directly from the bottle. He knew if Camilla had caught him, she'd have a hissy fit. Myles also knew he had to fix things with her and apologize for getting carried away. When he first introduced the fetish sex idea to her, she was hesitant, but eventually warmed up to it. After a while, Camilla couldn't get enough. Her orgasms were normally ferocious when asphyxiation came into play. But Myles realized this time she didn't even cum, which was another sign that something was off.

Nearly halfway into the bottle, Myles heard the shower stop then seconds later, the door opened. He quickly poured her a glass of champagne and met her at the door with it.

"What's this for?" she asked when he handed her the flute.

"A peace offering. I'm sorry about…"

"I just don't understand why I'm not worthy of your seeds," she said after yanking the flute from his hand causing some of the champagne to spill out.

Myles was completely confused. "I don't understand."

"Oh, don't act stupid. You pulled out of me."

"So, y-you're not mad about the choking thing?" he stammered.

"What? Oh…no! I loved that part."

"But you didn't cum."

"Yeah, I know. That was a bit weird, but I love it when you're freaky. Maybe we should even get some whips and chains."

Still shocked, Myles placed the bottle up to his lips. But before he could drink from it, Camilla yanked it from his hand then handed him her glass.

"Maverick, I just want us to be as one. I don't ever want you to pull out of me. Why did you do that?"

Myles shrugged his shoulders. "I don't know. I guess I was just caught up in the moment."

"Look, I don't want you to be afraid that I'm going to get pregnant or anything. Not only am I too old to have kids at fifty-six years old, but I could never bear children anyway. I've wanted kids all my life, but it just never happened for me. That's why I treat Brooklyn like my daughter." She lowered her head. "The hotels are my kids now. That's why I named this one, Bella. I always loved that name for a girl."

She'd never opened up about that before. Knowing she was at

a vulnerable state, Myles used that to his advantage.

"Maybe we can talk about adopting once we get married," he suggested.

Camilla's eyes lit up. "Really, baby?"

"Absolutely. Why should you go through life without being a mother?"

It looked like she wanted to cry. "I thought about adopting once, but just never went through with it."

"Well, don't rule it out just yet. I would love to have a child with you," he added. Myles planted a soft kiss on her lips. "And I'm sorry for pulling out. That will never happen again."

Camilla could feel her clitoris getting excited as Myles led her to the bed, pulled the covers back, then helped her inside. He slipped in behind her and wrapped his arms around her waist.

"I love you, Camilla."

"I love you, too, Maverick."

"Even though we're both super busy in our lives, I think you would make a great mom."

"Thank you, I appreciate that." Camilla slid her fingers between his. "Speaking of being busy, how did the modeling job in Toronto go last week?"

Myles coughed because he was caught off guard. Luckily, he was quick on his feet. "Baby, it didn't go well at all. You're not gonna believe this," he laughed. Camilla turned to him. "My agent tried to cast me in a damn dog food commercial."

She turned to face him. "Are you serious?"

"Yeah, I gave her a piece of my mind though. I told her that she'd better not ever pull another stunt like that again. I'm not some rookie trying to make a quick buck. I've worked fashion week in Paris and New York just to name a few."

"You told her, sweetie. Now, if you want, you can fire her and I can get you hooked up with a different agent; one that will definitely have your face all over the world."

"I love you for that, Camilla but I'm fine with the agent that I have."

"Well, when I become Mrs. Maverick Lewis, you can quit altogether because you'll never have to work another day in your life,"

Camilla stated before turning back over so that he could hold her. "Things are only going up for us, Maverick. It was more than fate that I met such a loving man."

At the mention of their first encounter, Myles took a stroll down memory lane. He was at the gym when the local news came on. He stopped running on the treadmill when Camilla's face filled the screen. Myles was instantly taken aback by her beauty and when she spoke, it was like music to his ears. She was visiting Charlotte to donate money to Carolinas Healthcare Foundation, an organization geared to help Levine Children's Hospital. Myles needed to investigate as to why this was a newsworthy story.

He ended his workout and hurried to his car to Google Camilla on his phone. Fireworks ignited as he learned that she was a serious, wealthy businesswoman. He was intrigued by her rags to riches story, but focused more on the riches.

Although he didn't want to be surrounded by a bunch of sick kids, Myles knew he had to suck it up to achieve his goal. He hurried home, freshened up and dressed to impress. He was happy that Kenya wasn't home. He didn't need his mission to be halted with questions.

Thirty minutes later, he arrived at the hospital. Apparently, there was an event going on for the kids because there were hundreds of people in the lobby walking around with toys, cotton candy and balloons. Looking through the crowd of several Sesame Street characters, Myles figured it would be a huge task to find Camilla. But luck was on his side. He spotted her a few minutes later, bouncing a baby in her arms.

Myles didn't waste any time. He immediately headed over and struck up a conversation with her. Like the professional liar he was, Myles told her that his modeling agency had sent him to the event to donate as well. Once Camilla found him intriguing, they ended up finding a quiet corner where they talked at least an hour. Camilla agreed to meet Myles later on that night over drinks at the Westin Hotel. By her third Dry Martini, Camilla was an open book. They eventually swapped stories about their abusive childhoods. Camilla's parents abandoned her along with her brother at the age of seven and she was bounced around from foster home to foster home until she landed in a group home. He could tell that her childhood was a touchy subject for her so Myles made sure to comfort her as much as he could. Several hours later, Myles was providing Camilla with the best orgasm she'd had in years. Just like he'd done with Kenya, he'd won Camilla over as well.

"I'm living out my dream," Camilla interrupted his trance. "It was a hard road trying to get here, but I'm here. I now own three hotels and I'm on my way to owning four. There's no stopping me, Maverick and I want you right by my side living this dream with me." Her words caused a cunning smile to form on his face and his dick instantly rose. "Baby, you're ready for round two already?" Camilla asked with a welcoming smile.

"He's always happy to be around you," Myles replied.

"Mav, Brooklyn keeps asking questions about you." Camilla breathed a bothersome sigh. She apparently wasn't ready for another round of sex.

Myles' hard-on softened at the mention of Brooklyn's nosiness. "What kind of questions?"

"Things like how much do I really know about you and she's been really adamant the past few weeks about me getting a prenup."

Myles' heart rate increased. "Oh really."

Camilla nodded her head.

"Well, baby, if she feels that strongly about it then maybe you should, but the decision is up to you." He prayed that the reverse psychology worked.

"Baby, I trust you. As much as I love you, I would never consider such a thing like that. I don't allow other people's opinions to get in my way. What is mine will be yours and vice versa. I know you won't do anything to hurt me like the others did."

Myles breathed a sigh of relief.

"Maybe Brooklyn shouldn't be in the wedding. It's obvious that she is jealous," he suggested.

"Maybe she is, but she's my niece, Maverick. I can't do that."

"Well, maybe we should forget about the big wedding in Anguilla and just go somewhere and elope?"

Camilla frowned. "Elope? Are you kidding me? I want the world to witness my happiness. I've put too much money into this anyway."

"I guess you have a point."

"Don't worry. Everything will be fine. Brooklyn will eventually come around."

She better or I'll make sure to get rid of that bitch if she gets in my way, Myles thought.

Chapter Six

The following afternoon, Myles and Camilla browsed around inside the Cartier jewelry store for Myles' wedding ring. For Myles, the task was tedious because everything seemed to spark her interest. He'd already picked out his ideal ring: a striking, white gold ring with paved diamonds and black ceramic.

"Baby, I would love to see this watch on your wrist," Camilla addressed after receiving the 18-karat Roadster Chronograph from the saleswoman.

The smile on Camilla's face gleamed bright as she presented the watch to Myles. She wanted to keep him happy because in the short time they'd known each other she was constantly showering him with gifts.

"Baby, I don't need another watch. You just bought me a Breitling, remember?" Myles reminded.

"Just try it on. A man shouldn't have just one watch," she convinced.

Myles naughtily shook his head at her as he grabbed the timepiece. It was a beauty, and he had every intention of accepting the ten thousand dollar gift. He just wanted her to feel like he wasn't the type of man who used women. That method always worked.

As Myles admired the watch, his eyes quickly widened. "Is the time on this correct?" he asked.

"Yes, it is," the saleswoman confirmed.

It was 1:35p.m. He'd missed his flight back to Charlotte.

"Shit," Myles stated under his breath.

He'd completely lost track of time. Also, he'd been so wrapped up with Camilla that it never even crossed his mind that he hadn't called Kenya. To make matters worse, after thinking about it even more, Myles realized that he must've left the white i-Phone he talked to Kenya with at home and that was why he hadn't heard from her.

"Is everything okay?" Camilla asked. "You look like you've seen a ghost."

"Everything is fine, sweetie," Myles said. He needed to secure another flight home. "Baby, can we go ahead and wrap things up...quickly?"

"Give me a few more minutes, Maverick. I want to check on this diamond bracelet that I've had my eyes on for a while."

Camilla whisked off to a different counter while Myles stayed back and tried to figure out what he would tell Kenya when he arrived home. While Camilla shopped, Myles secured a flight back to Charlotte on his phone that was due to leave in three hours. He needed to figure out a way to let Camilla know that he had to leave.

"Would you like for me to go ahead and wrap the watch for you, sir?" the saleswoman addressed Myles.

"Of course," Myles replied while smiling at her. "As a matter-of-fact, go ahead and add that one, too." He pointed to the stainless steel watch with the alligator strap. The saleswoman pulled it from the case and handed it to him.

"This particular one is $7,100.00," she informed.

"Oh, the price doesn't matter. Just wrap it up," he said while winking at her.

Forty-five minutes later, Myles and Camilla walked out of the jewelry store and entered her chauffeured, Mercedes Maybach. Once they were seated and en route back to the hotel, Kenya entered Myles' mind again. As much as he wanted her to sell the company, a part of him liked the fact that she'd missed the meeting. The last thing Myles wanted was for Kenya to be hanging around the house all the time knowing that he'd have to continue his trips to New York. With the wedding nearing, he knew Camilla would want to see more of him and would eventually convince him to quit the fake modeling job.

"Is there somewhere more important you'd rather be, Maverick?" Camilla interrupted his thoughts.

"Huh?"

44

"Is there someone else you'd rather be with because it seems you have checked out with me," she added.

"That's nonsense, Camilla and you know it. I was just thinking about how I was supposed to give my agent a call about a modeling job. You've had my undivided attention and I completely forgot about the call." Myles gently pulled her hand to his lips and kissed it. "You do that to me…make me forget things." As Camilla blushed, Myles pulled his private bat line phone from his pocket. "Shoot! I missed five calls from Dana," he said, making sure that Camilla couldn't see the phone screen. "I need to call her back in case she has a good job for me."

"No problem honey. Handle your business."

Myles turned away from her and pretended to make a call.

"Dana, it's My…Maverick." Myles regrouped quickly from nearly saying his other name. "Are you serious? When? Yes, go ahead and set it up…I'll talk to you soon, Dana."

"Sounds like good news," Camilla spoke solemnly because she knew Myles would be disappearing soon.

"Great news, baby! I just landed a shoot for Rag and Bone and need to leave for L.A. immediately," Myles continued to lie. He had to get home to Kenya and knew the only way to get away from Camilla was to pretend he had another job offer lined up.

"Rag and Bone? What the hell is that?"

Myles smiled, forgetting about Camilla's age. "It's Justin Timberlake's new clothing line."

"Oh…I see. Guess I need to be more hip, huh?" she joked before pouting. "Baby, I thought I'd have you for at least a few more days."

"In due time, you'll have me forever." Myles leaned over and pecked Camilla on the lips.

"I'm sorry for being so selfish and inconsiderate, Maverick. It's just that when you're with me, I want all of your attention and vice versa. This distance is killing me as well as your sporadic modeling jobs."

Myles kissed her again.

"Baby, I know your life has been filled with abandonment and disappointments, but things are different now. I'd never abandon you.

45

I'd never disappoint you. We've both experienced those things, but now we have each other to hold on to and love." Myles could tell that she was hanging on to every one of his words. "The distance and time away is killing me, too, but this is my life. I have to live it."

Camilla listened to each of Myles' words. Although she understood, she still wasn't satisfied. Myles was right; she had serious disappointment and abandonment issues. Her parents chose drugs over her. Going from one foster home to the next, she was even abused and molested in a few of them. She eventually settled in a group home where she shockingly found peace. Camilla was smart and sharp as a knife and landed a scholarship at a few prominent colleges. She chose Stanford University where she met, Dustin Lange, during her move into the dorm. His daughter was Camilla's roommate. Before he departed, Dustin requested that the two ladies join him for dinner. Camilla was adamant at first because she'd never been around Caucasian people, but the daughter, Rebecca, convinced her to join them.

Camilla learned that Dustin owned a chain of hotels and was rich. In the midst of the talks, laughter and get-to-know, Rebecca excused herself to use the restroom. Camilla was flattered and caught off guard when Dustin made a pass at her. Needless to say, they fooled around behind Rebecca's back and a few months into their secret courtship, Dustin asked Camilla to marry him. Camilla thought nothing of the age difference. She was eighteen and he was forty-one. She was in love so she agreed to the marriage, quit school and moved to Brentwood, California to be with him.

The marriage was all flowers and bunnies in the beginning until Dustin began to show his other side. He became verbally and physically abusive toward Camilla. He'd even bring women to their home and make Camilla sleep in the guest bedroom while he and his friend would sleep in the master. Camilla had nowhere to go. She didn't have a penny to her name and no family to fall back on. She dealt with the abuse for nearly ten years until one day she'd had enough when he caused her third miscarriage. She left and filed for divorce. She took him for nearly half of his estate and ironically, Rebecca helped her get it.

During her marriage to Dustin, Camilla learned a lot about Dustin's business affairs and decided to follow his footsteps and invest in the hotel chain business. The decision proved to be a prominent one. Although the money made her happy, Camilla still longed to fill the hole in her heart...love. She accepted two marriage proposals; one at the age of thirty-five and the other at the age of forty-three. She ended them both due to cheating, lying, thieving and neglect. She was done with finding love until it found her and Maverick was his name.

"Baby, did you get lost in your thoughts over there?" Myles interrupted her trance.

"No, baby, I'm still here. I understand what you're saying about your life, but in the meantime, why don't you move to New York with me. I've made that suggestion a few times before. That way, the distance won't be a problem. When you're home, you'll be home with me."

"Camilla, I told you, I'm old fashioned. I don't want to live together until we're married."

"Old fashioned? But we have sex!" Camilla laughed.

Myles knew he needed to skate through that particular conversation as he'd done on other occasions.

"Baby, just let everything continue to fall into place like they're doing. No need to rush. Now, let me make this flight reservation to L.A., but before I do, let me leave you with something so that you'll miss me when I'm gone."

After rolling up the frosted glass so Issac couldn't see, Myles took his hand and placed it under her body hugggging Emilio Pucci dress. He then pushed her panties to the side, and placed his thick middle finger into her nest. His lips curved upon witnessing Camilla's struggle to breathe while he moved his finger in and out at a slow pace. Seconds later, Myles pulled out. Camilla watched intensely as he brought the finger up to his mouth and placed it inside. He hummed before withdrawing. And all Camilla could do was shake her head. She was definitely in love.

Later that evening,
Myles pulled into his garage and frowned when he saw Kenya's black BMW X6.

"Damn!" he huffed loudly.

Myles hoped that Kenya was probably at Jada's house checking on her. He wanted a little time to himself before she ripped into him about not calling her and not returning home when he was supposed to. He wasn't ready to hear Kenya's nagging or Zoie's crying.

Myles pulled his duffle bag and rolling luggage from his trunk. He ended up having to purchase the luggage after all the new items he'd acquired on his shopping spree. After sighing one last time, he rolled the luggage into the house. The lights were out so he assumed Kenya and Zoie were asleep.

"Good. Maybe I can get a little peace after all," he mumbled before flipping on the lights in the kitchen.

Myles stopped dead in his tracks when he saw Kenya sitting at the table with a serious, yet angry expression on her face. He immediately dropped the bags.

"So what are you saying? You don't get any peace around here?"

"Kenya, I…"

"Save that shit! You lied to me, Myles. You gave me your word that you'd be here. I had to reschedule the meeting because of you. Zoie was whining so much, that I couldn't even take her with me."

"Kenya, I'm so sorry, baby," he pleaded. "But why didn't you just have one of the female employees look after Zoie while you were in the meeting? You shouldn't have missed it regardless. We just agreed on a purchase price. You don't want the potential buyers to change their minds, do you?"

Kenya was furious. "Are you serious right now? You've got a lot of damn nerve coming in here telling me what *I* should've done. What about you? What the fuck did you do today to make my life any easier? Did you make it here on time…no. Besides, I told you that Zoie was fussy. I don't like taking her out like that," she blasted. "And why are you late? Why didn't you bother to call?"

"Kenya…"

Before he could continue, Kenya slid his white iPhone across the table. He caught it before it hit the floor.

"So, did you leave your phone on purpose?" she continued her tirade.

"If you'd let me get a word in, I could explain." Kenya folded her arms and allowed him to speak his peace. "There was a layover due to bad weather. That's why I'm late, Kenya, I'm sorry, baby. I really am. I didn't know that I left my phone until this morning when I woke up. When I checked into my hotel last night I crashed after being so wrapped up into this kid all day who's a damn good point guard."

Myles realized that he'd made a major slip up and couldn't afford to make the same mistake of leaving his white phone again. Myles then panicked slightly when he didn't feel the wedding band on his finger. Evidently, Kenya hadn't noticed because she would've immediately called him on it. He turned around and knelt next to his carry-on bag. He then unzipped the pocket, retrieved the ring and slipped it on without her knowledge.

"You could've found a way to call me today *after* you realized your phone was missing, Myles. I can't believe you went all day yesterday and today without checking on your family. Plus, I never know what hotels you're staying in. Why is that?" Kenya continued to hammer.

"Most times, I never know what hotel I'm gonna stay at until I get there."

"That's a poor fucking excuse."

"Kenya, what do you want me to do? What do you want me to say? I made a mistake!"

"A mistake was accidently leaving your phone. Being a bad father is not a fucking mistake. That's a problem!" Kenya yelled.

"I'm not a bad father, Kenya. I just had so much going on, that's all. I promise I'll make it up to you," he replied. Myles knew at that point that he had to act like he cared. "So, where is my princess? Is she asleep?"

"No, she's not."

"Then where is she?"

"She's with Jada."

Myles looked displeased. "Why?"

"Why not? Jada is her Godmother."

"Why would you leave our daughter with someone who's

49

dying?" Myles questioned snidely.

Kenya's eyebrows shot up and her mouth widened. She couldn't believe him. Myles had gone too far.

"How dare you say that?" Kenya exclaimed. "You have no right to speak of my friend like that! She wanted to spend time with Zoie today, and I didn't see a problem with it. If she's well enough to come and get her to give me a break from time to time, then so be it. Hell, at least somebody besides me wants to spend time with her."

"It's true, Kenya and you know it. Jada can hardly take care of herself, so I don't understand why you would leave a newborn with her." Myles walked to the refrigerator and pulled out a bottle of apple juice. Kenya was outraged at his nonchalant attitude and insensitivity about her friend. Myles noticed her eyes filling up with tears. "What are you crying for? I'm only telling you the truth about Jada."

"That's not the only reason I'm crying, Myles."

"Then why are you crying, Kenya?"

"You...us," Kenya sniffled.

"What are you talking about?"

"You used to be this sweet, loving, sensitive man. Now, I don't seem to know you anymore. You've changed, Myles."

Myles drank from the apple juice bottle. He wasn't in the mood for the conversation, but knew he had to engage in it. Yes, he'd changed because his life was changing. Basically, he changed because the money changed.

"You talk about my weight, you make me feel insecure, and you seem so secretive lately." Kenya wiped the tears that rolled down her cheek.

"You're just paranoid, babe. When was the last time you talked to your doctor? You may be going through that postpartum depression shit. You need to find a hobby or something or go back to work full time instead of every now and then. Shit, maybe you shouldn't sell the company if you're gonna act like this."

Kenya didn't appreciate the undiagnosed illness. She also didn't appreciate the rush back to work suggestion either.

"There's nothing wrong with me, Myles," she snarled between sniffles.

"Baby, you're cooped up in this house all day with Zoie. You need to get out more."

"Maybe I am being a little crazy. I even feel like someone has been following me around lately. That's probably why I'm a little upset."

"Following you? Yeah, now I know you need to go back to work full time." Myles chuckled.

"I'm serious, Myles. I always see this silver Toyota following behind my car every time I go out, and it's making me feel a little eerie."

"Again...that's called paranoid, Kenya and that's a crazy reason to be upset. Do you know how many silver Toyota's are in this city?"

"You may be right. Why would anyone be following me anyway?" She shrugged it off.

Myles walked up to Kenya and pulled her in his arms. Myles knew he needed to work on Kenya's self esteem before her mind began to wander about other things. "Maybe you and Jada could take a vacation or something."

Kenya managed a smile.

"You'd do that, baby. You'd watch Zoie while Jada and I..."

"Hold up! I didn't say anything about keeping Zoie. She would definitely be going with you. You know I don't do diapers and shit," Myles added.

"I knew that idea was too good to be true," Kenya sighed as she eyed Myles' extra luggage. "Myles, you left here with only a carry-on bag."

"Oh, I bought a few things while I was in Chicago."

Kenya stepped away from him.

"I thought you were tired? So, you found time to go shopping, but you couldn't find a fucking phone to call your worried wife to let her know that you were okay?"

Myles knew he was digging himself a deeper hole. He needed to plug it before he was kicked into it.

"The high school wasn't far from the mall, so during a small break, I picked up a few things," he replied. Myles grabbed the rolling luggage piece, opened it and pulled out a small bag. "I picked this up for you while at the airport."

"The airport? So, you have Saks and Bloomingdale's bags and I get something from the damn airport?" Kenya was insulted when she pulled out a *Shape* magazine.

"There's a great article and tips in there about how to lose baby weight, I thought you'd like to read it." Kenya threw the magazine at him. "What in the hell is wrong with you?" Myles asked.

"Fuck you, Myles. I know I'm overweight right now, but you don't have to keep throwing it up in my face! You know I'm trying to get myself back together."

"It doesn't seem like you're trying hard enough to me."

Myles took another sip of apple juice. If Kenya's eyes could shoot bullets, he'd be dead.

"So, why is the mortgage company calling about past due bills?" Kenya questioned.

Myles choked on the juice. "What? When did they call?"

"It doesn't matter when they called. The problem is that they shouldn't be calling. So, are you not paying the mortgage?"

Myles looked at her with an 'are you kidding me look'. "Kenya don't insult me like that. Of course I'm paying the mortgage. I'm sure it's a mistake, but I'll check on it. Don't worry your pretty little head about it. Okay?"

He stepped up to Kenya and kissed her on the forehead. Kenya was still slightly worried about the call, but decided to leave it up to Myles to take care of it.

"Now, since all of that has been cleared up, can you tell me why you were in Aspen two days after Zoie was born when you were supposed to be in Cleveland?" she questioned suspiciously.

Myles' heart stopped beating and he nearly dropped the apple juice bottle.

Chapter Seven

The following day, Kenya and Jada decided to do lunch at Krazy Fish restaurant. One of Jada's cancer buddies introduced Jada to the spot and she, in turn, introduced it to Kenya. It was a little shabby for Kenya's taste, but it grew on her the more she and Jada visited. The fact that Jada loved it weighed heavy on Kenya's like for the establishment as well. She wanted to keep her friend happy and spend as much time with her as she could. Kenya even offered to pick Jada up to ride to the restaurant with her, but Jada declined. Kenya knew the day would be filled with laughter when Jada said to her, "Bitch, I ain't dead yet. I can still drive."

"Thank you," Kenya addressed the waitress when she placed their dishes in front of them. Kenya's eyes immediately locked onto Jada's bowl of shrimp and grits. "I don't know why I don't just get the shrimp and grits when we come in here. That looks so good."

"You're the one who keeps getting those crazy ass salads. Stop letting Myles put pressure on you about your weight," Jada replied before picking up a spoon full of grits. "Speaking of Myles, where is he now?"

"Playing golf." Kenya sighed as she glanced down at her dry looking chef salad.

"So, he couldn't even keep the baby while you went out for lunch."

Kenya shook her head. "I didn't even ask him; didn't want to hear his mouth."

"See, I have a real fucking problem with the fact that you just used the word, *asked*. You shouldn't have to *ask* Zoie's father to babysit."

Kenya looked like she wanted to cry after placing a fork full of lettuce in her mouth. At that moment, Jada decided to change the subject.

"Why don't you revisit the idea of opening up your own restaurant?" she asked. "You would blow a lot of these chefs out of the water with your cooking, Kenya."

"I really want to, but I feel bad about no longer wanting the family business. My dad is probably turning over in his grave," Kenya said then turned to Zoie when she cooed.

"That baby smells these grits I'm over here eating," Jada joked. "Seriously though, Kenya, it's time for you to start living *your* life and stop worrying about everybody else."

Jada's words caused Kenya to think about her parents' dream and how hard her father worked to build the only black owned marketing company on the east coast. She knew that if he was still alive, the thought of selling the company would never be an option.

"Why even feel bad about selling, Kenya when the company is not doing well anyway?" Jada continued. "You should want to get out of this while you still can and get some money out of it to start living your own dream."

"It's easier said than done, Jada," Kenya responded. "Myles wants me to sell, too but I'm just not sure. At first he was against me selling, but now he's pushing the idea."

Jada dropped her spoon into her bowl. "To hell with what Myles wants you to do," she barked softly. "It's *your* company, which means it's *your* decision. He's not affiliated with Creative Minds and don't give me that 'when you're married shit'."

"Jada, Myles and I have to be in agreement. We have to discuss things before decisions are made. That's how a marriage works."

"His ass wants you to sell because he knows his pennies don't amount to shit. Is his recruiting checks gonna keep you in that nice, four bedroom house out in Ballantyne? Or what about your nice cars and clothes when the company falls apart and you have to file bankruptcy?"

"Damn, Jada! You didn't have to take it that far."

"I'm just keeping it real because I care about you and Zoie.

When I leave this earth, I want to go knowing that you two are okay."

Kenya forced back tears as she listened to Jada's sorrowful words. She reached across the table to grab her friend's hand. "I hate when you talk like that."

"Well, it's the truth."

"What in the hell am I gonna do with you?" Kenya questioned.

"Not a damn thang." They both laughed. "I just want you to be happy even if that means getting rid of Myles so that you can get your life back."

"Speaking of Myles..."

"Ah hell!" Jada exclaimed while throwing up her hands to add to the effect. "Please don't let him ruin this lunch."

"It's not what you think, Jada. I called him out on that plane ticket receipt we found."

Jada leaned in closer.

"Oh now your ass is interested," Kenya said.

"What happened, Kenya? What lie did he tell this time?"

"It was a misunderstanding on my part."

Jada stared at her friend, then rolled her eyes. "There you go taking blame for shit. I really need you to stop being so damn naïve."

"No, seriously, it was a misunderstanding. I confused his Aspen trip with his Cleveland trip that was a few weeks after."

"I don't trust it. He *recruits* and *scouts* too damn much for me," Jada stressed suspiciously.

"Jada, you have to give him credit. The man's NBA dreams were crushed when he tore his ACL in college so he has to live out his dream some way."

"Have you seen the damn X-rays?"

Kenya couldn't help but laugh.

"I'm serious, Kenya. I don't have to give him credit for shit if there's no proof."

At that point, Kenya knew there was no way she would get Jada to agree with her so she changed the subject.

"Enough about me and Myles, what's going on with you?" Kenya asked after lifting Zoie from the carrier.

"Well, I didn't want to bother you with what I've been doing

55

since you have so much going on right now," Jada said while retrieving an iPad mini from her tote bag, then powering it on.

"I'm insulted. What's been going on besides the chemo and radiation treatments?"

"I started this blog about my experiences with cancer."

Jada handed the iPad to Kenya so that she could read the first few entries.

1/16/2013- Going into chemo this week was very nerve wrecking for me. I really didn't have a good reaction after the first one, and the one thing that I've been told by my doctors over, and over is that chemo builds in your system that's how it works. The worst part is that I'm still feeling side effects from the first round. Lord, I just want a week away from hospitals, and more time to spend with friends and family. I just want to pretend for ONE week that I'm not "sick." I've also been experiencing swelling in my left leg. I mean really can I please just catch a break. At this point anything that could make me remotely feel like a normal person I'll gladly take.

2/7/2013- I've been to the doctors enough times in the past six months to last me a lifetime. At this point you would think it would be a breeze, and that I never get nervous anymore. However, I hate to break it to you all, but that never happens. It's something about the name "Oncologists" that will never rest easy with me. In fact, every time I go to that office I read the name, thinking in my head I can't believe this is my life right now. As much as I would love to close this chapter in my life, I don't think it's ever going to be that simple. In fact, one of my biggest fears is the thought of me living in fear for the rest of my life.

3/4/13- Going into chemo is such a pain. In addition, it's very hard on your body, and your veins. I always have a hard time when the nurses try to set me up, because my veins never cooperate. During my last chemo they had to stick me four times, before they found one that hadn't collapsed. Wow...I honestly can't believe I have to go through this right now. I often wonder what I did to deserve this. During the many nights of crying myself to sleep, I tell myself how closing the chapter to chemo is gonna be another check off my list. But I can't wait until I get to check off the biggest one of all, which is getting to live. No matter how much pain I'm in, that's one thing I'm thankful

My Counterfeit Husband

for everyday...living. The little things mean so much more now, and everyday is an accomplishment in the long run.

"Look, bitch, dry up those damn tears. Do you see me crying?" Jada teased.

Kenya grabbed a napkin and wiped away the tears while laughing. Kenya felt sorry for her friend because Jada had always been the sister she never had. She hated to see her going through any type of pain. Kenya watched her friend eat the last of her shrimp and grits and wondered how she'd manage if Jada was no longer around.

"Well...well, look who's here," Jada said while looking over Kenya's shoulder. "Damn, he's fine. I wonder if he's into frail bitches."

When Kenya turned around, the Controller of Creative Minds, Julius was headed toward their table. Kenya had to agree with Jada. Julius was very easy on the eye. He was like a tall glass of cold water in the summer time. Kenya tried to resist the urge to stare at him, but his smooth, chestnut skin, low, tapered fade full of natural curls, and Crest smile were making it difficult to do so. Kenya glanced at Jada who smiled cunningly.

"Hey, Julius," Kenya spoke.

Jada noticed that Kenya had tensed up when she saw Julius. Julius' demeanor was a little off as well. The sparks between the two were so evident.

"Hi, Kenya. Hi, Jada," Julius spoke to them both before directing his attention back to Kenya. "Are you okay?" he asked with a hint of concern in his voice.

"Yes, why do you ask?"

"It looks like you've been crying. Your eyes are red," he responded. "Can I get you something?"

Kenya's heart warmed at Julius' concern. She smiled internally. Jada, on the other hand, didn't care who saw her smile.

"Oh!" Kenya said. "Jada had me laughing and you know how she can be. She'll have you in tears."

"Yes, I know. Before you had the baby, every time she came up to the office, she would have everyone in stitches," Julius agreed before turning to the female standing next to him then back at Kenya. "This is my friend, Alexia."

57

Immediately, Kenya wanted to crawl under a rock and die. Alexia was a bombshell. She was tall and thin like a model with a thousand dollar weave and eyes that would make any man dive into them.

"Hi, Alexia. I'm Kenya."

Kenya offered her hand to Alexia and she shook it with an 'I'm the shit and you're not' smile. Jada, on the other hand, didn't speak. She was too busy sizing Alexia up especially after seeing that wicked smile.

"She's getting so big," Julius spoke with a bright smile as he played with Zoie's hand. "And she's so pretty."

"Yeah, she's gorgeous, just like you," Jada boldly stated.

Kenya choked on her water while Julius tensed. Seconds later, Kenya kicked Jada under the table. Jada kicked her back.

"Umm, Kenya, I'm glad I ran into you. I wanted to let you know that the potential buyers had to reschedule the meeting to July 2nd." Julius did a good job at ignoring Jada's comment.

"That sounds great," Kenya replied.

"So, Kenya, that's a nice ring on your finger. How long have you and your husband been married?" Alexia questioned as she placed her arm in the crook of Julius'. She could see the obvious attraction Julius and Kenya had for each other.

Jada didn't give Kenya a chance to respond to Alexia's slight insult. "*Short* enough to be annulled," she sassed.

"Well, let's go ahead and get to our table," Julius suggested. As Alexia turned around and walked away, he locked eyes with Kenya one last time. "I'll talk to you soon."

"Okay," Kenya said as he walked off. She immediately turned to Jada. "You were so out of line."

"Whatever! Are you gonna just sit there and let that bitch walk away with my man like that?"

Kenya grinned. "He's not your man."

"Not now…but when I get rid of this cancer shit, he will be."

Kenya playfully rolled her eyes at Jada while staring back at Julius.

Twenty minutes later, Kenya sat in her car fumbling with the radio stations until she came across one of her old favorite songs that took her back to her and Jada's conversation.

"*Are you the man who loves and cherishes and cares for me? Is that you? Is that you?*" She sang along with Jennifer Hudson. "*Are you a guard in a prison, maximum security? Is that you? Is that you? Is that you?*

"Yeah, that is you, Myles," she said while pulling out of the restaurant's parking lot.

Jennifer Hudson's throwback song, *Spotlight* made Kenya realize that what Jada had been saying all along was true. Myles was controlling, but she loved him.

A few blocks into her drive, Kenya glanced into her rearview mirror so that she could cross into the turning lane. She didn't want to miss her turn. She paused when she noticed the silver, Toyota Avalon that she'd seen in her neighborhood a few times. She'd also seen it while running errands around the city but thought nothing of it until it started showing up around her house. She knew it was the same car because of the crack in the windshield. She became nervous and scared. She took small breaths to avoid an asthma attack. Kenya fumbled inside her purse for her inhaler in case something unexpected happened. Once located, she placed it in her lap. Kenya glanced in the backseat at Zoie. She was asleep. Moments later, Kenya quickly swerved into the right lane. She became frantic after the car swerved into the lane as well. Kenya picked up her phone and called Myles.

Hi, this is Myles Whitaker. Sorry I'm unavailable at the moment...

"Your ass is never available!" Kenya cursed at the phone when the voicemail came on.

Kenya's eyes were glued at the car in the mirror.

"Who are you? What do you want?" she asked the driver as if he or she could hear her.

Kenya was so distracted that she'd missed her turn and didn't even realize it.

She tried to call Myles again. But still...no answer. As she was about to call Julius, it dawned on her that he was on a possible date and didn't want to bother him. Instead, she called Myles again as she watched the car. To her surprise, this time he picked up.

"Why the hell do you keep blowing up my phone? I'm trying

to concentrate on this course," Myles barked.

Before Kenya could respond, she panicked after realizing she'd driven through a red light. Out of the corner of her eye, she saw a black SUV driving full force toward her within seconds.

"Mylessssss!" she screamed before the SUV made contact.

Chapter Eight

"I'm going to check on the patient in room 2256," a stout nurse informed as she walked away from the other nurses. Once inside the room, she checked the vital signs on the machine and the IV drip. "Hey there. I see you finally decided to wake up." The nurse smiled at Kenya as she watched her slowly open her eyes.

Kenya fought with the fluorescent light in the room as well as the sunlight beaming through the window. "W-Where am I?" Kenya asked. Her voice was scratchy and hoarse as she glanced at the blood pressure machine.

"You're at Mercy Hospital. You were involved in a pretty bad car accident."

"A car accident?" Kenya questioned. Suddenly, fear took control of her body. "Zoie! Zoie!" Kenya yelled. "Where's my daughter?"

Kenya tried to sit up, but the pain in her back and the excruciating headache caused her to fall back onto the pillow. She grabbed her head, hoping that would subdue the pain. No such luck.

"Where's my daughter? She was in the car with me!"

"Kenya, calm down," Julius said when he rushed to her side.

Kenya was startled by his presence. "Julius, what are you doing here? Where's Zoie? She was asleep in the backseat!"

"Ma'am, I'd like to give you a sedative to calm down," the nurse suggested.

"I don't want a damn sedative!" Kenya barked. "I want my daughter! Now, where is she?"

Julius stopped Kenya as she tried to yank the IV from her arm.

"Ma'am, I'll try and calm her down, but can you be on standby if we do need the sedative?" Julius said to the nurse. The nurse nodded. "Can you give us a little time alone?"

"Sure," the nurse agreed. She checked to see if the IV was secure then stepped out.

"Why do we need time alone, Julius? What are you about to tell me? Where is Zoie?"

Kenya's tears poured from her eyes like a running faucet. She fought Julius as she tried to sit up. He held her down.

"Kenya, please calm down."

"Is she dead? Oh God now, please don't tell me she's dead!" Kenya's voice was extremely loud.

"Ssssh. No, Zoie is fine," Julius assured. "She's downstairs in the cafeteria with Jada."

Kenya continued to cry…tears of happiness this time. "Are you sure?"

"Yes, I'm sure. Zoie didn't have a single scratch on her. The SUV that hit you, hit the driver's side not the passenger side so Zoie was lucky and so were you for that matter."

"What do you mean by that?"

"The doctors said that although you had a bad concussion, an asthma attack and several lacerations to your forehead from the shattered glass and airbag, things could've been a lot worse."

Kenya cried as she reflected on her parent's fatal accident.

"It's okay, Kenya. You're alive. Zoie is alive and I'm here." Julius stroked her hand.

"I'm just thinking about my parents being crushed by that 18-wheeler," Kenya said in a low tone.

Julius tried to comfort her. "Don't think like that, Kenya."

"I can't help it. I could've died the same way that they did."

"But you didn't. That's all that matters."

"I miss them dearly." Kenya's eyes instantly watered.

Julius stroked her bandaged forehead. "I can only imagine what you're going through. And I know it still hurts, but you have to stay strong for your daughter."

Kenya and Julius locked eyes as he gently squeezed her hand. Kenya felt slightly odd with Julius staring at her while she was bruised and bandaged. Kenya's breaths were fast. Julius intense, loving gaze was the culprit behind the state she was falling into. He needed to stop looking at her like that before she had another asthma attack.

"I'm just happy that you're okay, Kenya."

Before Kenya could repspond, Jada walked into the room with Zoie.

"You would think hospitals would have a better food selection since it may be some folks last meal," Jada joked.

Kenya was so happy to see the two of them. "Didn't you just eat?" she reminded after reaching out for Zoie. Her face grimaced from the pain.

"Girl, I threw all that shit up when I saw that SUV hit you. By the way, you owe me for a car cleaning." Jada laid Zoie next to Kenya so that she could be close to her daughter.

"Thank you, Lord?" she prayed.

"That is exactly who you need to be thanking." Jada laughed. "And this lil' feisty heifer almost yanked my scarf off of my head when we were in the cafeteria." Jada pretended to spank Zoie's thigh.

"So, you saw the accident?" Kenya asked ignoring Jada.

"Yes. I was a few cars behind when you ran that red light."

"I ran a red light?"

"Yes, but keep that on the hush hush. Rumor has it that the driver of the SUV had been drinking and thinks he ran the light and hit you," Jada informed.

"Is he okay?"

"He's fine, but the accident caused a chain reaction. It was like some final destination kinda shit. What made you run that light? Were you distracted?"

Kenya shook her head. "No...well I guess I did. I freaked out because I think someone's been following me. Did you see a silver Toyota Avalon behind me?"

"Yeah, I did. That was the only car able to avoid the accident actually. The person driving hauled ass too as soon as you made impact," Jada informed. "Why the hell didn't you tell me that shit, Kenya? I would've chased the damn car down if I'd known that."

Kenya wasn't up for the discussion since she didn't have any proof that the Toyota was actually following her. "Did anyone get hurt?" she questioned.

"Don't worry, everyone is fine," Julius said as he rubbed

Kenya's arm. "All that matters is that you're okay, too."

"Yeah, girl, I'm happy you're okay. You scared the shit out of me. I'm the one who's supposed to be laid up in the hospital with IVs and shit, not you."

Kenya smiled at Jada and squeezed her hand. "Where's Myles? Has anyone called him?"

Jada shook her head at the mention of Myles' name. "I called him several times, but he didn't answer. I was so pissed that I didn't even leave a message."

"Didn't leave a message? Then how is he supposed to know where I am?" Kenya looked around the room. "Where's my phone? Maybe he called me."

"Honey, your phone is probably still in your BMW and that's been towed," Jada answered. "He should've had enough sense to realize something may be wrong when my number popped up on his phone. I never call his ass to socialize. It doesn't matter though. The right man answered the phone. A real man is gonna come to your rescue." Jada winked at Julius.

"Jada, I'm not in the mood for this Myles bashing segment," Kenya moaned as she tried to shift positions. "Can you get Zoie? My back is killing me."

Jada lifted Zoie from the hospital bed. "So, where's your little girlfriend?" she questioned Julius.

"She's not my girlfriend, Jada."

"Then who is she?"

Julius smiled, showing a dimple in his left cheek. "Just a friend if you must know."

Before anymore words could be exchanged, Myles suddenly burst into the room in his green and yellow, Travis Mathew polo shirt with matching cap and dark grey slacks.

"What happened?" Myles asked, walking straight toward Kenya. "Are you okay? Are you hurt?"

Jada was surprised to see him and wondered how he knew Kenya was in the hospital. She gave him an 'I can't stand your ass' look as he showed an overly excessive concern toward Kenya. Jada felt that it was all an act since Julius was in the room.

"I called you over twenty times. Why didn't you answer the

phone? She could've been killed today," Jada interrogated. "Better yet, how did you know that she was here?"

Myles returned the look when he turned to answer Jada. "Not that it's any of your business, but one of my golf buddy's daughter works here. She called him when she saw Kenya being wheeled into the ER."

"You would've known she was here if you had answered my calls," Jada returned. "What took you so long to get here anyway? Kenya's been here for over two hours."

"Are you my fucking mother?" Myles growled.

"No, but I'm your wife's best friend."

"And you think that gives you the right to question me?" Myles fired back.

"Someone needs to question your shady ass since you have Kenya afraid to do so."

Myles barged over to Jada and snatched Zoie from her arms. "I don't want my child around your sickness."

"Cancer is not contagious, dumb ass," Jada retaliated.

"Dumb ass?" Myles laughed. "That cancer must've spread to your damn brain if you think you can talk to me like that."

"If anything, I'm speaking the truth and you hate that shit."

Myles stared at her with an evil set of eyes. If looks could kill, Jada's casket would be picked out. "When did the doctor say you're supposed to die because your demise is taking too damn long?"

"Now, that was uncalled for, Myles" Julius suddenly defended. He caught Jada in midair when she charged Myles.

By this time Kenya was in tears.

"First of all, why are you even here?" Myles questioned Julius while sizing him up. Ever since Julius was hired, Myles had never been too fond of him.

"I called him," Jada answered boldly. "Kenya needs a dependable man in her life not one who has to finish eighteen holes of fucking golf before coming to check on his wife and daughter."

"I'm not getting into this," Julius spoke.

"You should've never been here in the first place," Myles spat.

"If you had answered your phone, he wouldn't be," Jada spewed.

"I've had enough of your dying ass!" Myles spewed back.

"I think it's best that I leave," Julius stated.

"Yeah, that's a great idea," Myles agreed before turning to Jada. "You should leave, too, Sicko."

Jada was about to flip out on Myles again until she caught a glimpse of Kenya. She looked worn out and sad as she folded tissues to wipe her tears. Jada decided to hold her peace.

"I'm outta here," Jada added. She walked up to Myles to give Zoie a kiss, but Myles stepped back.

"My child doesn't need your germs."

"Myles, please…just stop it," Kenya finally said. "You're being an asshole!"

"Oh, don't worry about it Kenya. Me and this muthafucka will meet again," Jada threatened.

"Do you think you'll be around long enough to see that day?" Myles joked. Jada balled up her fists, bit her bottom lip then left. Myles then turned to Julius. "Now, it's your turn."

Julius huffed then walked over to Kenya.

"The door is the other way, dude," Myles spat.

Julius ignored Myles' remarks and faced Kenya. "Feel better soon. I'm here if you need me."

Kenya smiled and nodded as Julius walked out. "I really wish you and Jada would make peace with each other somehow," she said to Myles when he walked back over to her.

Kenya was caught off guard when Myles grabbed her by the neck and squeezed tightly. Her eyes widened in disbelief as she struggled for air. She tugged at Myles' arm and hands, but he wouldn't let up. Zoie playfully squirmed about in Myles' other arm while her mother fought for her life. Kenya didn't know what was going on and why it was happening. Myles had been verbally abusive at times, but never physical. Myles leaned into Kenya's ear.

"If you ever disrespect me in front of another nigga or your sick ass friend again, I will end you, bitch" he growled before releasing his grasp. *You don't want me to do a repeat of what I've done before*, he thought. Thinking about his past, Myles quickly removed his hand. Seconds later, he left the room with Zoie, leaving Kenya fighting for air.

Chapter Nine

Brooklyn sat in front of her computer scrolling through photos while waiting for one of the seamstresses from the Reem Acra boutique to come back to the phone. Brooklyn thought about the possibility of her getting married and if she'd act as crazy as Camilla or the girls on the show *Bridezillas*.

"Hello, Brooklyn?" a lady with a thick, Russian accent spoke into the phone.

Brooklyn clicked back onto Camilla's calendar. "Yes, Sasha, I'm here."

"You ladies put me in quite a pinch having to repair this dress at the last minute. I had to juggle a few customers around. Thankfully, they were all patient and understanding. But of course I had to fib a little." She chuckled.

"We apologize for that, Sasha, but my aunt will compensate you for your time."

"I know she will."

"Is the dress ready?"

"Ms. Ellington's dress will be finished tomorrow."

Brooklyn smiled and nodded her head as if Sasha could see that she was pleased. Brooklyn turned to the door when she heard it open. It was Camilla carrying a beautiful flower arrangement.

"We thank you so much for your services, Sasha and like I said, you will be compensated accordingly."

When the two ladies ended their call, Brooklyn typed the information onto Camilla's calendar.

"Aunt Camilla, your dress will be ready tomorrow."

Camilla set the bouquet on the table. "Great! Brooklyn, I don't know how I can ever repay you for helping me out since Lilly is on vacation. I'm happy you stay on top of things."

"I wear many hats, Aunt Camilla. I guess that's why you gave me the Director of Operations title."

They both laughed. Camilla picked through the flowers as if trying to make a decision.

"I can't decide between white orchids or peonies to go with my white, antique roses," Camilla spoke as she pulled an orchid from the array.

Brooklyn wasn't interested in the flowers. She wanted to know about the dress.

"When your dress arrived two weeks ago, it was perfect when you tried it on for me. What happened to it?"

Brooklyn cut her eyes at Camilla to find her lips slowly curving upward as if she had something to hide. Brooklyn had an idea there was more to the dress. Camilla's smile confirmed it for her. Camilla thought back to the night the dress was torn and blushed.

"I'm assuming Maverick had something to do with the dress being ruined?"

Camilla's smile moved upward a little further at the mention of Maverick's name.

"You act like a giggly schoolgirl whenever his name is mentioned," Brooklyn stated while slightly shaking her head. Brooklyn couldn't believe how her aunt acted over a man at her age.

"Brooklyn, I can't help it. He makes me so happy. I haven't been this happy in years."

"Don't you think you can be happy with someone around your age?"

Camilla frowned. "So, you think because I'm over fifty that I can't be happy with a man in his thirties?"

"I'm not saying that, Aunt Camilla. I'm just concerned because you're established and he's not. I think you may be in over your head."

"In over my head?" Camilla questioned and frowned harder.

"I feel that you may be rushing things because of your age and the failed relationships in your past."

"And all of this is coming from a woman who never goes out on dates," Camilla shot back.

"I'm not trying to upset you, Aunt Camilla. I..."

"Well, you have upset me!" Camilla yelled.

Brooklyn knew she should've left well enough alone after hearing the anger in Camilla's voice, but she couldn't. She was looking out for her aunt's safety and money. She'd watched nearly every Lifetime movie about a younger man taking advantage of an older woman and they ended in either, death, broken homes, broken hearts or poor.

"Aunt Camilla, didn't you say that Maverick worked for IMG modeling?"

"Not that it's any of your business...but yes." Camilla took out her frustration on the flowers. She tugged, pulled and yanked.

"Come over here for a sec," Brooklyn requested before clicking on the computer link she was looking at prior to speaking to Sasha.

Camilla blew a loud, drawn out sigh. She was tired of Brooklyn's *Inspector Gadget* ways and wondered why she wouldn't stay out of her relationship. It was more than evident that she was happy, so why couldn't Brooklyn be happy for her, too?

"What is it, Brooklyn?" Camilla questioned. She stood next to her niece and watched her scroll through several male model photos. Camilla was outraged. "Are you serious? Why are you doing this?"

"Aunt Camilla, just hear me out, please. Look at these pictures. I can't find Maverick anywhere. He's nowhere on the cover of those magazines you say he shot for either."

"Maybe you made a mistake. Maybe I misunderstood and it's not IMG modeling. Maybe it's something else," Camilla defended.

"Okay, I can deal with that, but what about the magazine covers?"

"I probably misunderstood about those too or you probably made a mistake."

Brooklyn was slightly insulted that Camilla would think that she could've made a mistake.

"Aunt Camilla, come on now. I don't make mistakes when it comes to things like this and you know it."

My *Counterfeit* Husband

"Everyone makes mistakes, Brooklyn," Camilla seethed.

"And maybe you're making one of them with Maverick."

Camilla was bothered by the aggression in Brooklyn's voice.

"Brooklyn, I don't want to fall out with you about this. I love you dearly. So, to keep from destroying our relationship, maybe you need to find something better to do with your time."

"I'm just trying to look out for you."

"And I certainly appreciate it. But why are you so concerned about this anyway? Answer that for me before we end this."

"I just don't want to see you get hurt. My mother has only been dead for a year and my father has already gone through two girlfriends who stole from him. And look what happened to you."

Camilla didn't want to travel back in time with her failed relationships.

"I appreciate that honey, but I'm not your dad. I learned my lesson. My brother is looking for someone to replace his wife. They were together for nearly thirty years. I can't fault him for that."

"Well, he's going about it the wrong way. He hasn't grieved. The women that he's been meeting are young and money hungry. They know that my dad is a high profile divorce attorney. It's no secret that he invests in residential and commercial property as well. He is stacking major paper. He's being stupid about things and I want him to stop before things get out of hand." Brooklyn's eyes filled with tears.

"Your dad is a grown man, Brooklyn."

"I know that and you're a grown woman. But that still doesn't mean I can't be concerned about you. Maverick is just as young as those women my father deals with and I don't want you to be blind to the fact that he may be doing the same thing."

"I get the sense that something else is bothering you about your dad."

"The night of the party for Bella Grand, my dad said that he wasn't going to be able to come because of a case, remember?"

Camilla nodded.

"And his girlfriend was supposed to show up, but didn't. She was actually on her way."

Camilla nodded again.

70

"Well, I found out that the reason she didn't show up was because he called and told her to meet him at his house in the Hamptons. He caught her before she arrived at the party. He was supposed to be there for us. I was so proud of Bella Grand because we both put a lot into it, but he decided to make other plans! That shit couldn't have waited! He chose that bitch over me again… and you for that matter; all because of some ass!"

"I know you're upset, but watch your mouth," Camilla disciplined.

Camilla knew all about her brother's sudden plans and ripped him a new one when she learned of them. Brooklyn had lost one parent. She didn't need to lose another one. Her brother Pierce was so busy chasing ass that he never made time for his daughter.

"Brooklyn, let your dad make his mistakes. He's a big boy. Trust me, at some point he'll come around."

"And what about you?" Brooklyn worried.

"Don't worry about me either. I'm handling my business. Listen, I know nothing or no one will ever replace your mom, but maybe you need to think about getting you some *business* as well."

Brooklyn knew what Camilla was insinuating…a man.

"You need to stop working so late and get out and mingle," Camilla suggested after glancing down at her watch and realizing that it was 7:50 p.m. "The office closes at five, and you're still here. Now, what's wrong with that picture? Plus we're in the middle of Manhattan, surrounded by several bars and nice restaurants. Why don't you go have a drink and loosen up a bit?"

"You're still here aren't you and a few other employees are as well."

"Well, all of your asses need to get out and mingle. You see…I don't have to because I have a man," Camilla responded.

Brooklyn rolled her eyes. There was a knock at the door.

"That's probably someone who doesn't have a man or woman either," Camilla teased.

Brooklyn didn't find the remark funny and decided to ignore it. "It's open," she said to the person on the other side of the door.

"Why are you still here, Derrick?" Camilla questioned one of her accountants.

71

"You're not serious, right?" he laughed. "Do you want me sleeping on your money?"

"No, I wouldn't want that."

They both laughed.

"I don't know why the call came to my line, but Maverick is on line one for you."

"Thanks, Derrick. My cell phone is in my office. He's probably called it a million times," Camilla boasted and smiled.

Camilla gathered the flower arrangement and walked to the door. "Life is too short, Brooklyn. You need to start living instead of worrying about me and my brother."

"That's because you and your damn brother are both stupid," Brooklyn mumbled after Camilla left.

Brooklyn turned back to her computer and pulled up the Google search engine again. She typed in the words *male model Maverick Lewis*. Again, nothing.

"I will find out why your ass is nowhere to be found, Maverick," Brooklyn said before finally shutting her computer down.

Camilla rushed to her office and answered the line before Myles hung up.

"Hey, baby," she said.

"I've called your cell a dozen times."

Camilla picked up her phone from the desk and smiled. He didn't lie. "I'm sorry. I was in Brooklyn's office checking on my dress and showing her the flowers."

"I've got some great news." Myles ignored her excitement.

"Do tell!" Camilla wanted him to know that she was just as excited as he was.

"The modeling job in L.A. went very well. So well, that Dana set up another job in Atlanta. I just landed in ATL about an hour ago." He released a fake yawn. "Man…it's only eight o'clock and I'm beat. I need to get some rest."

Camilla's smile turned upside down. She knew what was coming next. "Oh really?" she responded.

"Yes. The bad part about that is it'll probably be another week or two before we can see each other again."

With Kenya ordered to stay in the hospital overnight for observation, Myles knew he had to stick around for a while. But at the same time he also knew Camilla was getting tired of his absence.

"Maverick, this is getting ridiculous. Will you even at least be available for our damn honeymoon?"

"What kind of question is that, Camilla?"

"I'm gonna fly out to Atlanta. I have to see you."

Myles sat up straight on the sofa after hearing Camilla's intent. "That's not a good idea."

"Why not? Don't you want to see me?"

"Of course, I do, baby. But having you at the shoot may be a distraction. Besides, the companies that I'm modeling for may think that's a bit unprofessional."

Myles knew there was nothing that would stop Camilla from hopping on a plane. But he had to try his best to convince her otherwise.

"I wasn't asking to sit with you at your job. I could've stayed at your hotel and waited for you to get back," Camilla informed.

"Yeah, but I still don't think it's a good idea."

"Why don't you just quit already? I can afford to pay for all of your little modeling jobs and then some."

Camilla wasn't taking no for an answer. Myles had to come a little stronger.

"Little modeling jobs. Listen Camilla I know you're rich and powerful, but don't belittle what I do because I don't have your kind of money." He tried to sound pissed.

Myles crossed his fingers and prayed that his reverse psychology worked. Instantly, Camilla felt like the scum of the earth.

"No, I wasn't trying to offend you, baby, and if that's the way it came across then I apologize. I just miss you holding me. I miss dining with you. I miss you."

"Sounds to me like you're horny," he joked.

"This is serious, Maverick even though what you said is true. I am horny."

73

"Then maybe we can do something about that now."

"Like what?" Camilla asked. Her body was immediately filled with excitement. She stood up then walked to her door to lock it. "Does it involve the webcam again?"

"No, not today," Myles answered quickly. "I'm unzipping my pants now. What are you doing?"

"I just lifted my skirt and sat down. Now, I'm sliding my lace panties to the side," Camilla moaned softly.

"Good. Now, imagine your fingers are my tongue and slide two fingers inside."

Camilla tossed her legs on top of the desk as he coached her on what to do.

"You feel me, baby?" Myles asked as he stroked his shaft.

Camilla's breaths were labored as she slowly fingered herself. She was unable to answer him.

"Baby, tell me how I feel?" he asked as his strokes increased.

"Oh Maverick...baby..."

"I know how you feel, Camilla," he moaned and stroked. "I can almost feel your wet pussy on top of me."

Both of them were into the phone sex when all of a sudden, Zoie began to cry. With his love pipe exposed, Myles jumped off the sofa. He snatched up Zoie's carrier and quickly placed her into the office.

"What was that noise?" Camilla asked as he returned back to the living room and zipped up his pants.

Shit, he thought. "That's just the TV, baby."

Zoie's loud cries floated into the living room.

"So why do you have the TV up so loud? It's distracting if you know what I mean."

"I'll call you right back."

"What...Why is..."

Myles hung up before Camilla could finish. He stomped into the office.

"You almost fucked things up!" he yelled at Zoie. "I should've let that dying bitch, Jada keep your crying ass."

Zoie cried even louder. Myles glanced at his watch. He knew she was hungry, but he refused to feed her. He wouldn't even pick her up. Each time he stuck the pacifier in Zoie's mouth she spat it out.

"Since your stupid ass mama was in an accident, now I have to be bothered with you. Well, you're just gonna have to wait until I can get a babysitter or someone over here to watch you. That's your mother's job. Not mine."

He forced the pacifier in her mouth again. This time, Zoie accepted it.

He walked back to the living room to call Camilla again. He'd missed at least three calls from her after deciding to hang up. But before he had a chance to make the call, there was a knock at the door.

"Now, what?" he huffed while marching toward the foyer.

Myles dropped the phone in shock as soon as he opened the door.

"What in the hell are you doing here?"

My Counterfeit Husband

Chapter Ten

"Have you lost your damn mind? How the fuck did you find out where I live?" Myles panicked.

"That's not important right now. Aren't you gonna invite me in?"

Myles glared at the person at his doorstep. "Krystal, what the hell are you doing here? What do you want?"

"Let me in and I'll tell you."

Krystal leaned against the threshold and twirled a lock of blonde hair around her finger. She lifted her leg and pressed her foot against the wooded frame, revealing her toned thigh.

"I don't know what the hell is rattling through that head of yours, but I'm not letting you into my house."

"Why are you being so mean? You never acted like this when I was sucking your dick," she struck back.

"What the fuck do you want, Krystal? This shit is foul and you know it."

Myles' irritation was evident.

"I want *you*, baby." When Krystal rubbed her hand across Myles' chest, he knocked her hand away.

"Don't be like that, baby. You know you like when I touch you."

"Not anymore. Don't tell me you're that stupid. You know how it goes. The pussy is gotten and you're forgotten."

"Oh yeah," Krystal egged him on.

"You need to leave before I call the cops and have you arrested for trespassing."

"The cops?" she laughed demonically. "Now, that was funny."

Myles raised a curious eyebrow as to why that comment didn't make her uncomfortable. "Krystal, this is…"

"Enough of the idle threats," Krystal interrupted and lowered her leg. "Do you want me to cause a scene out here?" She glanced around the neighborhood. "You seem to have some decent neighbors. I don't think you'd want to be known as *that neighbor* who slept with a teenaged girl."

Myles didn't want to admit it, but Krystal had him by the balls. He didn't need any unwanted attention. Myles finally caved in and allowed her inside. But just before closing the door, he glimpsed around the neighborhood to make sure no one was watching.

"You have a nice home, Malik."

Myles glared at Krystal as she walked in with her small studded clutch bag that had a long shoulder strap and admired the beautiful decor.

"Okay. You're in. Now, what do you want? And how the hell did you find out where I live?" Myles didn't waste any time. He wanted to get to the reason for her unwanted and unexpected visit.

"I followed you the last week. You remember? The last time we had sex."

Myles' eyes bulged. "Are you fucking crazy? You followed me?"

"Yes. You act like that's a bad thing. I wanted to know where my man lived."

Myles wanted to pinch himself to make sure he wasn't dreaming. "*Your man*? When did that happen?"

"The night I told you that I loved you."

Myles laughed heartily. Krystal frowned.

"Little girl…"

"*Little girl?*" Krystal felt insulted.

"Look, I can have you kicked out of school for showing up here like this."

"If you had the power you could, but since you don't, you can't."

"How do you figure that I can't?"

"We'll get to that later. How's your wife?"

Myles' right eyebrow rose like The Rock's. "M-My wife?"

"Yeah, I know you're married, Malik or should I say, *Myles*."

Myles swallowed the hard, thick lump that was lodged in his throat.

"I'm the reason she's in the hospital," Krystal continued.

"What? What do you mean?"

"She was trying to get away from me when I was following her as I'd done several other times. I didn't mean for her to get hurt though. Is she alright?"

Myles wondered what he'd gotten himself into.

"You need to get your crazy ass out of my house! Why would you be following my wife?"

"I needed to see the woman who I'd be replacing."

"Yes, it's official. You're certified fucking insane," Myles stated as he looked around the room for a weapon. As unstable as Krystal seemed, he wanted to be prepared.

"You know what?" Krystal paused for effect. "Let me stop playing your game, *Myles*."

Myles just stood there wondering what was about to come out of her mouth next.

"I went through your mail. That's how I know your real name."

Myles felt trapped and wondered how far Krystal was willing to go. Better yet, he wondered what she was after.

Myles had met Krystal in a Starbucks six months ago. From the thick fishtail braid she wore in her hair, nerdy glasses, and baggy sweatpants from Victoria Secret, he could tell she was young. At that point, Myles knew it wouldn't take much to strike up a conversation and wheel her in. He learned that she was a nineteen-year-old UNC Charlotte college student majoring in Engineering. He in turn told her that he'd just left the campus helping the basketball coaches with recruiting.

Myles could tell that Krystal was fascinated with his life after telling her all the places he'd been to recruit players and all the NBA players he'd met over the years. It wasn't long before he followed her to an unoccupied parking lot where they had sex in the backseat of her car. During their conversation, Myles knew that she was broke, but for once he didn't care. At that particular moment, he was horny and itching for something younger. Myles also wanted to see what it was like to be with a white girl. She was like a young Taylor Swift, and that turned him on. He didn't however expect it to continue months after that first encounter.

"So, why haven't you been answering any of my calls, Malik…I mean, Myles. I feel like I'm the only one in this relationship."

"Bitch, you really are a dumb blonde. You have no right to question me."

"I need more of your attention." Krystal stepped up to Myles and tried to kiss him. He stepped back. "Don't be like that, baby."

Krystal kicked off her Tory Burch flats and removed her t-shirt. She then quickly removed her distressed denim shorts and panties. Fully naked, she stepped up to Myles again and grabbed his hand; placing it between her thighs.

"You see how wet I am for you."

Myles yanked his hand back, then pointed toward the door. "You need to leave."

"Don't tell me you've never fantasized about having sex in the house that you share with your wife before?"

"I have…just not with you."

Krystal approached Myles again. "I know you want me."

He looked at the patch of freckles on her left shoulder. "Krystal, face it. You were just a fuck. Now, do us both a favor and disappear."

Krystal was about to approach him again then stopped when she heard Zoie's cries. She gave Myles a puzzled look. Gazing at her naked body turned him on.

"You have a kid?" Krystal questioned curiously as she walked towards the cries.

When Myles grabbed her, Zoie's cries quieted again.

"You need to leave now, Krystal, and never come back," Myles threatened.

"I've got a better idea. How about we go into the room with your daughter and you can see who cries the loudest while you're fucking me. I'll sure I'll win though."

This bitch is truly crazy, Myles thought.

"Your baby's little brother or sister needs to be fed anyway."

Myles stared into her eyes that were the color of bleached jeans. "What in the hell are you talking about?"

"Don't play dumb Myles. You know what I'm talking about. I'm pregnant."

Myles' heart seemed to stop pumping blood, but he figured Krystal was lying.

"Whatever."

"I figured you wouldn't believe me, so I brought the pregnancy test with me. At that point, Krystal reached into her purse and pulled out an EPT test that was inside a plastic bag. The first thing Myles could see was the big blue plus sign.

"I took one again this morning, so I would be sure. Isn't it great?" Krystal beamed.

He had to think of a way to get out of this quickly. "Who do you think you're fooling? If you are pregnant, it's probably not mine anyway. Look how quick I fucked you so it's no telling how many other dudes you're screwing."

Krystal jerked her head.

"I would never claim or take care of a baby that wasn't mine."

"It is yours. You can even use the credit card you stole from my purse to buy pampers and milk when the baby is born."

"What are you talking about?" Myles played dumb.

"I know you took it the last time we were together. You were the only one who has been in my dorm room. Besides, I'm an Abercrombie & Fitch type of girl, not Louis Vuitton. Hope you liked your belt and shoes," Krystal said. "My father gave me that card for emergency use only and now, he suspended it. He reported it stolen and may even press charges."

Myles was a bit worried, but didn't show it.

"I want my child to have a father. I don't know how you plan to swing it with your wife, but you're not leaving me alone in this. If you refuse, I'll tell my daddy that I know who stole his card and I will tell your wife about all the devious things that you've done."

"Devious?"

"You do remember me telling you that I've followed you,

right?"

Again, Myles began to worry.

"Why do you go and check that P.O. Box once a week? Why doesn't all your mail come here?" Krystal questioned "What other secrets do you have besides me and your unborn child? Does your wife allow you to do the things in bed to her that you do to me? If not, how do you think she will react when she learns that her hubby is a sadistic freak...choking me on the brink of your orgasm and all that other crazy ass shit. Need I continue?"

Myles glared at Krystal as she listed his acts and angrily redressed.

"What in the fuck do you want, Krystal?"

"Let me finish. I know that you're not a recruiter. My cousins play basketball for UNC Charlotte and my brother plays for Michigan. I asked them about you and they asked their coaches and basketball buddies from different schools. No one has ever heard of Malik James or Myles Whitaker for that matter. Is Myles even your real name? What last name will I give our son or daughter?"

Myles was furious and caught. Steam blazed from his nostrils as Zoie's abrupt screaming added fuel to the raging fire.

"Again, what do you want?"

"I want you to tell your wife about me and our unborn child. Better yet, I'll tell her. I know what hospital she's in."

Myles' chest rose and fell in anger.

"So, do we have a deal?"

All Myles could do was stare at her as she tapped her foot in patiently.

"Okay fine." Krystal snatched her purse from the floor and headed toward the door. With Myles not prepared to have any of his alternate life exposed, he hurried to Krystal and snatched her arm.

"I thought you'd see it my way." Krystal smiled deviously when she turned to face him. She knew she'd won. At least, that's what she thought.

"Fuck you and fuck that imaginary baby!" Myles barked before wrapping his hands around her neck and throwing her to the floor. He dove on top of her and forced her thighs apart. With one hand still wrapped around her neck, he used the other to unzip his pants and force himself inside of her.

"Is this what the fuck you want, bitch?" Myles growled. He pounded and choked her at the same time. "Blame this shit on my dad! I try hard not to be like him, but you bitches be trying to ruin my life!" Myles squeezed harder as he thought back to his father doing the same to his mother. "I'm not like him! I'm not like him!"

The truth was, Myles was exactly like his father. Even after experiencing what he did as a child, Myles was following directly in his father's path; a verbal abusive murderer who had the same violent behavior and no respect for women. It was in his DNA. He hated following in his father's footsteps, and most times blamed his behavior on all the built up anger inside of him. He was emotionally unstable. He was also someone who refused to get attached to anyone. In Myles' mind, there was no such thing as love.

Krystal clawed at his hands and tried to wiggle from underneath him. Myles watched her facial expression turn from triumphant to terror in a matter of seconds as he applied more pressure. The more she fought, the harder he squeezed and banged. Tears leaked from her eyes and soon, they rolled upward. As Krystal's face turned red, she swung violently trying to break free.

"Who you gonna tell now? Huh? Huh," Myles asked.

Krystal kicked wildly until she couldn't fight anymore.

"Ahhhhhhhhhh!" Myles bellowed as he unloaded a large amount of cum inside of her. "Let the baby feast on that."

Myles hopped to his feet and stared at Krystal's lifeless body then just like that, he snapped to his senses. Shock showered his entire body.

"What the hell did I just do?"

He placed his hands on top of his head and immediately began to pace the floor; realizing that he'd snapped. The more he paced, the more Myles couldn't believed that he'd just raped and killed Krystal while Zoie screamed to the top of her lungs in the other room.

"Zoie, will you shut the fuck up!" he screamed while pacing the floor around Krystal's body.

"You stupid bitch! You should've left well enough alone!" he shouted at Krystal's corpse. He zipped up his pants. "It needed to be done. She was going to expose me. I couldn't have that." Myles tried to convince himself. He paced more while scratching his head. "I didn't do anything wrong. She was asking for it. She was asking for it just like that other bitch did in Connecticut," he said, thinking about his troubled past. Myles had placed that memory far back into his brain and now the episode was clear; like it had just happened yesterday. He quickly shook off those thoughts, then stopped abruptly. "Shit! What am I gonna do with her body?"

Within minutes, Myles picked up his private phone and dialed a number. "I need your help," he said when the person on the other end answered.

Chapter Eleven

"Do you know what time it is?" Jada barked at Myles when she answered her door at 2 a.m. in a pair of flower printed, cotton pajamas.

Myles stared at her and grimaced. He'd never seen Jada without a wig or scarf. It took everything in him to not say something horrible to her about her bald head. Since he needed her help, it took everything in him to hold his tongue. He couldn't stomach the sight of her, so he turned his head as she continued her rampage. He also began to think about Krystal again.

After killing her, Myles tormented himself about his actions, but he knew that was just the beginning. He had to get rid of Krystal's body. Once that realization was made, he thought about how Krystal arrived at his house. With those thoughts in mind, Myles bolted out of the door and to the end of his driveway. That's when he spotted Krystal's Toyota Avalon at the end of the street. Myles knew he'd have to get rid of the car as well. Lucky for him, ideas of getting rid of Krystal and her car popped in his head after rushing back inside the house.

"Did you hear me? Why the hell do you have Zoie out at this time of night?" Jada asked, disrupting his reflection.

"I need you to watch her for a while. I have an emergency that I need to take care of," Myles answered.

Jada eyed Myles, who held Zoie and the carrier in his hand. She was asleep.

"Watch Zoie? For what? I'm not watching her so that you can go screw around on my friend?" Jada rolled her neck and smacked her lips.

Myles knew that it wasn't going to be that easy, but it had to be done. He glanced back at his car then back at Jada.

"Nobody's cheating on Kenya, Jada."

"You come to my house at two in the morning with my God-daughter while my friend is laid up in the hospital, and you expect me to think otherwise? You never come to my house. You don't even like me."

Myles blew a long, hard wind. He needed to get going. Myles tuned Jada out as she bickered at him while pointing her slender finger in his face. He reverted back to Krystal doing the same thing a few hours ago and where her actions landed her.

You don't know how bad I wanna slap the shit out of your bald headed ass so you'll shut the fuck up, he thought.

"I wish Kenya would leave your ass!" Jada continued.

She was prolonging what he needed to do. His momentum and adrenaline pumped hard, but her yapping slowed them down. When Zoie made a noise in her sleep, Myles glanced down at her, and thought back to how difficult it was to take care of her while trying to deal with the Krystal situation. Back home, he ended up having to feed and change her diaper so she would finally stop screaming. Myles had never changed Zoie's diaper before so that task was difficult. It took him nearly twenty minutes to master it. Zoie wouldn't take the cold breast milk from the refrigerator either, which pissed him off even more. Luckily he had sense enough to place the bottle in the microwave for a few seconds which worked like a charm. Zoie went right to sleep once all her needs were met. But Myles knew he couldn't go through that again.

After his unwanted fatherly duties were done, that gave him time to get rid of Krystal's car. He drove it to the shopping center that was five miles from his home, then parked the car in the lot. He figured the car would be less noticeable in a busy shopping center as opposed to some deserted road. After wiping his fingerprints off everything he touched, Myles tossed the keys in a nearby ditch then sprinted back home. He was in shape so the sprint wasn't bad and it gave him a few minutes to think about his actions. Krystal would still be alive if she'd just kept her mouth shut and boarded up her emotional attachment to him.

My Counterfeit Husband

Myles knew it was a bad idea to keep things going with Krystal because she showed signs of clinginess early on. But it was hard for him to kick her to the curb because she allowed him to act out his sexual fantasies no matter how demented they were. Plus, her pussy was always nice and tight. He always wanted to cum as soon as he got inside of her. She had that 'call out sick to work' type of sex.

When Myles arrived back home minutes later, Zoie was still asleep, but his private phone rung nonstop from Camilla's constant calls. Knowing he had a bigger issue to handle, Myles quickly snatched a comforter from the hall closet. After wrapping Krystal's body along with her purse and clothes inside, he carried the one hundred and fifteen pound frame to his car and placed it inside the trunk. Afterwards, he ran back inside, snatched up Zoie and the carrier, then placed her in the backseat of the car. He couldn't figure out how to buckle the carrier down so he placed it on the floor then jetted to Jada's where he knew he'd be walking into a F-5 tornado.

"Look, Jada, I don't have time for this! I've got shit to do!" Myles interrupted her tirade.

"The only shit you can be doing at this hour is laying up inside some pussy. You ain't recruiting this time of night."

Myles wanted to strangle and toss her in the trunk along with Krystal.

"I'm not keeping Zoie for you! Besides, I thought you didn't want your child around my germs, remember?" she reminded.

"Jada, you know it must be important if I'm asking you to do this."

"Again, I'm not keeping her for you to go catch an STD and transmit it back to my friend. You…"

"You have no other fucking choice!"

At that moment, Myles set Zoie's carrier down on the porch then walked off.

"You're wrong for this shit!" Jada belted as she followed him to his car.

Myles shut her out when he hopped inside his car, then closed the door in her face. Jada continued her rant and beat on Myles' window until he backed out of her driveway. He sped off and prepared himself for the drive to South Carolina.

My *Counterfeit* Husband

Myles passed the Lancaster, South Carolina sign at exactly 3:04 a.m. He figured if Krystal's body was found, the authorities would think she was murdered in their state, then spend unnecessary time and resources searching for someone else. A few cars accompanied him on the road as he continued to drive on the Interstate. He allowed each of them to pass, and also made sure to abide by the speed limit. Getting pulled over for speeding wasn't in his plans, and he couldn't take that chance. Lying to steal, deceive and cheat was completely different from lying to conceal the fact that there was a dead body in the trunk of his car.

Myles was surrounded by woods; woods that he knew no one in their right mind would walk into, woods that freaked him out. It was extremely dark and he knew he'd have to walk deep into the blackness. He could only hope the rodents, brush and bugs would speed up the decomposition of Krystal's body.

After glancing at the digital clock, Myles decided it was time to put his forced plan into action before the sun came up. After getting off on an exit, then turning down another dark road, Myles finally pulled over onto the side and stopped the car. Looking around and not seeing one soul in sight, he hopped out, popped the trunk and dashed to the back of the car. He then pulled the body out.

"Shit!" he said when Krystal's shoe hit the ground and a pair of headlights headed his way.

Myles threw Krystal's body back inside the car along with the shoe. He waited impatiently for the driver to pass, but instead, the driver stopped.

"Now, ain't this some shit," Myles mumbled angrily. "Of all the fucking roads, I choose this one. Besides, what asshole pulls over nowadays with all these crazy ass people in the world?" He quickly closed the trunk.

"Is everything okay?" the tall, burly man asked after stepping out of his Ford F150.

Myles could hardly see his face. The headlights of the man's truck were blinding him.

"Yeah, everything's okay. Had a flat, but I took care of it. Thanks for stopping though," Myles rambled, trying to hurry the Good Samaritan along.

"Are you sure?"

Myles wondered if the driver was one of those crazy people that he spoke of. He slowly walked to the driver's side of his car, prepared to hop inside if the man decided to make a move.

"Yeah, I'm fine," Myles assured.

"Okay. You be careful around these parts," the man replied.

These parts? Does he know something that I don't, Myles thoughts started to get the best of him until the man pulled off.

He sat back inside his car for a few minutes until the man was completely gone. Unbelievably, Camilla was still calling and texting him on his private phone.

Why the hell aren't you answering my calls or responding to my text messages? What's going on, Maverick? Call me! I need to know that you're okay!

Myles knew that he'd have to dig deep into his bag of lies to get out of this one, but he couldn't entertain any of that at the moment.

"Why the hell is she still up?" he said to himself.

Looking around once again and realizing he was all alone, Myles hurried to the trunk again and lifted Krystal's body out for the second and hopefully final time. He grabbed her shoe, and a flashlight he'd taken from his house. He took a deep breath before stepping forward. Those steps quickened when Myles thought he heard something. Before long, his steps turned into a quick dash. Myles stepped on twigs as he walked further into the woods. And as each twig snapped, it caused him to jump and pay even closer attention to his surroundings.

When he didn't see his car anymore, Myles knew he'd walked far enough. He placed Krystal on the ground, then tossed several twigs and broken branches over her body. Satisfied with her burial, he stood up.

"This shit is all your fault," Myles said as if Krystal would talk back.

Moments later, he headed back to his car. He took a deep breath and brushed a few leaves from his shirt after jumping back into the driver's seat. He took a long look at himself in his rearview mirror. Myles was somewhat bothered by the fact that he was able to deal with his bad deeds so easily.

"It had to be done though, she was going to ruin my life," Myles spoke to his reflection wishing it would speak back and tell him that everything was going to be okay.

When Myles cranked his car, a call from Camilla stopped him from pulling off. Myles turned on the AC to cool himself off then answered the call.

"Hey, baby," he spoke in a low tone. He wanted her to think she'd woke him up.

"Don't you *hey baby* me!" Camilla wasted no time biting his head off. "You hung up in my face, Maverick! I've been calling and texting you for hours! Are you cheating on me? Who were you with?"

Camilla wouldn't allow Myles to get a word in.

"You said you'd never hurt me like everyone else did! How could you?" Camilla cried.

"Camilla, baby, calm down. I dropped my phone in the toilet earlier. That's why I never called you back," Myles stated. "I had to let it dry out to see if it would work again, so in the meantime I fell asleep. I just put the battery back in."

Camilla's silence could've gone one of two ways; she believed him or she didn't. Myles crossed his fingers that it was the former. He'd been chewed out enough for the day.

"Well, I'll see you in Atlanta." Camilla abruptly changed the subject.

Myles turned the AC on full blast when Camilla voiced her intent.

"Camilla, I told you. You can't come."

"No one tells me what I can or can't do, Maverick. I want to see you and I'm going to see you."

Myles knew that she was serious. When Camilla put her mind to an idea, there was no stopping her.

"Baby, I don't barge in on your business so why do you wanna barge in on mine?"

"I'm catching the 1:45 p.m. flight out tomorrow. I'll call you when I arrive."

Myles tried everything to keep her grounded in New York. "Baby, let's talk about this. You're obviously upset."

"Is there something you need to tell me? Are you fucking someone else?"

"No, not at all."

"Then I'll call you when I arrive in Atlanta."

Camilla didn't wait for a response. She ended the call. The roles quickly reversed. This time Myles blew up her phone. But each of his calls went to voicemail.

"Damn it, Camilla!"

Myles threw the phone down on the passenger's seat. He then put his car in drive and made a forceful u-turn. He drove like a mad man headed back toward Charlotte. This time, he didn't care about getting pulled over. He needed to get back home.

"Camilla, you're seriously tripping! Now, you're making me spend unnecessary money to intercept your ass!" Myles frowned at the thought of having to fly out to New York.

My Counterfeit Husband

lyn didn't want to upset her, but she knew that was the path they were going down.

"Let's not complicate things. I'll just give you the key back."

Leelia sighed. "You're missing the point. I don't want the key back."

Suddenly, Brooklyn's phone rang. She was happy for the interruption until she saw the name pop up on the screen. It was her dad. She rejected the call.

"That's not what I want, Brooklyn," Leelia continued.

"So, what do you want?" Brooklyn snapped. She was so tired of having the same conversation over and over. It was like a broken record.

"I want us to be a real couple. You treat me like a secret, Brooklyn. We don't go out. If we do, it's late at night…club atmospheres and shit like that."

"We go out to dinner."

"That's just it. Everything is at night. You even refuse to sit by the window at the restaurant or eat outside. It's crazy."

"I'm working all day and so are you so I don't see your point."

When Brooklyn's cell phone rang, she rejected it once again. She couldn't be bothered with him at the time, not now anyway. Leelia shot a questioning look at her.

"I just told you my point, Brooklyn." Leelia frowned.

"Look, I can do without all of the dramatics, Leelia. I came to your house for peace and because I wanted to be with you. I didn't expect to receive the third degree."

"Brooklyn, I can't go on with this one sided relationship."

"One sided?" Brooklyn questioned with a curious look. "I love you, Leelia. That's all that should matter."

"Then show me how much you love me. I want to meet your family."

"That's not happening," Brooklyn replied sharply while 'ling out the bed.

"You're keeping something from me. Is it another woman?"

"Don't be ridiculous," Brooklyn laughed at the thought.

"Well, is it another man? Is that him who keeps calling?" a questioned with a hint of jealousy.

Chapter Twelve

"Lee! Lee! Oh my, goodness! Lee!" Brooklyn moaned and arched her back with each flick of Lee's tongue on her pussy.

Brooklyn pressed her feet against Lee's shoulders. She wanted to push away from Lee's tongue of fury, but couldn't. Lee's arms were locked tightly around her thighs so she couldn't get away even if she truly wanted to.

"Lee! Baby! Stop! No! Yes! No!" Brooklyn fought with her sexual emotions. She hadn't seen Lee in a few weeks, so her body had been denied the pleasure. Her own wants and needs were neglected due to the grand opening of Camilla's hotel. Brooklyn wanted to make sure that every I was dotted, T crossed, napkin folded and fork spot free. Her efforts were proven to be worthwhile due to the many reservations that were booked for the rest of the year. Now, since that was over, she needed some playtime.

"Turn over, baby," Lee ordered.

"Nooooooo! I wanna stay right here," Brooklyn whined.

"Baby, I'm gonna give you what you want. Now, turn over on all fours."

Lee helped Brooklyn into the position then licked and lapped her goodies from the back. Brooklyn clawed at the comforter.

"Oooooooo, baby…Yeeeeessssssssss!" Brooklyn howled as she rolled on Lee's tongue "Oooooooo, God! You know what I like, baby!"

Brooklyn reached between her legs and fondled the outside of her clit while Lee's tongue took care of the inside.

"Baby, I'm not ready to cum! It's too soon!" Brooklyn begged as she felt her insides about to explode.

Lee pulled out and flipped Brooklyn onto her back. Their eyes locked as Brooklyn's heart raced as she anticipated what was about to happen next.

"You're so beautiful, Brooklyn," Lee spoke then pushed a few loose strands of Brooklyn's hair from her forehead. "I'm sorry for diving right in. But I've missed you, baby. With you dealing with your job and me dealing with my brother's legal issues, I forgot to *enjoy* you...fully."

Brooklyn's eyes rolled to the back of her head as Lee's tongue and lips traced their way from her chin to her neck to her breasts to her belly button. Lee's kisses were so tender, and her touch was like silk against Brooklyn's skin. Brooklyn's body danced with the mute rhythm. When Lee met her face to face again, Brooklyn's eyes begged to taste the lips. Lee heard them loud and clear. Before the sexy tongue wrestling match took place, Brooklyn breathed the words, "I want you." Their lips locked and six inches slowly eased inside of her.

"Tell me when you want all of it, baby," Lee whispered in Brooklyn's ear.

"I want it all! I want it all now!"

At that moment, Lee grabbed Brooklyn's hands and placed them over her head. Seconds later, Brooklyn heard a lock. Lee had cuffed her right wrist and when there was no resistance, the left one was cuffed. Brooklyn wrapped her legs around Lee's waist and rolled her hips. She was ready for whatever Lee had in mind for her. Lee pulled out of Brooklyn. Brooklyn stared in wonderment as she watched Lee's tongue reenter her. Brooklyn yanked at the cuffs as Lee's tongue action became pleasurably unbearable.

"You know I can't take this like this, baby!" Brooklyn said as she kissed Lee to mute her loud moans,

However, her pleas were ignored.

"Yummy. Just like I like it...wet," Lee cheered before diving back in.

Tears of pleasure rolled from Brooklyn's eyes as she allowed Lee to take over her body. Seconds later, Brooklyn began to thrust harder on Lee's tongue. Lee knew what that meant and seconds later, ten inches reentered Brooklyn.

"God, help me!" Brooklyn begged through tears as Lee pounded her. "Baby, it's happening! I'm cumming! I'm cumming!" She'd never experienced such intense, yet sweet lovemaking all at the same time.

The moment her orgasm ended and her body stopped trembling, Brooklyn collapsed...Lee did as well. Brooklyn rolled onto her side when she felt Lee climb out of bed.

"What are you doing?" Brooklyn asked as she watched Lee remove the strap on dildo.

"I think I tightened it too tight this time," Lee replied once the strap on was removed.

"Come back to bed. I need you to hold me," Brooklyn whimpered.

Lee smiled then rejoined Brooklyn.

"Baby, how long do you plan on keeping me a secret?" Lee asked while pulling Brooklyn into the spoon position. "We've been seeing each other for almost a year and I have yet to meet any of your family. You've met the majority of mine."

Here we go again. I didn't ask to meet them, Brooklyn thought. Brooklyn prayed that she wouldn't have to revisit that conversation for at least another week. For one, she was tired of it and two, there was no way her family would ever meet Lee.

"Leelia, must we talk about this now?"

"Yes, we must. I'm tired of sitting back in the shadows like you're ashamed of me or something."

I am and I'm even ashamed of myself for being conf[used] who I want; a woman or a man, Brooklyn thought. She tu[rned to] Leelia and kissed her on the tip of her button shaped nos[e.]

"I'm not ashamed of you, baby. It's just not the [...]

"Not the right time? How many times am I go[ing...] Brooklyn? You have a key to my place, but I don't [...] How do you think that makes me feel?"

"But when I come here, I knock."

"That's just it, you don't have to knock [...] key!" Leelia fired back in her raspy voice.

Brooklyn rolled over and gazed into [...] brushed the back of her hand across her br[...]

The two ladies locked eyes. Leelia knew about Brooklyn's exploits with men, but was able to look past the idea of her being with them. Brooklyn was very convincing that she no longer desired men so Leelia took a chance with her.

"Why would you think that?"

"Because you keep hitting the decline button."

"It's my dad, Leelia. I just don't want to talk to him right now, so that's why I'm not answering."

"Well, I see how you reacted with the dildo. I only brought in the dildo action at your request. You already know how I feel about them and men. They don't play a role in my life, but I did it for you. Do you know how hard that was for me? Do you miss being with men?" Leelia badgered.

Who said I ever stopped being with them, Brooklyn thought. Feeling a slight draft, she picked up her undergarments from the floor and slipped them on. Before she could answer Leelia's question, her phone buzzed again. This time it was a text message.

I know you see me calling you. Dinner. Tomorrow. I left details on your voicemail.

Brooklyn could hear her father voice the demands of the text. She knew he was only inviting her to dinner to showcase his new fling who Brooklyn despised just like the others. But not showing up wasn't an option, especially if she didn't want to hear her father's mouth.

"Earth to Brooklyn. Did you hear me?" Leelia chimed in.

Brooklyn had zoned out after reading her father's text.

"Leelia, you need to stop thinking so much. Just let things fall into place."

"Why can't you just give me a yes or no answer? And don't think I haven't noticed that you only call me *Lee* when we're having sex. I feel like you have to convince and force yourself to perform oral sex on me when you do. It's like you want the perks of being with a lesbian, but you don't want to *be* with a lesbian."

Brooklyn knew that Leelia would eventually pick up on that. All of the other women she'd dated in secret had done so, too.

"You're trying to twist things around, Leelia."

"No, I'm just trying to understand them. I've been through this

97

before with a woman who fought with her feelings and the man eventually won. I vowed to only deal with lesbians after that. Then you came along and swept me off my feet."

"Maybe you'd understand if you'd ever been with a man."

Leelia gave Brooklyn a detrimental glare that Brooklyn knew she deserved. Leelia never desired to be with a man so Brooklyn's comment warranted whatever Leelia decided to throw at her.

"So, you're admitting it. If you're having those feelings tell me now so that I won't invest anymore time and energy into this relationship."

Brooklyn stared at Leelia who was on the brink of tears. She didn't want to hurt Leelia, but their relationship wasn't that easy. Plus, Brooklyn's family despised homosexuality. Her father was strong about his traditional beliefs that a woman should be with a man and vice versa. To make matters worse, her father was waiting for a grandson to follow in his footsteps and possibly take over his law firm in the future. Even though Camilla had a slew of homosexuals working for her, it still seemed as if she wasn't a fan of homosexuality either. If Brooklyn's family were more open like Leelia's then things would definitely be different. Brooklyn's love for Leelia was truly genuine, but she couldn't lose her family over her relationship.

"Leelia, I love you and one day, you will meet my family, but now is not the right time. I've told you before, my father is old school and this news would probably get me removed from his will." Brooklyn chuckled to try and lighten the mood, but it didn't work.

"Soooooooo, money is the culprit or are you just making that up so I'd say something like *that's a good reason for hiding your secret love interest?*" Leelia was extra animated.

"I see your acting classes are paying off," Brooklyn joked as she thought back to the day she met Leelia.

They literally collided in downtown Manhattan. Brooklyn was rushing to the bank and Leelia was rushing to an audition. They quickly sparked each other's interest. No words were spoken. Actions spoke for them instead. Brooklyn shocked herself by making the first move in asking for her number. They swapped digits and went about their merry ways.

"I'm not playing games with you, Brooklyn. You're either

with me completely or you're not. It's fucking 2013. Your father needs to stop being so damn close-minded and learn to respect your decision. It's your life, not his. Besides, if your family loves you it shouldn't matter if you're gay or not."

"You can't change people who don't want to be changed, Leelia"

"I guess you can't."

Brooklyn knew that shot was pointing directly at her. She walked to the side of the bed when Leelia got up.

"What's the big deal about having people in our business, Leelia? Our business is our business, right?" Brooklyn questioned softly.

"If you say so," Leelia answered halfheartedly.

"Don't be like this, baby. I love you."

Leelia stared at Brooklyn. "Only when it's convenient for you."

She walked past Brooklyn and slipped on her silk robe. Brooklyn couldn't help but stare as she skimmed Leelia's luscious body before it was covered. Leelia was thick in all the right places, especially her ass. She had a Serena Williams booty with thick hips to match. Brooklyn even loved the small belly pouch that Leelia acquired during a bout of depression due to a woman she used to be in love with. Although it was before Brooklyn's time, she didn't want Leelia to go through that pain again.

Leelia made her way toward the bathroom.

"Baby, let me try and ease this on my dad before we make a decision to introduce you to him," Brooklyn tried to convince. She waited for Leelia to turn around and show her the flawless smile she'd grown to love, but Leelia never stopped walking.

"Words don't mean shit to me, Brooklyn. Leave my key on your way out," Leelia replied before slamming the bathroom door.

Carla PENNINGTON

Chapter Twelve

"Lee! Lee! Oh my, goodness! Lee!" Brooklyn moaned and arched her back with each flick of Lee's tongue on her pussy.

Brooklyn pressed her feet against Lee's shoulders. She wanted to push away from Lee's tongue of fury, but couldn't. Lee's arms were locked tightly around her thighs so she couldn't get away even if she truly wanted to.

"Lee! Baby! Stop! No! Yes! No!" Brooklyn fought with her sexual emotions. She hadn't seen Lee in a few weeks, so her body had been denied the pleasure. Her own wants and needs were neglected due to the grand opening of Camilla's hotel. Brooklyn wanted to make sure that every I was dotted, T crossed, napkin folded and fork spot free. Her efforts were proven to be worthwhile due to the many reservations that were booked for the rest of the year. Now, since that was over, she needed some playtime.

"Turn over, baby," Lee ordered.

"Nooooooo! I wanna stay right here," Brooklyn whined.

"Baby, I'm gonna give you what you want. Now, turn over on all fours."

Lee helped Brooklyn into the position then licked and lapped her goodies from the back. Brooklyn clawed at the comforter.

"Oooooooo, baby…Yeeeeesssssssss!" Brooklyn howled as she rolled on Lee's tongue "Oooooooo, God! You know what I like, baby!"

Brooklyn reached between her legs and fondled the outside of her clit while Lee's tongue took care of the inside.

"Baby, I'm not ready to cum! It's too soon!" Brooklyn begged as she felt her insides about to explode.

Lee pulled out and flipped Brooklyn onto her back. Their eyes locked as Brooklyn's heart raced as she anticipated what was about to happen next.

"You're so beautiful, Brooklyn," Lee spoke then pushed a few loose strands of Brooklyn's hair from her forehead. "I'm sorry for diving right in. But I've missed you, baby. With you dealing with your job and me dealing with my brother's legal issues, I forgot to *enjoy* you...fully."

Brooklyn's eyes rolled to the back of her head as Lee's tongue and lips traced their way from her chin to her neck to her breasts to her belly button. Lee's kisses were so tender, and her touch was like silk against Brooklyn's skin. Brooklyn's body danced with the mute rhythm. When Lee met her face to face again, Brooklyn's eyes begged to taste the lips. Lee heard them loud and clear. Before the sexy tongue wrestling match took place, Brooklyn breathed the words, "I want you." Their lips locked and six inches slowly eased inside of her.

"Tell me when you want all of it, baby," Lee whispered in Brooklyn's ear.

"I want it all! I want it all now!"

At that moment, Lee grabbed Brooklyn's hands and placed them over her head. Seconds later, Brooklyn heard a lock. Lee had cuffed her right wrist and when there was no resistance, the left one was cuffed. Brooklyn wrapped her legs around Lee's waist and rolled her hips. She was ready for whatever Lee had in mind for her. Lee pulled out of Brooklyn. Brooklyn stared in wonderment as she watched Lee's tongue reenter her. Brooklyn yanked at the cuffs as Lee's tongue action became pleasurably unbearable.

"You know I can't take this like this, baby!" Brooklyn said as she kissed Lee to mute her loud moans,

However, her pleas were ignored.

"Yummy. Just like I like it...wet," Lee cheered before diving back in.

Tears of pleasure rolled from Brooklyn's eyes as she allowed Lee to take over her body. Seconds later, Brooklyn began to thrust harder on Lee's tongue. Lee knew what that meant and seconds later, ten inches reentered Brooklyn.

94

"God, help me!" Brooklyn begged through tears as Lee pounded her. "Baby, it's happening! I'm cumming! I'm cumming!" She'd never experienced such intense, yet sweet lovemaking all at the same time.

The moment her orgasm ended and her body stopped trembling, Brooklyn collapsed...Lee did as well. Brooklyn rolled onto her side when she felt Lee climb out of bed.

"What are you doing?" Brooklyn asked as she watched Lee remove the strap on dildo.

"I think I tightened it too tight this time," Lee replied once the strap on was removed.

"Come back to bed. I need you to hold me," Brooklyn whimpered.

Lee smiled then rejoined Brooklyn.

"Baby, how long do you plan on keeping me a secret?" Lee asked while pulling Brooklyn into the spoon position. "We've been seeing each other for almost a year and I have yet to meet any of your family. You've met the majority of mine."

Here we go again. I didn't ask to meet them, Brooklyn thought. Brooklyn prayed that she wouldn't have to revisit that conversation for at least another week. For one, she was tired of it and for two, there was no way her family would ever meet Lee.

"Leelia, must we talk about this now?"

"Yes, we must. I'm tired of sitting back in the shadows. It's like you're ashamed of me or something."

I am and I'm even ashamed of myself for being confused about who I want; a woman or a man, Brooklyn thought. She turned to Leelia and kissed her on the tip of her button shaped nose.

"I'm not ashamed of you, baby. It's just not the right time."

"Not the right time? How many times am I gonna hear that, Brooklyn? You have a key to my place, but I don't have one to yours. How do you think that makes me feel?"

"But when I come here, I knock."

"That's just it, you don't have to knock. You have a damn key!" Leelia fired back in her raspy voice.

Brooklyn rolled over and gazed into Leelia's eyes then brushed the back of her hand across her bronze colored cheek. Brooklyn didn't want to upset her, but she knew that was the path they were going down.

"Let's not complicate things. I'll just give you the key back."

Leelia sighed. "You're missing the point. I don't want the key back."

Suddenly, Brooklyn's phone rang. She was happy for the interruption until she saw the name pop up on the screen. It was her dad. She rejected the call.

"That's not what I want, Brooklyn," Leelia continued.

"So, what do you want?" Brooklyn snapped. She was so tired of having the same conversation over and over. It was like a broken record.

"I want us to be a real couple. You treat me like a secret, Brooklyn. We don't go out. If we do, it's late at night…club atmospheres and shit like that."

"We go out to dinner."

"That's just it. Everything is at night. You even refuse to sit by the window at the restaurant or eat outside. It's crazy."

"I'm working all day and so are you so I don't see your point."

When Brooklyn's cell phone rang, she rejected it once again. She couldn't be bothered with him at the time, not now anyway. Leelia shot a questioning look at her.

"I just told you my point, Brooklyn." Leelia frowned.

"Look, I can do without all of the dramatics, Leelia. I came to your house for peace and because I wanted to be with you. I didn't expect to receive the third degree."

"Brooklyn, I can't go on with this one sided relationship."

"One sided?" Brooklyn questioned with a curious look. "I love you, Leelia. That's all that should matter."

"Then show me how much you love me. I want to meet your family."

"That's not happening," Brooklyn replied sharply while rolling out the bed.

"You're keeping something from me. Is it another woman?"

"Don't be ridiculous," Brooklyn laughed at the thought.

"Well, is it another man? Is that him who keeps calling?" Leelia questioned with a hint of jealousy.

Chapter Thirteen

Kenya sat up in her hospital bed and dialed Myles' number for the millionth time with no response. She'd filled his voicemail with so many messages that now it was completely full. She didn't have her cell phone to see if he'd called her back on that line because he certainly hadn't called the hospital room.

"And he could've waited to give me these," Kenya mumbled as she glanced at the pink roses that lay next to her on the bed.

Around ten that morning, one of the nurses came into her room with the dozen of roses and a huge smile. Kenya also displayed a huge smile when she read the card until she got to the last line. She lifted the card off the bed and read again it for the hundredth time:

Baby, there's no apology or excuse for what I did to you.
You're the light of my life and the reason my heart beats.
I don't know what came over me.
I promise to never raise a hand to you again.
Kenya, I love you!
P.S. I hope you're not too mad at me when you find out what I did.
Myles

"I'm waiting on the doctor's discharge papers then you'll be all set to go," the nurse said to Kenya after peeking inside the room.

Kenya nodded then tossed the card on the bed. At this point, she was livid. Myles knew she was getting discharged at noon today so she didn't understand why he wasn't there. She also didn't know what the last line of the card meant. Kenya was still in disbelief at the move Myles pulled when he choked her. She went back and forth in her head trying to justify his actions.

"If he'd disrespected me in front of another woman, I probably would've done the same thing," she defended to herself. *Hell, I have issues; issues that keep me up at night*, she thought. "But my mama and daddy raised me to believe that a man should never put his hands on a woman…no matter what."

Kenya glanced at the card and flowers again.

"Okay, I have your papers." The nurse bounced back into the room. "Just sign by these X's and you'll be all ready to go." When Kenya signed her name, the nurse handed her the copies. "Is someone coming to pick you up?"

"Yes," Kenya responded even though she didn't know how true that statement was.

"Okay, I'll wheel you down once your ride gets here."

"Oh no! I can handle it." Kenya forced a smile. Her blood boiled again at the fact that Myles wasn't present. She felt that if Myles really wanted to show her how sorry he was, he'd do it in person, not send some flowers. To pour salt on an already open wound, she hated roses and told Myles that on several occasions.

"It's actually hospital policy," the nurse informed. "Just hit the call button when you're ready."

When the nurse exited the room, Kenya called Jada. She hated to bother her friend. Kenya assumed Jada would probably be tired or medicated, but she needed to get home to Zoie as fast as she could.

"Girrrrrrrrrrrrrrrrrl, we have a lot to talk about," Jada started in as soon as she answered the phone.

Kenya really didn't feel like hearing about Jada's issue at the moment. She wanted to get home. She was worried about Zoie and Myles.

"Jada, can we do this another time? I'm at the hospital and need a ride home. Can you pick me up?"

"Wait…so that asshole didn't come and get you!"

Before Kenya could reply, she heard a baby's whimper.

"Is that Zoie?"

"Yeeesssss! That's what the hell we have to talk about! That asshole husband of yours dropped her off at two this morning."

Kenya jumped off the bed. "Jada, come and pick me up. Now!

I'll be waiting outside."

Kenya didn't even wait for Jada's response before she jetted to the elevator, leaving the roses and card behind. Luckily, the nurse who'd just left her room was with another patient, so Kenya was able to get to the elevator without being stopped.

"Myles, what in the hell are you up to?" she mumbled after riding the elevator down to the first floor.

Twenty minutes later, Kenya flagged down Jada's car when she saw her pull into the parking lot. As soon as she stopped, Kenya hopped into the backseat.

"Jada, what's going on?" When Kenya looked up at Jada, she noticed that her friend wasn't looking too well. Jada looked weak...weaker than she did the day before. "Sweetie, you look tired. Let me drive," Kenya insisted.

"Girl, I'm fine. I can drive."

"Put the car in park," Kenya ordered.

Jada did as she was told then climbed into the passenger's seat. Kenya listened to her moan in pain as she did so. After carefully inspecting Zoie who was sound asleep, Kenya climbed behind the wheel of Jada's white Infiniti FX35.

For her 31st birthday, Jada bought the new ride as part of the bucket list she created after learning about her condition. It didn't take long for her to blow through half her savings like a teenager with free reigns of her parents' credit card. Jada traveled everywhere she'd wanted to visit in a year's time. Just like Kenya, Jada's father left her mother a hefty life insurance policy that the mom split with her when he passed away. The only difference in the deaths was that Jada's father passed due to natural causes. Her father suffered a heart attack in his sleep.

"Jada, before you tell me why you have Zoie, are you okay?"

"I told your ass that I'm okay. Now, can we leave this hospital? I hate hospitals now."

Kenya adjusted the driver's seat, rearview and side mirrors. "I don't know why you're lying to me. I know you're not feeling well," she said pulling off.

"Okay! Okay! Okay! Damn! I'm not feeling well. I've been throwing up all morning and my pain medication doesn't seem to be working. On top of all of that, I had to take care of Zoie. I did the best I could under these circumstances, but she may need to be changed."

Kenya's anger tipped the scale. She wanted to murder Myles for leaving Zoie with Jada.

"Jada, why do you have my daughter?"

"Because that son-of-a-bitch showed up at my house in the middle of the night saying he needed me to watch her. He said it was an emergency, and that his bitch ass had something to do."

Kenya couldn't help but smile. Although she was extremely ill, Jada was still feisty and foul mouthed. "What did he have to do? Do you know where he is?"

"The hell if I know! When I tried to stop him, he cursed me out and left Zoie on the porch."

"He did whaaaaaaat!"

"On top of that, he didn't have any diapers for her, no change of clothes or milk," Jada fumed. She needed to get things off of her chest. "I know you give her your titty milk, but she drank Similac this morning. I had to drive to Walmart early this morning to get that along with some diapers and a onesie."

Kenya's face turned redder than a fire truck. "Jada, why didn't you bring Zoie to me or call the hospital?"

"Because, you needed to get some rest that's why. I held it down."

"Jada, I'm so sorry that you had to…"

"No! No apologies from you. You didn't do shit wrong. If anyone is going to apologize to me, it's gonna be your sorry ass husband. You need to poison that muthafucka."

"I called him a million times, but he didn't answer. I know he got my messages," Kenya huffed. "Then he had a nerve to have some flowers delivered to me this morning with a card that said, he hopes I'm not that mad after finding out what he did."

"I'm telling you Kenya. He's doing something he has no business doing or showing you how pissed he is that Julius was at the hospital."

He showed me alright, Kenya thought. She wanted to tell Jada about the choking incident but decided not to. With Jada going through so much already, Kenya didn't want to add anymore drama to her plate.

"He's a bitch ass!" Jada continued her disgust toward Myles. "What grown ass man plays games like that?"

"I'll deal with Myles when he gets home, Right now, I need to get to the car rental place and pick up a car. Hertz has one waiting for me."

"Hell, they don't pick you up like Enterprise?"

"Girl, stop!" Kenya laughed.

Zoie woke when they arrived at the rental car location on College Street minutes later. Kenya eagerly scooped Zoie into her arms. They were both happy to see each other. Kenya wasn't able to really hold her like she wanted when in the hospital, so she showered Zoie with extra kisses and hugs.

Kenya walked inside the office with Zoie cradled in her arms while Jada stayed in the car. She gave the customer service rep her info.

"They're pulling the Chevy Aveo around for you now, ma'am?" the rep said a few minutes later.

"The what?"

"It's a compact vehicle."

"I'm not going from a midsize SUV to a compact car. I have an infant with a car seat and diaper bags."

"Well, the insurance company is only obligated to give you an operable vehicle while yours is being repaired or replaced. Now, if you desire something larger, you can pay extra and I'll just adjust."

Kenya thought long and hard. She'd grown accustomed to the SUV life and couldn't go back.

"Okay. Give me a SUV. Like a Chevy Traverse or an Equinox. I'll even take a Cherokee. "

The rep checked to see if any trucks were available. When she located one, Kenya handed over her credit card.

"Ma'am, I'm sorry but your card was declined," the rep informed.

Kenya scowled "What do you mean *declined*? No, that's impossible. Run it again, please."

After four failed attempts and not wanting to bother Jada with a materialistic issue, Kenya opted for the compact car that the insurance company had originally approved. Completely humiliated, she stomped out of the building when the tiny car was pulled around. She yanked Zoie's seat from Jada's car.

"What in the hell is wrong with you?" Jada asked when she noticed that Kenya's face was blazing like the gates of hell.

"I don't know, but I'm about to find out."

Kenya hugged and thanked Jada, secured Zoie in the rental car, then drove off. Kenya's first instinct was to rush to the bank, but Zoie killed that idea. She was completely irritated and needed to be changed. Kenya could smell the soiled diaper up front. At that point, Kenya hurried home to tend to her child so that she could get to the bottom of her credit card declining.

Kenya was furious and worried when she saw the garage door open when she pulled into her driveway and Myles' car wasn't there.

"Where the hell is he?"she mumbled.

After parking the car and removing Zoie, she walked inside the house. She frowned when she noticed one of Zoie's dirty diapers lying on the floor. It was open, exposing a pile of green feces.

"Are you fucking serious Myles?" Kenya yelled.

With a major attitude, she disposed of the diaper in the kitchen trash then took Zoie upstairs to change her. Once that was done, Kenya dashed back downstairs into the office with Zoie latched on to her nipple. Kenya sat down in front of the Mac desktop prepared to check her credit card statements.

"What do you mean *incorrect passcode*?" she addressed the computer.

She tried a few more codes, but none of them worked. Enraged, she shoved the keyboard across the desk, just before a light bulb went off inside her head. She still had her old Dell laptop that was stored away in a box in the guest bedroom. She hurried into the room and laid Zoie on the bed. As soon as she took her breast away, Zoie wailed.

"Baby, please give me a minute." Kenya hoped her words would soothe her daughter. But no such luck. "You're just gonna have to cry for a few minutes." Kenya hurried to the closet and pulled out a few boxes. "Thank goodness."

The laptop was in the second box she pulled out. It was heavy and bulky, but still powered up. Once she plugged it into the wall, Kenya then sat down on the floor. When Zoie's cries began to lessen, Kenya figured she was falling asleep.

It took a while for the dinosaur laptop to completely power up, but once it came to life, Kenya began her investigation. Her Amex card was first on the list since it was the one that had declined at the car rental office.

"Incorrect passcode? What the hell? I've had this account for years. I should know the passcode," she spoke to the laptop as if it would mysteriously tell her what the issue was. She typed it in again. Same message. "What in the hell is going on?" Next, Kenya went to the PNC bank website only to receive a different yet same message. *The Online ID or passcode is incorrect.*

"I know good and damn well Myles has not locked me out of my money." Kenya tossed the laptop on the floor and hopped to her feet. "Good," she cheered softly when she walked over to Zoie who was off in la la land.

Kenya dashed into her bedroom and into Myles' closet. She pushed through his clothes until she reached the safe. The passcode that he'd given her months ago popped in her head. After pressing in the four digit code, she tried to turn the latch. It didn't budge. She attempted the same action again. Nothing. Kenya walked back into her bedroom and sat on the bed. She was in a twilight zone. There was no way she was oblivious to what was going on in her own home. She reached for the cordless phone and dialed Myles' number. Voicemail.

"Who the hell did I marry?" she screamed.

My *Counterfeit* Husband

Chapter Fourteen

"Move it, asshole!" Myles' aggressive cab driver yelled to the car in front of him as he whizzed his way through the Manhattan streets. He was on a mission to get to the Bella Grand Hotel by a certain time since Myles offered to give him an extra tip if he did.

Myles had to catch Camilla before she left for the airport. A bad feeling brewed inside his stomach that she'd already left. When it came to flying, Camilla was at the airport well in advance. But that was a chance he was willing to take; especially since Camilla wasn't answering any of his calls or text messages.

During the ride, Myles thought about Kenya and the numerous calls she'd made to him from the hospital. He couldn't deal with her at the moment. The flowers and card were enough. There were more pressing issues to deal with. He couldn't wait for Kenya to hurry up and sell the company so that he could make his move and bounce. He was beyond tired of her and Zoie. Plus, all of the back to back, first class flying was taking its toll on his funds. The recent last minute ticket to New York alone was nine hundred and twenty dollars. His funds were depleting…fast. Myles knew that he needed to push things along with Camilla since Kenya was taking her sweet time.

Her fat ass moves way too slow for me, he thought.

Myles didn't allow the cab to come to a complete stop after arriving at the hotel ten minutes later. While still rolling, Myles tossed three twenty dollar bills at the cabbie and jumped out like a professional stuntman. He ran through the hotel lobby disregarding the guests. His run came to an abrupt stop when he tripped over a piece of luggage and slid across the newly waxed marble floor.

"Oh my goodness, are you okay?" one of the guests asked.

Myles didn't have time to thank the man who assisted him back to the vertical position. He needed to get to the penthouse. He dashed to one set of elevators, and quickly pressed the up button.

"Come on. Hurry up," Myles barked at the shiny steel doors while staring at his reflection. "Damn! I never realized how slow these elevators were before."

As if they heard Myles' complaint, the doors suddenly opened. Myles hopped on, placed his special key card inside the slot, and pressed the PH button. However, as the doors were closing, he spotted Camilla stepping off the adjacent elevator with Issac who was carrying several pieces of luggage. Myles grabbed the doors and pushed them open.

"Camilla?" he called out after jumping off.

Camilla turned to him. She couldn't believe her eyes. "Maverick? How? Why? What are you doing here? I was on my way to you."

"I canceled the shoot," Myles pretended. "I realized you mean more to me than these damn magazines and shit." He poured on his charm. It worked.

"Oh, baby! I love you!" Camilla jumped into his arms and sprayed him with kisses.

"I love you, too, Camilla. That's why I jumped on the first flight. I didn't even bother to pack."

"Don't worry about that. We'll take care of that later."

I know, Myles thought. He retrieved her luggage from Issac. He even grabbed Camilla's Charcoal Hermes Birkin bag from her arm, too. "We don't need you now," Myles said to him.

But Issac didn't budge. He turned to Camilla. "Ms. Ellington, will you need me?"

Myles didn't appreciate the step-over.

"Yo, I told you that we don't need you anymore," Myles spoke defiantly. He'd never had any issues with Issac before, so he couldn't understand the problem.

"With all due respect, sir, Ms. Ellington is my employer. I do what *she* tells me to do."

Myles sized him up. Issac may have sounded like the actor, Ving Rhames, but he was nowhere near Ving's build. Myles figured he'd give Issac a run for his money if it came down to it.

"Isaac, Maverick is about to be my husband," Camilla stepped in. "So, please do not treat him any differently than me."

Isaac nodded. "Yes, ma'am. I understand."

"So, as I said before, we no longer need you." Myles had to get the last word. "As a matter-of-fact, take the rest of the day off."

As if Camilla hadn't spoken a word, Isaac turned to her for approval.

"Actually baby, I'll need Issac later on tonight." Camilla turned to her long time driver. "Issac you can take the rest of the day off, but come back around eight."

"Yes, Ms. Ellington," Issac replied.

Camilla grabbed Myles'arm and pulled him onto the elevator when she saw that he was about to say something.

"Baby, you need to check that nigga." Myles was bothered by Isaac's disrespect.

"Isaac means no harm, Maverick. He's been with me for over fifteen years and has only taken orders from me. Give him time, he'll get used to you."

"Well, he needs to do it quick."

"Why are you so uptight? Is everything okay?"

"Yeah, I'm fine. So, what's going on tonight?"

Before Camilla could respond, his white iPhone rang. However, Myles couldn't answer it because it was the phone he used for Kenya.

"You changed your ringtone?" Camilla questioned.

"Yeah, but I'm gonna change it back because I really don't like this one." Myles always tried to stay quick on his toes.

"Well, aren't you gonna answer it?"

"I'm sure it's just my agent, Dana calling. She's probably pissed that I canceled the shoot without telling her," Myles responded. He reached inside his back pocket and turned off the phone. "She'll be okay, though. I had to get to my baby." He leaned over and kissed Camilla's shoulder.

"So, are you gonna tell me what's bothering you?"

Myles was hesitant for a moment. "I have to leave later tonight."

Camilla frowned. "But you just got here, Maverick."

"Baby, I know, but my townhouse is being shown tomorrow. I need to be there to make sure everything goes well. Besides, I haven't been home to Florida in forever. You do remember me telling you about me putting my house on the market, right?"

Myles had lied so much that he was starting to believe them. Besides, although he didn't want to leave, he had to get back to Kenya and face the hell she'd have waiting for him.

"I remember, but can't your realtor handle that?"

Myles could tell that Camilla had an attitude. "Yes, but I really wanna go and check on everything. Plus, I wanna make sure all my valuable items are safely put away. I don't remember doing it before I left."

"Well, can you at least take an early morning flight? I'm meeting my brother for dinner tonight. It's about time you two meet."

Myles thought long and hard. He was opposed to meeting her brother, but knew he had to keep Camilla happy. "Does it have to be tonight?"

"Yes, it does."

Myles saw the anger in Camilla's eyes. It was at that moment when he realized that Kenya would have to suffer a little while longer.

Myles smiled. "Sure…anything for you, baby."

When the elevator doors finally opened on the top floor, Myles stunned Camilla when he scooped her up into his arms. She giggled.

"Shouldn't you save this move for our wedding night?"

"So, do you want me to save all the moves that I'm planning on showing you?"

Camilla giggled again. "Well, you can give me a sneak peek."

"Now that I can do."

After opening the door to Camilla's fabulous residence, Myles carried her to the bedroom and laid her down on the 400 thread count bedding. He hovered over her for a few seconds before pressing his lips against hers. Myles slowly removed her heels, and clothing.

"Camilla, do me a favor?" Myles asked while on his knees and discarding his shirt.

"Wh-What is it, baby?"

"Watch me eat you."

Camilla turned to the huge mirror that was positioned on the wall in front of the bed. Their bodies were laid horizontal across the bed so she had a perfect visual of butterscotch and caramel meshing together.

"Oh Maverick?" she whimpered when Myles' tongue made entry into her honey dip.

Camilla watched his head wind and glide as she moved her hips. As he hurled her legs over his shoulders, she placed her hands atop of his head and watched herself slowly massage his scalp.

"Maaaaaav, right there, baby," Camilla cooed. "I see what you're doing to me, baby. I feel you. I see…you," she wheezed.

Myles reached under Camilla's ass and massaged her cheeks. Camilla enjoyed the feeling as well as the show. Myles cut his eyes at Camilla's reflection in the mirror. His lustful look intensified the moment for her. Camilla looked away from his oral action for a brief moment. Her eyes then followed his hand. Myles anxiously unzipped his pants and whipped out his python. Camilla was ready to receive its poison, but Myles had other plans. He pleasured himself.

"Baby, I want…it," Camilla begged. "Don't be stingy."

Myles flicked his tongue a little faster. He knew what Camilla wanted, but he wasn't ready to give it to her yet.

"Please Maverick. Pllllease," Camilla whined. She pressed Myles' face further and thrust her love harder. "Yes, Oooooo, Yes!"

When Myles felt Camilla's body twitch, he heaved his body on top of hers and glided his pipe inside her pussy.

"Damn, you're so wet," he voiced his appreciation.

Myles massaged every curve of Camilla's body and stopped when he reached her neck. Camilla's eyes gave him the go ahead. But instead of his hand, Myles pressed his forearm against Camilla's neck. She gave him a concerned look.

"It'll be okay, baby. Just breathe through your nose," Myles coached. "Relax. I got this."

The harder Myles pressed, the stronger his thrusts were. Camilla didn't know what to think as she watched Myles transform into a different person right before her eyes. As her heart raced, the nose breathing technique didn't seem to work. She clutched her hands around Myles' arm and pulled, but he didn't budge. She even kicked uncontrollably. However, all of her efforts to break free were useless. Myles was in complete control over her body. Once Camilla's eyes rolled to the back of her head, he pressed even harder against her neck. Myles enjoyed seeing the control he had over her and the visual took him back to the Krystal incident. He was highly turned on knowing that Camilla was at his mercy.

Camilla couldn't understand how her vagina could be pleased with Myles' actions. Her walls began to contract. Her nails dug deep into Myles's arm until they broke skin. Her body jerked and twitched outrageously. Suddenly, they both climaxed at the same time. But instead of staying inside of her, Myles pulled back and shot his seeds all over Camilla's chest. When Myles finally removed his arm from Camilla's neck, she slapped him.

"What the hell?" Myles was stunned by her actions.

Camilla shoved him off of her and jumped off the bed. She shot fiery daggers at Myles with her eyes. "Are you crazy? You could've killed me!" she screamed.

Myles sat on the side of the bed and pulled Camilla between his legs. She tried to break free but couldn't.

"But I thought you liked it when I got naughty."

"I do, but you're starting to get carried away with it."

"Well, if I tried to kill anything, it was your tasty pussy," he joked.

"I'm serious, Maverick. That was way over the top and you know it."

"Didn't you cum?"

"Yes, but…"

"But nothing. Aren't you breathing?"

"Yes, but…"

"But nothing," he interrupted her again.

"Stop cutting me off," Camilla chastised. "You know what I told you about the abuse in my past. Your actions are reminding me of that shit and it's starting to bother me. The small stuff was fun, but you're taking it to another level now."

"Baby, I apologize but don't you love the intense orgasms you get from it?"

114

"Maverick, I can deal with our normal rough sex, but from this point on, that extra shit is off limits." Camilla put her foot down. "Things can get carried away and I don't want to fall victim to it."

Myles stared into Camilla's eyes and hoped that she wasn't serious. He released his hold from her waist and stepped back. "No problem."

"I'm gonna go get in the shower. You're welcome to join me if you like," Camilla offered. "We don't have time to go out shopping for any clothes. I just realized that I have a few suits and some other things for you in the closet."

Myles nodded. "I'll join you in a sec."

Once Camilla disappeared into the bathroom and turned on the shower, Myles hurried to his back jean pocket and pulled out his white cell phone. He turned it on. There were numerous calls from Kenya. Myles stepped into the second bedroom to call her.

"You have a lot of fucking nerve, Myles! Where are you? How could you leave our child with Jada and no one knows where you are? And why weren't you at the hospital to pick me up?" Kenya roared.

He took a deep breath before speaking the words, "I'll be home tomorrow." His voice was cold as ice. He ended the call as Kenya went ballistic, then turned the phone off. "I'll deal with that shit when I get back to Charlotte."

As Myles walked back into the master bedroom, he looked into the bathroom and watched Camilla wash her toned body with a loofah sponge. It wasn't long before he could feel his stiff dick standing at attention.

"I'm ready for part two baby!" he yelled out with an enormous smile.

115

Carla PENNINGTON

Chapter Fifteen

The ride to Mr. Chow restaurant was slightly awkward for Myles as Isaac periodically cut his eyes at him during the drive. Myles returned the eye bullets, but decided not to make a scene since he was trying to get back on Camilla's good side for his sexual aggression earlier. Surprisingly, she wouldn't even have sex with him in the shower earlier, which was odd. To keep calm, he rolled up the tinted window separating them; blocking Isaac's view. When Myles placed his hand on Camilla's thigh, she shifted.

"So, you're not in a playful mood, huh?" Myles asked.

"No, I'm not. I just want to get through this dinner, get back to my suite and go to bed. I feel a bad headache coming on."

"Don't be like this, Camilla. I'm leaving in the morning and probably won't see you for another week or so. What more do I have to say or do to show you how sorry I am?"

Camilla turned to him. "I forgave you back in the suite. Can we please leave it alone?"

Myles knew by Camilla's demeanor that his actions stirred up past memories of her abuse. He had to get *his* Camilla back. He poured two glasses of champagne, handed one to her and moved closer.

"You know you can't stay mad at me forever, baby. I'll do whatever it takes to warm up that cold shoulder that you're giving me."

Camilla shifted again then sipped from her glass.

"So, are you gonna act like this when we get inside the restaurant?" Myles continued.

Camilla teasingly rolled her eyes. "We'll see when we get there."

Myles moved back to his side of the car and emptied his glass. He knew Camilla would come around eventually so he left her alone. Fifteen minutes later, the car stopped in front of Mr. Chow on Hudson Street. When Isaac stepped out and opened the door for Myles and Camilla, he extended his hand to assist Camilla out of the car. However, when Myles stepped out behind her, Isaac moved back. Myles was so happy when Camilla walked ahead of him because he had a few choice words to say.

"Nigga, I don't know what your problem is, but you need to check your attitude with me." Myles didn't expect Isaac to react being that he was an employee.

"My problem with you is that I don't like you. I don't trust you. I've seen your kind before. I know you're using Ms. Ellington. What real man enjoys spending a woman's money?"

Myles was thrown for a loop. He didn't expect the recoil.

"You need to watch yourself, old man," Myles threatened.

"You do the same," Isaac returned then walked back to the driver's side.

"Maverick, are you coming?" Camilla called out to him.

Myles slit Isaac's throat with his eyes then trotted to Camilla. She held out her hand and smiled at him. Myles smiled back. He knew she'd come around.

"Baby, before we go in, I need to ask you something," Myles said.

"What is it?"

"As a man, this is hard for me, but do you think you could spot me a few dollars until I get back home to pay you back? I lost my debit card on the way here. I think I left it at the airport when I was rushing trying to get to you. I promise...I'll pay you back with interest. I don't want to walk around..."

"It's okay, baby. You don't have to explain yourself. What's mine is yours, remember? Just remind me when we get back to the suite."

Those words were music to his ears. As they were about to

enter the restaurant, suddenly Camilla's phone rang.

"I never get calls from blocked numbers," she spoke softly after glancing at the screen then answering the call. "Hello?"

"Camilla Ellington?" the female questioned.

"Yes, this is Camilla Ellington. How may I help you?" she asked curiously.

"I know something you don't know," the female replied sadistically.

"Excuse me? Who are you?"

Myles noticed the odd, uncomfortable look on Camilla's face and wondered who was on the other end of the phone.

"You'll find out who I am in due time, especially when secrets are revealed," the female spoke.

"When secrets are revealed? What are you talking about?"

The caller hung up.

"What was that about?" Myles questioned.

"I don't know. Some woman talking about she knows something that I don't know. It was really weird."

Myles became nervous as he wondered who the woman could've been. He knew that she could've easily been someone that he deceived. "What was her name?"

"She didn't give me one."

"Don't worry about it. It probably was a wrong number."

"She said my name, Maverick, so it couldn't have been a wrong number," Camilla looked slightly worried.

"It was probably a prank call, baby. Don't worry about it." He needed to get Camilla's mind off of that call especially since he was slightly concerned about who the woman was, too. "Come on. I'm starving."

They entered the restaurant hand in hand. After informing the hostess who she was, the tall brunette woman ushered them to the appropriate table. Camilla smiled once they walked up. However, Myles grimaced when he saw Brooklyn sitting there. He shot Camilla a 'why didn't you tell me' look. Before they could even sit down, Myles could feel the tension between Brooklyn and her father.

"Well, hello, dear sister," Camilla's brother addressed her. He stood up, hugged and kissed her on the cheek.

"Hi, Pierce. I didn't think you'd actually join the dinner party although it was your idea."

"Come on, now. I have to see my other two favorite girls from time to time," Pierce spoke of Camilla and Brooklyn.

When Brooklyn huffed, Pierce turned to her.

"Not tonight, Brooklyn and get your elbows off the table. Where do you think you are? A ghetto buffet?"

Like a trained little girl, Brooklyn did as she was told. Pierce turned back to Camilla and Myles. He sized Myles up from head to toe.

"So, who's your little friend, Camilla? Someone who works for you?"

Myles was up on Pierce's game and he was definitely ready to play. Myles' first thought was that Pierce needed to shave his head completely bald. His receding hairline could've been the brunt of all comedic jokes. Pierce and Tyler Perry were probably the same height and both men rocked neatly trimmed beards. He was dressed in a custom made Italian suit, and Myles had already spotted his gold Presidential Rolex.

"Pierce, I told you..." Camilla tried to say.

Myles extended his hand. "I'm no friend, Pierce. I'm Maverick...Camilla's fiancé."

Pierce took his seat without shaking Myles's hand. Myles was insulted, but kept his cool. "What is it that you do, Myrick?" Pierce questioned.

"It's Maverick," Myles corrected as he assisted Camilla in her seat, then sat down himself.

Pierce grinned. "Okay. What is it that you do, *Maverick*?"

Myles turned to Brooklyn who looked as though she was enjoying the show and happy that her father's undesired attention turned to someone else. Myles was now in the hot seat.

"I'm a model."

Camilla and Brooklyn jumped when Pierce burst out laughing. "You're kidding me, right? A model? Are you gay?"

"That's enough, Pierce," Camilla warned.

"No, baby it's cool," Myles said. "No, I ain't gay. And since you're so busy prying into my life, what is it that *you* do?" he questioned.

Brooklyn was instantly uncomfortable at the mention of the word *gay*.

Pierce leaned across the table. "I make money, son," he answered boldly as if that was all that Myles needed to know. "And I don't pry. I pay people to do that." He leaned back into his seat and waved the waitress over.

Camilla needed to get the heat off of Myles. "Pierce, where's…"

"Here she comes," Brooklyn interrupted knowing that Camilla was about to ask about her father's girlfriend.

Pierce stood up when his new fling rejoined the table.

"Honey, I'm sorry about that. I got caught up on the phone," she apologized from behind Myles.

Myles immediately froze when he heard her voice and nearly flatlined when she stepped to the side of Pierce.

"Dear, you've already met my sister, Camilla. This is her fiancé Maverick. Maverick, this is the love of my life, Gabrielle," Pierce introduced.

Gabrielle nearly fainted when she saw Myles. When she tried to sit down, she nearly missed the entire chair.

"Are you okay, dear?" Pierce asked Gabrielle when he caught her arm.

"I'm okay, Pierce. I can't believe I almost tripped myself." Gabrielle tried to laugh it off.

As soon as Gabrielle was seated, a paparazzo walked over to the table. Myles immediately tensed.

"Ms. Ellington, Mr. Warrick, can I take your photo?" he asked politely.

"Oh my goodness, by all means," Camilla cheered as she leaned closer to Myles.

"Any publicity is good publicity," Pierce added after wrapping his arm around Gabrielle.

Brooklyn gagged. "I guess I'm not part of the family photo, huh?" she voiced her dismay.

"Move in closer to Gabrielle, honey," Camilla suggested.

When Pierce didn't offer to place his other arm around Brooklyn's shoulder, she didn't move. At that point, she didn't care if she made it in the photo or not.

"Camilla, you know I don't like taking pictures that I'm not paid for," Myles whispered in her ear. He turned his head.

"Baby, please turn around, this will be great PR."

As soon as the paparazzo raised his camera, Camilla leaned in and kissed Myles on the cheek.

"Damn it, Camilla!" Myles wailed.

Everyone at the table turned to him.

"Is there a problem?" Pierce asked.

"No, there isn't," Camilla responded with a pinch of embarrassment in her voice.

"Why'd you do that, Camilla? I've told you over and over that I don't like taking pictures and you go and pull a stunt like that?" Myles roared.

"But what's the problem? You're about to be my husband," Camilla responded.

Pierce stared at him. "Son, are you okay?"

Myles sliced Pierce with his eyes. "I'm not your son. Get that straight. Now, will you please excuse me, I need to use the restroom."

Myles stood up. Camilla looked slightly hurt as he leaned down and kissed her on the forehead then hurried to the restroom. He pushed the doors open forcefully and jolted inside. Not caring who was inside, he paced back and forth cursing out the photographer and Camilla.

"I need to find that fucking photographer asap," he mumbled after turning on the faucet to splash water on his heated face. "Get yourself together," he addressed his reflection.

Myles dried his face then bolted out of the door to locate the photographer. Although he was in New York, he couldn't risk any chances of Kenya finding out before his mission was complete.

"You told me your name was Mitchell and that you were some kind of recruiter!" Gabrielle said when she bumped into Myles outside the restroom. "And did you forget to mention the fact that you're engaged to be married?"

He glared at her with disbelief. "First of all, you need to lower your damn voice and second, what did it fucking matter? We didn't expect to ever see each other again anyway," Myles retaliated as he glanced around the restaurant and pulled Gabrielle to the side.

"So, what are we gonna do? If they find out about…"

"We ain't gonna do shit and they're not gonna find out about us," Myles interrupted. "You need to calm your ass down at the table before someone starts asking questions."

"How in the hell can you ask me to calm down? I'm sitting next to my boyfriend and across the table from a stranger that I had a one night stand with. Oh yeah, that makes me feel real comfortable."

"Gabrielle, calm the fuck down before you get us both exposed! I would think that you'd be able to keep shit together since you were the one who initiated everything between you and me in the first place. Does your man know that you go around fucking men in airplane bathrooms? I hope you don't think I believe that our encounter was your first time doing something like that."

"This is different! It's too close for comfort!"

"I don't give a damn how close comfort is!" Myles stepped in Gabrielle's face that exuded terror. "Calm your ass down before you fuck things up for me. You don't want that," he threatened viciously.

"This is crazy and you know it," Gabrielle said as she placed her hand on his chest. "I'm actually getting turned on right now."

Myles removed her hand. "See, that's what got us in trouble."

"I would love to fuck you right now." Gabrielle had gone from nervous to horny in sixty seconds. She softly touched Myles' chest once again; this time using both hands. "Damn, you feel so good. I've been thinking about your dick ever since we…"

"What the hell is going on here?"

Both Myles and Gabrielle turned to see Brooklyn standing there with wide eyes. Myles quickly removed Gabrielle's hands from his chest.

"Nothing's going on," Myles answered before storming off.

A few hours after dinner, Myles paced the floor in the penthouse and reflected on the night's events and how Gabrielle was a nervous wreck the entire night. She'd cut her eyes at him, shift in her seat and refill her champagne glass after taking a sip or two. If that wasn't bad enough, Myles couldn't believe how Brooklyn watched the two of them the entire night. She could barely eat her food.

Myles stopped pacing and killed the scene in his head to check on Camilla. She'd complained about a headache the entire drive home, but still jumped his bones when they arrived back at the hotel. Myles knew he laid it down with Camilla although Gabrielle was on his mind. He made sure that nothing was different about his sex game. In fact, the incident proved to be a slight turn on knowing that he'd slept with Pierce's new lady. After the way he'd treated him at dinner, Myles figured Pierce deserved it.

"Pre-Karma," Myles mumbled before gulping from the champagne bottle that he and Camilla opened after their wild sexcapade.

Myles peeped inside the master bedroom and found Camilla passed out under the covers. There were three empty glasses of champagne on the nightstand along with a bottle of prescribed Naproxen. She'd taken two pills for her headache, then eventually went to sleep. Myles leaned against the threshold and watched Camilla as he drank from the bottle. Myles contemplated how he could talk Camilla out of the extravagant tropical island wedding that she'd poured tons of money into. He needed to speed things up with Camilla because the situation with Kenya seemed gloomy by the minute. Suddenly, a knock at the door interrupted his thoughts. Myles glanced at his watch.

"Who in the hell can this be at damn near midnight?" he questioned while snatching his white t-shirt and slacks from the floor then putting them on. Closing the bedroom door, he couldn't help but wonder who it was as he headed towards the front of the suite. He took another swig from the bottle, then opened the door without bothering to look through the peep hole.

"What's going on between you and Gabrielle?"

Stunned, Myles spat the champagne from his mouth. Without receiving an invite, Brooklyn bounced inside then turned to face him. She secretly gawked at Myles' abs that printed against his wife beater. The unbuckled belt dangled from Myles' waist as he walked from the door to the kitchen where he set the bottle on the counter.

124

"Do you know what time it is?" Myles questioned with authority. "What in the hell are you doing here? Did you even go home? You have on the same dress from earlier?"

"Where's my aunt?"

"She's asleep and that's where I'm about to go."

"Doesn't look like it to me," Brooklyn replied while glancing at the champagne bottle."Looks to me like you have something heavy on your mind."

Myles swallowed the lump in his throat that seemed to take its time going down. "I don't know what you're talking about, Brooklyn."

"I think you do. Gabrielle had her hands all over you. I even caught the two of you cutting your eyes at each other several times over dinner. So, did you sleep together? How do you know her?"

"You know at some point you have to get a fucking life," Myles shot back. "Now, to answer your questions...no, I don't know her. I've never seen her a day in my life so how could I possibly have slept with her?"

Myles hoped his words were convincing.

"I don't believe you. Tell me why she had her hands on you?"

"The hell if I know. Maybe she wanted some young meat instead of that freezer burned dick your daddy is serving." He smiled.

"Maverick, I know you're some kind of slickster."

"While you're busy trying to throw salt in my game, you need to worry about your daddy issues."

Myles turned the tables and knew he'd struck a nerve when Brooklyn jerked her neck to show her disapproval towards his comment.

"I don't have daddy issues."

"Yes, you do. You're mad because Gabrielle is taking your place now. You're pissed about it so you're trying to fabricate a story to get her kicked to the curb and be number one again."

Brooklyn rolled her eyes. Myles knew he had her and found a way to get the heat off of him.

"I know what I saw, Maverick."

"So, you came over here to tell Camilla what you *think* you saw? Whose story do you think she's gonna believe? The love of her life or the jealous niece?"

"No, I came here to tell her that you're a fucking liar. I've been investigating you. You're no damn model! You're nowhere to be found. I've called my contacts in New York and California. No one has ever heard of a *Maverick Lewis*. You're a fraud. So, what's the deal? What do you want from my aunt?"

It took a lot for Myles to keep his cool when in actuality he wanted to wrap his arms around her long neck and apply tons of pressure. "You think you have it all figured out, huh? You think you have me backed in a corner, huh? Where's your proof? Like I said, who do you think Camilla's gonna believe, me or you?"

"Let's see."

Brooklyn charged toward Camilla's bedroom, but Myles pulled her back. Instead of snatching away, Brooklyn surprisingly turned to him then threw her tongue down his throat. Myles didn't resist. Although they seemingly despised each other, the sexual tension and attraction was evident. Suddenly, Brooklyn ripped Myles wife beater down the middle then squeezed his chest pecs. She'd missed the smell, feel, looks and sounds of a man as he barreled down on her. Myles forced her black Alice & Olivia peplum dress up then ripped off her thong.

"What if my aunt wakes up?" Brooklyn breathed through their heated lip lock.

"It's too late for that now, don't you think? You didn't have to put on this act. If you wanted to fuck me, all you had to do was ask."

Myles spun Brooklyn around and bent her over the arm of the sofa. Seconds later, he was inside of her. Brooklyn wanted to scream but couldn't out of fear that Camilla would hear her. The sofa cushion received punishment as she clawed and scratched. The dildo Leelia used didn't have anything on his massive dick.

"Maverick! Maverick!" she called out softly.

"Don't talk," Myles ordered as he watched the bedroom door.

Myles knew he'd just opened up a whole new can of worms, but couldn't deny himself the pleasure of having Brooklyn. He'd lusted after her long enough. It was only a matter of time before their bodies eventually met. He never in his wildest dreams thought they'd meet while his fiancée was in another room though.

"Damn, Brooklyn! Shit!" he moaned. "You're soaking wet."

Brooklyn reached backward and pinched Myles' thigh to let him know to be quiet. Moments later, Myles pulled out of Brooklyn and maneuvered her on the sofa.

"I've wanted to taste this for a while now," Myles spoke seductively while sliding to his knees then disappearing between Brooklyn's thighs.

Brooklyn grabbed one of the throw pillows and bit into it while thrusting on his tongue and lips.

"Maverick, this isn't right! This isn't right!" Brooklyn said as if she'd suddenly gained a conscious. But her body spoke a different tune as Myles pleasured her and himself as well. "Maverick, go faster! Faster!" she cried out.

Myles followed her commands. His Johnson requested the same orders and he maneuvered his tongue even faster. When Brooklyn's body told him that it was about to erupt, Myles hopped to his feet and pulled her face to his hardened dick. Brooklyn gladly accepted his offer. He watched Brooklyn's lips reach the base of his rod with ease and no hesitation. He also continued to watch the bedroom door and wondered how Camilla would act if she caught the two of them in the mix. All of a sudden, she pulled away from him.

"No, you've gotta finish this, baby. I wasn't done," he said.

Brooklyn leaned her head forward and allowed him back inside her mouth.

"That's right. Take all this dick."

He thrust his dick deeper and faster. Brooklyn pulled away once again when she realized that he was about to cum.

"You're not cumming in my mouth, Maverick," she breathed heavily.

"Just spit it out."

When she wouldn't budge and allow him back inside, he forcefully reentered her wetness again.

"Oooooo, Maverick! Maverick!" Brooklyn whimpered. She couldn't deny how good he felt. It seemed like forever since she'd been pleased by an actual man.

"Ooooh shit. Ooooh shit," he repeated.

Moments later, Myles unloaded a large amount of cum directly into her nest. Having every intention on pulling out, he was pissed at himself when his orgasm finally came to an end. No words were spoken as they took turns cleaning themselves in the bathroom. Brooklyn stayed a little while longer and stared at herself in the mirror. Shame filled her body. She couldn't believe what she'd done. She'd deceived and betrayed the one person who she loved more than life itself. To make matters worse, having sex with a man only added to the confusion about her sexual orientation. As tears began to stream down her face, Myles tapped on the door.

It took her a few moments before she finally opened it.

"Camilla is still asleep, but I think it's best that you leave," Myles advised while pulling a new wife beater over his head. "I just ordered room service. Too bad you can't stay."

Brooklyn sniffed. "I was about..."

Knock! Knock! Knock!

Myles glanced at his watch. "Damn, I know this is a bomb hotel, but room service couldn't have been that quick."

Brooklyn followed him to the door, grabbing her purse and keys along the way.

Myles looked through the peephole. When he saw a woman standing on the other side, he figured it probably was room service even though he didn't see a tray in her hand. As soon as he opened the door, the uninvited guest stormed inside.

"Oh my, God!" Brooklyn gasped. "Leelia, what are you doing here?"

"I followed you here after you left my apartment."

Brooklyn was in complete shock. "How the hell did you get up here without a key card?"

"Let's just say, I know how to get things done," Leelia bragged.

I'm making sure everyone on this shift is fucking fired, Brooklyn thought.

"Whoa! Who are you?" Myles spoke while grabbing Leelia by the arm and walking her back toward the door.

"Get your damn hands off of me!" Leelia yelled after yanking her arm away.

"Brooklyn, I don't know what the hell is going on, but you

need to handle this shit," Myles scolded. "And calm her ass down before she wakes Camilla up."

Brooklyn was at a loss for words.

"Who is he, Brooklyn?" Leelia questioned while staring at Myles.

"Who the hell are you?" Myles returned.

"I'm her girlfriend," Leelia answered aggressively.

Both Myles and Brooklyn were stunned. Brooklyn frowned while Myles produced a huge smirk.

So this bitch is gay, huh, he thought. *No wonder I never see her ass with a man.*

"Now, that I've answered your question, who are you?" Leelia addressed Myles again.

"I'm her aunt's fiancé."

Leelia shot daggers at Brooklyn. "So, you're cheating on me with your aunt's man?" Her voice cracked.

Brooklyn knew she had to speak up before things spun even more out of control. "Leelia, it's not what you think. My aunt is in the other room asleep. I stopped by to check on her because she had a headache earlier. Then Maverick and I started talking about their upcoming nuptials."

Brooklyn turned to Myles for assistance. Myles stood frozen at the news of Brooklyn having a girlfriend, but knew he needed to help out to take the heat off of him as well.

"She's right. We were discussing my upcoming marriage to her aunt," Myles aided. "Camilla's in the other room if you want to peep inside."

Leelia turned back and forth to the both of them then walked up to Brooklyn. "Baby, I'm sorry. You know how jealous I get when I think you're fooling around on me," she apologized while stroking the back of her hand against Brooklyn's cheek.

"Please don't do that," Brooklyn responded. She was beyond devastated. She had to get out of there. "Umm…Maverick. Tell my aunt to call me in the morning about the food for the cocktail hour," she said. Brooklyn watched as Myles shook his head at her like he was disappointed. She wondered how he could judge her after what they'd just done to Camilla.

129

Leelia turned to Myles and apologized to him. "I'm real sorry about that."

Myles walked them to the door. "Oh, it's no problem. I completely understand. I'm actually glad you came by." He stopped Brooklyn before she walked out and leaned into her ear.
"Now, we both have secrets," he whispered sinisterly.

Chapter Sixteen

The next morning, Kenya pulled a load of Zoie's clothes from the dryer and quickly dropped them in the basket when she heard her phone ring. She rushed to the living room to answer it. After learning that it was Julius, Kenya smiled. She turned to Zoie after hearing happy sounds pour from her mouth. Zoie kicked and punched at the air while in her swing. The characters from the *Phineas & Ferb* cartoon on the Disney channel seemed to be the culprit behind Zoie's contentment. Each day, Kenya learned new ways to keep her daughter occupied while she tended to house duties. She kissed Zoie on the forehead before answering the phone.

"Hey, Julius."

"Hi, Kenya. How are you doing?"

"I'm doing well. Thanks for asking. I just finished a load of Zoie's clothes."

"She keeps you busy, huh?"

"If only you knew. But motherhood is worth it though."

"Well, I won't hold you much longer," Julius responded. "I've got great news. Remember the meeting we were supposed to have a few days ago with the potential buyers for Creative Minds."

Kenya instantly felt bad. "I apologize again for missing that meeting. I know how much you're trying to help me with this acquisition. I also wanna thank you for dealing with all the lawyers and red tape. I feel awful that I haven't been there as much as I should. Are you calling to reschedule, again? I thought we decided to have the next meeting on July 2nd."

"Actually, I'm calling to let you know that everything in regards to selling the company is a go...one hundred percent. The meeting we were supposed to have was so the buyers could sit down and speak with you about a few more things before they made a final decision, but they obviously changed their minds. The deal is a go."

Kenya squeeled. "Oh my goodness. Are you serious?"

"Yep. Now, the only thing that they wouldn't agree to is you receiving 100% of the purchase price in cash. They agreed to 25% and the rest will have to come in the form of stocks," Julius informed. "If you agree to that, the paperwork is done. You can come to the office and sign all of the forms in three days."

"Of course I agree. Julius, I don't know how I can ever repay you. I thank you so much."

"No need to thank me, Kenya. It's okay. I'm always willing to help you."

"It's not okay, Julius. I should've been more involved on this. I haven't been much help at all."

"Kenya, I've got your back. Although, it looks like I'm gonna be out of a job soon, I'm still willing to help out in whatever way I can."

Kenya felt bad once again. "I know, Julius. You don't understand how much I appreciate your loyalty to me. You haven't even been at Creative Minds that long and you still went above and beyond what your job title is, so I'm truly grateful. I couldn't have done this without you, so I'll do whatever it takes to help you find another job. Hell, I'm thinking about opening up a restaurant so maybe you can come work for me again."

Julius laughed. "I would like that."

Kenya sighed. "This all happened so fast."

"I thought that's what you wanted?"

"It was but..."

"What's going on, Kenya? I can hear it in your voice that something's wrong. Is everything okay? Are you having second thoughts about selling? I can understand if you are. This was your dad's business. I can retract the sale. Just give me the okay and it's done."

Kenya listened to Julius' concern for her, a quality that Myles seemed to have forgotten. Kenya questioned where she and Myles went wrong and what had happened in their marriage to drive an imaginary wedge between them.

"Kenya, are you still there?" Julius asked, breaking Kenya's chain of thoughts. "Talk to me. What's wrong?"

Kenya didn't want to involve Julius in her problems, but she had no one to talk to. She didn't want to bother Jada with her issues. Although Jada informed Kenya that she would always have an ear for her, Kenya knew it was best not to get Jada involved. Jada didn't need to get worked up about her problems when she had her own to deal with. Before Kenya could attempt to tell Julius what was going on, Zoie began to whine. Kenya lifted Zoie out of the swing and rocked her while placing the pacifier in her mouth.

"It's not about the sale. I actually wanna get this over with. At first I thought I would go back and forth about my decision, but I'm actually fine with it."

"Then what is it."

"Julius, I just don't know what to do. Can you believe Myles didn't pick me up from the hospital when I was released yesterday afternoon?" Kenya felt a sense of relief once she let everything out.

"Stop playing."

"I wish I was playing. He didn't come home last night either."

"Are you serious?"

"Yes..." Kenya paused. "I don't need to be telling you my problems, Julius. I'm so sorry. This is embarrassing."

"Nonsense. Who else are you going to tell? You need to talk to someone with a level head. Jada will just go off the deep end and be ready to fight. Talk to me, Kenya. I'm a big boy. I won't repeat this to anyone."

Kenya closed her eyes then exhaled. "My mind is heavy. I can't help but wonder where he is and what he's doing. I know he's gonna probably blame it on his job, but things just don't add up."

"Well, I can't and won't offer an excuse for his actions because they're foul, but I can do this. Let me take you and Zoie out to lunch to get your mind off of things. You have a lot on your plate."

"Julius, you know Zoie can't eat table food yet." Kenya giggled and blushed at his offer.

"Well, I have another suggestion. How about a walk in the

park so we can talk? We can have the stroller for Zoie and I can get a nice picnic basket together."

Although Julius' offers sounded nice, Kenya knew that it was best to decline with all that was going on between her and Myles. Kenya glanced down at Zoie when she heard her whine. The pacifier had fallen out of her mouth and rolled under the sofa.

"Julius, as much as I would love to have lunch with you, I don't think it's a good idea at this time."

"It's okay, Kenya. I understand. Just remember that I'm a phone call away and my door is always open."

"What about the Alexia girl? Wouldn't she be mad if she saw you out with your boss?"

"There's nothing there, so it wouldn't matter if she got mad or not."

"Did you even give it a real chance? She seemed happy to be with you."

"Actually I didn't. The more we dated, the more I realized that she just wasn't my type."

Kenya wanted to ask what his type was but decided the leave that conversation alone. It was already inappropriate. When she finally glanced under the sofa to retrieve the pacifier, Kenya saw what appeared to be a card holder sitting next to it. She pulled out both items.

What the hell is this, she wondered while staring at the black Michael Kors card holder. Kenya could hear Julius talking, but she wasn't listening. Curiosity had gotten the best of her. Instead of going into the kitchen and rinsing off the pacifier, she wiped it across her shirt then placed it inside Zoie's mouth. Her inquisitiveness and nervousness kicked into full drive. The small wallet didn't belong to her and it definitely didn't belong to Myles. Kenya walked over to Zoie's swing and placed her back inside.

"Yeah, you're right." Kenya tried to continue the conversation with Julius without letting on that something else had her attention. No such luck.

As soon as Kenya pulled out the North Carolina driver's license, she immediately dropped the phone and covered her mouth. She was in shock while the woman named *Krystal Turner* smiled back at her.

After hanging up on Julius without a proper goodbye, Kenya cried hysterically for at least thirty minutes at the thought of Myles having another woman in their home. Kenya felt that she was in the middle of a twilight zone. She glanced at the ID again.

"Oh my, God! She's only nineteen, Myles! A baby! A fucking baby!" Kenya panicked frantically after learning Krystal's age.

She paced around the living room for a few seconds before sifting through the rest of the wallet.

UNC Charlotte college student? He must've met her while recruiting, she thought. *Fucking child molester.*

Kenya grabbed her phone and called Myles for the tenth time. She didn't want to leave a voicemail, but her anger wouldn't allow her to hold back this time.

"How could you, Myles? How could you? In our home…in our damn home!" She hung up.

Kenya wanted to leave the message as evasive as possible. She wanted to have the conversation face to face. Kenya also called Jada a few times against her original decision, but the calls to her went unanswered as well. The calls from Julius were directed to voicemail. She couldn't involve him in any more of her drama. She needed Jada. At that point, Kenya decided to go to her. She needed her friend especially after realizing that her suspicions about Myles were right. His strange behavior was due to another woman.

After lifting Zoie out of the swing, Kenya dropped Krystal's card holder inside of her purse then left. Backing out of the driveway, Kenya prayed that Jada was okay. It wasn't like her to not answer the phone even if she was feeling bad. While rushing out of her neighborhood, Kenya called Jada again. No answer.

"Jada, what's going on with you?" Kenya mumbled after ending the call when the voicemail picked up.

While driving, Kenya spotted a PNC bank a short mile away from her house which quickly prompted her thoughts back to the mortgage company calling, declining credit card and the changed passwords on the accounts.

"Let me make one quick stop before going to Jada's," Kenya mumbled again before making a quick right turn and pulling into the bank parking lot.

Minutes later, Kenya walked inside the bank with Zoie clutched in her arms.

"Welcome to PNC. How may I help you?" the short woman with a choppy bob haircut asked when Kenya walked in.

"Good afternoon. I'd like to check on my account. I forgot my password and can't seem to get online," Kenya said while handing the employee her ID. She then walked over, grabbed a blank deposit slip, then wrote down her account number on the back.

"Sure, let's go over to my desk," the woman said. "Technology is going to be the death of us." The two ladies laughed. As soon as the woman sat down and smiled, Kenya knew the woman was getting ready to engage in some bullshit conversation.

"So, how is your day going?" the woman asked.

"Fine."

"That's wonderful. It's a beautiful day. Actually, the sun is out now, but I think it's supposed to rain around four."

Instead of responding, Kenya just sat there, never saying a word.

"So, what's that beautiful babies' name?"

"Hey, I'm kinda in a rush if you don't mind," Kenya responded.

Finally taking the hint, the woman typed the information into her computer. "I have your account pulled up." She typed a few more things. "Oh, Mrs. Whitaker. How are you? Your husband comes in here all the time."

Kenya eyed the woman who reminded her of the actress, Wendy Raquel Robinson. "Can you tell me the balance, Candice?" she asked looking at the woman's nametag.

"Yes, it's two thousand, five hundred dollars."

"Excuse me? What did you say?" Kenya thought she heard the numbers incorrectly.

"Two thousand, five hundred dollars," Candice reiterated.

"Wait a minute, that can't be right. Can I see the screen?"

Kenya's hands trembled and heart pounded as the woman turned the screen toward her. She skimmed the list.

"Are you sure this is my account, Candice? I see a lot of withdrawals."

She turned the screen back to her so that she could see it clearly. "Yes, it's the right account. There are at least three withdrawals every time there's a deposit from something called Creative Minds. "

"But there are deposits from several different colleges, too, right? Like there might be one from UNC Charlotte or NC State?"

Candice slowly shook her head. "No, I don't see anything like that, just the deposits from Creative Minds."

Kenya pulled out her inhaler from her purse and squeezed life into her lungs before she passed out.

Where has all the money gone? What has Myles done, she wondered silently. "Are there any debit transactions?"

"No, ma'am I don't see any checkcard transactions, only withdrawals."

"So, are you sure there are no deposits from any *job*?" Kenya stressed.

"No, ma'am," Candice answered while scrolling through the account.

He's been lying to me all this time, Kenya thought. *I clearly remember Myles telling me that he had direct deposit for his checks. Now, where the hell is all the money?"* Kenya worried a little harder. At that point she wondered if he even had a job.

"Are you okay?" Candice asked when Kenya zoned out.

"Can you close the account, please?"

"We've changed our policy so the bank manager will have to help you with that."

"I don't care who does it, as long as it's closed. And I'll take the twenty-five hundred in cash please."

"No problem."

"Oh, I almost forgot. What about my money market account? What's the balance on that? Even though his name is not on that account, I just want to double check. It should be 1.2 million in there."

Candice punched the keyboard. "Yep. It's all there."

Kenya breathed a sigh of relief. That was the money from her parents' life insurance policy. It was also an account that he knew nothing about. *You're not the only one who can keep a secret, Myles. Actually you'd be surprised by the secrets I keep,* she thought.

"Thank you for helping me with this, Candice."

"No problem ma'am. Tell your husband I said hello."

Kenya didn't like the way the women said those words, but quickly shrugged it off. She fought back tears of pain, mistrust and dishonesty after hearing the news. She walked over to a small waiting area and took a seat as Zoie squirmed in her arms. After ten minutes with the manager, Kenya closed the joint account, got the twenty-five hundred dollars in cash and stormed out of the bank.

"How much more of our fucking marriage is a lie, Myles," she huffed as she stomped to the car.

138

Chapter Seventeen

Later that night, Kenya waited impatiently for Zoie to fall asleep. All of the investigating she planned to do was interrupted due to her need for attention. If she didn't need to be fed, she needed to be changed. If she didn't need to be changed, she needed to be held. However, around nine, Kenya received her big break. After a warm bath and warm bottle, Zoie finally decided to cooperate.

"It's about time," Kenya huffed while placing Zoie in her crib.

No sooner than Zoie was covered with her pink polka dot blanket, Kenya quickly turned around and dashed to her room. She was extremely livid about the account and just as livid that he still wasn't answering her calls. The only thing she felt good about was finally finding out that Jada was at her mother's house resting. When Jada never answered the door once Kenya went to her house, Kenya eventually called Jada's mom, Mama Dorothy who assured her that Jada was okay.

Kenya walked into Myles' closet. "So, you wanna spend all my damn money, huh?" she ranted while yanking several suits from the racks and tossing them along with countless pairs of shoes on the floor. "You have more damn clothes than me! Of course you do. You're spending all my money to buy 'em! Who needs fucking four thousand dollar suits?"

Kenya continued to yank, pull, toss and snatch. Her hair was a scattered mess and her tank top strap drooped over her shoulder exposing part of her breast.

"I oughta burn this shit like Angela Bassett did in *Waiting to Exhale*," she fussed as she kicked at the clothes.

My Counterfeit Husband

Kenya used the back of her hand to wipe the tears from her puffy, red eyes. She'd cried so much that she could hardly see. Her vision was blurry as well as her mind. Kenya turned toward her iPod dock station when she heard Mint Condition's *You Don't Have to Hurt No More*. The song added fuel to an already blazing fire. Kenya picked up one of Myles' shoes and threw it at the iPod. Even though it fell off the table, the song continued to play. Deciding not to waste any more time, Kenya continued to toss out more garments.

"I can't believe you, Myles! Huge withdrawals and no deposits! There's gonna be hell to pay when you come home!"

Kenya stopped her tirade when her eyes landed on Myles' safe. She dropped to her knees and stared at the small keypad.

"Let's see what other secrets you have."

Kenya tried Zoie's birthday as the four digit code, but it didn't work. Next, she attempted her own birthday. No luck.

"What in the hell can it be?" she snarled after attempting Myles' birthday.

The sound of the doorbell halted any further attempts.

"Now, who the hell can this be?"

Kenya hopped to her feet then bounced downstairs. She then yanked the door open without asking who was on the other end.

"Julius, what are you doing here?" She was surprised to see him.

"Are you okay?" Julius asked as he stared at her hair and restless eyes.

"Julius, wh-wh-what are you doing here? H-How did you find out where I lived?" Kenya stammered.

Julius conveyed a sexy smile. "It wasn't hard, Kenya. You do remember that I pay the bills for the company, right, including your cell phone bill. Even though your phone bill is in the company's name, it has this address on it. You might want to change that by the way."

Kenya just shook her head.

"So, again is everything okay with you?"

"Not really."

"And that's why I'm here. I'm sorry for showing up unannounced, but I was worried when you hung up on me and wouldn't

140

answer my calls."

"It's been a crazy day, Julius. I don't know if I'm coming or going."

Kenya turned and took a few steps backward, allowing him to step inside. Julius could see the hurt and pain in her face.

"I can see that you've unraveled, Kenya," he said after walking up to her and gently grazing the back of his hand across her cheek. Kenya closed her eyes and welcomed the soft touch. "Talk to me. I don't like seeing you like this. I hate seeing you cry."

"I don't even know where to begin. It's just so much."

"Well, if it takes all night, I'll be here to listen. You know Myles doesn't deserve a woman like you."

"So, I don't deserve her, huh?" Myles suddenly barked from behind.

Kenya and Julius turned toward the door at the same time. Kenya backed away from Julius then stared at Myles. He was holding a vase of red roses along with the infamous blue bag from Tiffany & Co. Myles hoped to surprise Kenya with a peace offering, but it was he who received the surprise. Although she was mad, Kenya couldn't help but to become nervous after seeing her husband standing there. She hadn't even heard his car pull up.

"Look, I didn't come here for any trouble," Julius stated.

"You caused trouble as soon as you stepped foot inside *my* house, nigga. What in the fuck are you doing here?"

"I came to check on Kenya."

"For what?" Myles asked while glaring at his wife. "What's going on, Kenya?"

"Maybe you two should talk," Julius suggested.

"I'm talking to you right now…man to man. This is the second time that I've found you with my wife. There's no telling how many other times y'all have been together behind my back."

"You're way off track, Myles. Slow down," Julius responded.

"Slow down? Nigga I just started," Myles fired back.

"Like I said before, I didn't come here for any trouble." Julius turned to Kenya. "Take care, Kenya. We'll talk soon."

"No, I don't think so. You stay the hell away from my wife or next time things aren't gonna end up like this," Myles shot back. He and Julius locked eyes until Julius made his way out of the door.

"What the fuck was he doing in my house?" Myles started in on Kenya. *So me choking your ass out wasn't enough, huh*, he thought.

"It's not what you think. Julius just worries about me and…"

"And why the hell would he be worried about you? Here I am, coming home to surprise you and this is the shit I walk into. I saw the car in the driveway, so that's why I parked across the street. I wanted to sneak up on your ass to see what you were up to."

"Spare me, Myles! You have no room to question anything that I do at this point after all the lies that I've learned about you today."

"Lies? What lies? What the hell are you talking about?"

In a fit of rage, Kenya charged Myles and slapped him, causing the vase to fall and shatter. Water splattered on Kenya's bare feet. She stepped away from the broken glass. When Myles followed her, Kenya slapped him again. Myles dropped the Tiffany's bag, grabbed Kenya by the wrists and penned her against the wall.

I wouldn't keep doing that if I were you, Myles thought. "What in the hell has gotten into you, Kenya? I come home to find another nigga in my house and you want to hit me? It should be the other way around."

"So, now what? You want to hit me or do you want to choke me again like you did in the hospital? By the way, I hate fucking roses. And I know that I've told you that before."

Myles released her and backed up. He tried to act as if he was concerned about putting his hands on her, but it was all just a performance.

"Kenya, I told you that if I could go back in time and change that, I would. You know I'd never hurt you, baby. I don't know what came over me that day. Jealousy maybe. Seeing another man by your side instead of me." Myles approached Kenya again and tried to kiss her, but she moved away.

"I don't know what to believe anymore, Myles."

"What do you mean? I'm telling you the truth, baby."

"Then tell me where all of our money has gone? Tell me why our mortgage is four months behind? Tell me why your checks are not being deposited in our account? Last but not least, tell me who the hell Krystal Turner is and why did I find her little wallet in my damn house?"

Myles wanted to crawl under a rock and die at the thought of him leaving Krystal's wallet behind before he dumped her body.

How could you be so damn stupid, he thought. *What else does she know?* "Baby, where is all of this coming from?"

"Don't try and sweet talk your way out of this one, Myles. Answer my damn questions!"

As Kenya started wheezing, Myles gently grabbed her arm and led her to the sofa.

"Baby, let me get you a glass of water or do you need your inhaler?" Myles hoped she would ask for either one so his departure would buy him some time to think. No such luck.

"I've got it under control, Myles," Kenya wheezed. "Now, answer me. What is going on? Who the hell is Krystal Turner?"

Myles knew there was no way out of the conversation, but he was prepared.

"Kenya, sweetie, you know how much I travel. That shit adds up: flights, car rentals, hotels and sucking up to potential players can be costly. I have to take them out to eat, fly them places as well, buy them shit, anything to secure the deal."

"Okay, that's all fine and dandy, but where are your checks from the recruiting? I went to the bank today…there were no deposits made into our account from *your* job."

"Baby, I never told you that I'd deposit my checks into that account. I have a separate account for that."

Kenya looked confused. "So, you decided to spend all *my* hard earned fucking money instead of spending your own? Not to mention, I never knew anything about this so called separate account."

"It's not like that, Kenya and you know it. That account was set up before meeting you. I just never got around to closing it."

"Myles, there was only twenty-five hundred dollars left in that account, which means you spent all of my money!"

"Baby, calm down. If you want, I can close my personal account at Suntrust and deposit all of the funds into our joint account over at PNC. That's not a problem." He lowered his head. "You're right. After taking out your portion of the bill money, I shouldn't have taken any additional money without your permission. It's just that when I'm on the road, I get so caught up in spending money to impress these young guys that I dip into your money every now and then when my funds get low. But it's only right that I pay you back every dime."

"Every now and then?" Kenya had to laugh. "How is spending all my damn money considered every now and then? You're fucking delusional."

"Kenya, I can fix it. I promise."

She shook her head with disappointment. "Why didn't you just ask me for the money?"

Myles lowered his head again. "I was scared that if I asked you would say no."

Kenya paused for a moment. "What about the mortgage? Why aren't you paying that?"

"Now, that must be a mistake," Myles tried to convince. "I'm gonna take care of that first thing tomorrow morning. Those payments are supposed to be automatically drafted out of our joint account."

Kenya stared into Myles' eyes. He had a plausible answer for everything. "Maybe they couldn't take it out because there wasn't enough money in there!" she roared. "So, here I am trusting you to take care of our finances and you're not even paying the bills on time! Oh, you can cancel that shit now. From here on out, I'll be paying the bills."

"That's fine," Myles agreed even though internally he was fuming.

"Who's Krystal, Myles?"

Myles took a deep breath but didn't break a sweat. "I hate you had to find out like this."

Kenya's eyes bucked. "So, it is true. You're fucking around on me with a damn nineteen year old white girl!"

"No, that's not it at all. I figured you'd need help after leaving the hospital so I interviewed a few people to help keep Zoie. I know how exhausted you've been lately, so I figured a nanny could help out. She must've dropped her wallet here the day I interviewed her. Hiring her was supposed to be a surprise, too." As soon as Myles saw

My Counterfeit Husband

Kenya lightening up a bit, he decided to turn the tables. "I can't believe that you're questioning me about all this shit when I should be questioning you."

"What do you mean *you should be questioning me*? I'm not hiding anything."

"Sure you aren't. This is the second time I've seen that nigga Julius around. You must be fucking him! Did my presence interrupt you from riding his dick?"

"What? Have you lost your damn mind?" Kenya was appalled by Myles' accusations.

"Is he Zoie's dad? Is that why he's been coming around so much?"

Kenya's mouth dropped. She couldn't believe her ears. It didn't take long for her to burst into tears. She hopped up from the sofa and glared at her husband.

"I've never cheated on you, Myles! I love you! Julius was only here to tell me that the deal to sell the company is a go. I sign the paperwork in three days."

Myles smiled internally. Kenya's words were music to his ears. At that moment, he walked up to her. When she backed away, he followed her until the wall stopped them from going any farther. Kenya turned her head away from him as Myles placed his forefinger under her chin. He turned her face back toward him. Myles wiped away Kenya's tears.

"Baby, I'm so sorry. I didn't mean what I said," he apologized. "Stop crying. Please."

"Myles..."

"Shhhhhhhh. All you need to know is that I'm sorry and I didn't mean anything that I said. I love you, Kenya. You mean the world to me. I know you'd never do anything to jeopardize our marriage."

Kenya jumped when Myles slipped his hands inside her leggings.

"I love you, baby," Myles continued as he pulled her leggings off and discarded them slowly then lowered to his knees. "I love you, Kenya...with all my heart." Myles disappeared between her thighs.

Kenya counted the red numbers on the elevator display as it ascended upward. She couldn't believe the day had come that she'd be selling off her father's company. Although she had Myles by her side, she needed Jada as well. Kenya felt bad that she hadn't checked on her friend again in the past three days, but it was for a good reason. She was too busy making up with Myles. One night, Myles even showed off his skills in the kitchen by cooking an exquisite meal.

"How many times are you going to call her?" Myles asked.

"Myles, it's not like Jada not to answer. I haven't spoken to her in days. The last time I heard anything was when I called her mother. She told me Jada was fine, but I feel bad that I haven't called and checked on her since then. I hope she's not mad." Kenya ended the call only to call right back.

"Has it occurred to you that she may want some time alone?"

"You may be right, but I need her to tell me that. She might be thinking that I'm the worst friend in the world by now, so I wanna tell her how sorry I am if she feels that way."

Kenya repeated her previous actions. She beat herself up for having so much fun with Myles over the past few days while her friend was ill. Kenya enjoyed having Myles at home. He even took the liberty of turning off his phone so they wouldn't be disturbed. Kenya's cheeks flushed red at the thought of them having sex in their Jacuzzi tub; something they hadn't done since they first met. It nearly brought tears to her eyes. He'd occupied her body and mind that she didn't give much thought to the reasons she was angry with him. Myles took the cake when he brought up the idea of the family taking a vacation to Aruba. Kenya was floored when he included Jada in the trip saying that he knew how much Jada meant to her. Kenya desperately wanted her husband and best friend to get along because they meant the world to her.

During the exquisite dinner, Kenya informed Myles that she was still slightly uneasy about the money situation and advised him once again that she'd be more hands on going forward. She wanted to see what his reaction would be since he had no clue that she'd closed the account. Myles informed Kenya that he had no problem with her decision and that she should've been part of their finances all along.

146

The only thing left for him to do was call the mortgage company with Kenya on the phone to clear up the misunderstanding. With all the sex going on, they hadn't gotten around to that task yet, but Myles assured her they would do it directly after the meeting.

Kenya was amazed at how much attention Myles showed Zoie. He even took care of her a few times while Kenya snuck in a nap. Kenya loved the direction her family was headed.

"Here's our stop, Zoie, the 5th floor." Myles peeped inside her stroller and smiled as he pushed it off the elevator. He then turned to Kenya. "Are you coming?"

"Myles, I'm really worried about Jada. Maybe we should stop by her house when we're done." Kenya ended another call.

"Look, enough about Jada, she's fine. You need to get your head in the game, baby. Today is the big day. Let's do this," Myles cheered.

"You're right, but I still wanna stop by her house once this is over."

"No problem, baby. Whatever you want."

"Thank you."

Kenya kissed Myles on the cheek then kissed Zoie on the forehead just before her secretary, Grace came around the corner. She held a big smile on her face as she looked at both Kenya and the baby.

"It's so good to see you, Mrs. Whitaker. "And I'm glad you brought that beautiful baby with you," Grace said. She walked up to Kenya and gave her a huge hug.

"It's good to see you, too, Grace."

Just like with Julius, Kenya felt bad when employees like Grace were going to lose their job once she signed on the dotted line. Grace had been with Creative Minds for the past nine years, so it was gonna be tough to let the employees know that the new owners had their own staff and didn't plan on keeping any of the current workers. It was definitely a bittersweet moment.

"So, how have you been, Mrs. Whitaker?" Grace asked. "You know Lance came to visit us yesterday. He asked about you."

"I thought fired employees weren't allowed to come back on the premises?" Myles questioned.

Kenya immediately felt uncomfortable. Even though Myles

had yet to admit it, she knew he didn't care for any of her male employees. She quickly changed the subject. "So, Grace how is your grandson doing?"

As Kenya and Grace talked, Myles thought back to Camilla's text that morning asking when he was coming back to New York and why he hadn't answered her calls over the past three days. He tried to comfort her by saying that he was handling some very important issues and didn't feel like having a conversation. Myles also told her that he hoped she understood and that he would explain everything later once he got back to New York within the next day or so. After informing Myles that she understood but needed to hear his voice soon, Camilla ended the last text with, "I love you." Myles couldn't wait until Kenya received the money from selling her company, so he could finally leave. Even though Camilla was content for now, he didn't know how long that attitude was going to last.

When Myles looked back at Kenya and Grace, they were still talking. "We have to go Kenya," he said with authority.

"Yes, I have to go Grace. I'm already a few minutes late. We'll chat once I come out of the meeting," Kenya informed as Myles rolled the stroller over to Grace. "I just fed and changed her in the car, so all she might need is a bit of cuddling."

"Okay," Grace replied before they both headed towards the conference room.

When they arrived, Julius sat at the table along with several other men. Kenya felt at home again when all of the men stood up. Myles took a seat as she headed to the head of the table.

The man standing next to Julius reached over and shook Kenya's hand. "Good afternoon, Mrs. Whitaker."

"Good afternoon, Mr. Freeman," Kenya responded to her company's attorney. She then looked at each of the buyers one by one along with their attorney and nodded her head. "Good afternoon to all you gentlemen."

"Good afternoon," they all said in unison.

"Do you know how long this is going to take?" Myles suddenly asked.

Both Kenya and Julius gave Myles a horrified look.

"It shouldn't take long. All of the paperwork has been looked over thoroughly. All we need now is Kenya's signature," Julius replied. He couldn't believe Myles' outburst and wondered why Kenya didn't ask him to stay home.

"Where's the paperwork?" Myles questioned.

Suddenly, Kenya wished Myles had stayed home, too. His behavior was uncalled for. When Julius slid the tan envelope over to Kenya, she opened it. Her lawyer walked over to her side.

"The X marks all the lines where you need to sign, Mrs. Whitaker," he informed.

Kenya grabbed the pen that Julius handed her. She wanted to get the deal over with so that she could get Myles out of the conference room before he continued to embarrass her. As soon as she pressed the pen to the first line, her cell phone rang. Kenya was desperate for it to be Jada so she placed the pen down and went to retrieve her phone.

"This is more important, Kenya. Whoever that is can wait," Myles scolded.

Kenya ignored him and looked at her phone. Her heart stopped when she saw that it was Jada's mom.

"Excuse me for one second gentlemen while I take this call," she said to everyone. "Hey, Mama Dorothy, is everything okay?" Kenya was beyond concerned.

"Baby, you need to get to the hospital. Jada's surgery didn't go well."

"Hospital? Surgery? What surgery?"

"I can tell you once you get here, but you need to get here quick. It doesn't look good," she replied.

"Oh my God. I'm on my way!"

Before Mama Dorothy ended the call, Kenya heard her crying. Without a second thought, she quickly apologized to everyone, then bolted out of the conference room, like the Roadrunner. In her mind, she would apologize for her behavior later on and once again reschedule the meeting. She hadn't made it very far before Myles ran up to her.

"Are you crazy?" Myles asked, pulling her arm. "Why did you just leave like that?"

"Jada's in the hospital!"

149

"Okay and…what does that have to do with you right now. You need to get back in that conference room and sign those papers, Kenya."

"Myles, I don't give a damn about that right now. My friend is in the hospital. I need to get there. Her mother said that it doesn't look good! Go get Zoie from Grace and meet me at the car." She turned around to walk away, but he pulled her back again.

"Well, I don't know how you're gonna get there because I'm not taking you, especially if you leave here without sealing this deal."

Kenya couldn't believe her ears. She quickly wondered what happened to the man she'd just spent three wonderful days with. She also thought about how they'd driven together in his car.

"I don't have time for games right now, Myles."

"Neither do I," he answered in a serious tone. "Do you think I care about some bitch with cancer right now? We worked too hard on this deal for you to just walk away and expect those buyers to keep waiting on you. What if they change their minds?"

"Well give me your keys then. I'll have one of my employees give you a ride home," Kenya suggested.

Myles chuckled. "You're joking, right?"

"Kenya, what's wrong?" Julius asked when he walked up.

"She needs to go sign those damn papers. That's what's wrong," Myles responded spitefully.

"You're so damn heartless!" Kenya's mascara ran with her tears.

"What's going on?" Julius questioned.

"Jada is in the hospital and Myles won't take me unless I sign the papers," she cried. "Julius, can you just let the buyers know how sorry I am? I can't do this right now."

Julius looked at Myles with disgust. "So, you're gonna sit back and let your wife go through this alone?"

When Myles turned around and threw up two fingers, displaying the peace sign and headed in the opposite direction both Julius and Kenya were in complete awe.

"Let's go," Julius said, as he grabbed Kenya's hand and hurried her to the elevator.

Chapter Eighteen

After walking into Presbyterian Hospital twenty minutes later, Kenya called Mama Dorothy to find out what floor Jada was on. Kenya held back the tears after learning that Jada was in the ICU. Julius stopped Kenya before they went inside.

"Kenya, look at me," Julius gently ordered as he watched Kenya completely unravel. "You don't want Jada to see you like this. You know she's gonna curse you out."

Although she didn't want to, Kenya laughed at the thought. She knew Julius was right.

"Mama Dorothy didn't sound too good on the phone," Kenya cried.

"Well, you still shouldn't think negatively. Right now, you just need to be by Jada's side."

"I can't go through this again." Kenya thought back to her parents' deaths.

They fell into a long embrace that allowed Kenya to revisit the day her parents died. Her mother was pronounced dead on the scene, but she was able to see her father before he transitioned to the afterlife. He spoke through his eyes because he was unable to verbally talk. He and Kenya shared tears before he closed his eyes for good.

She wiped the streaming tears from her eyes. "Okay, let's go."

As they were about to walk through the doors, a text came through from Myles.

The buyers are willing to be here tomorrow for you to sign the papers. So, I reset the meeting for 2pm. Don't fuck up this time!

Julius noticed the displeasing look on Kenya's face and

grabbed her phone. He read the text message and his face immediately fumed.

"Don't let his ignorance upset you."

"I just don't understand, Julius. He couldn't even bring me to the damn hospital. Why is he…"

"Kenya, fuck Myles! Jada's waiting upstairs. She's your priority now." Julius redirected her thoughts.

Kenya knew Julius was upset because of the time she'd known him, he rarely cursed. Evidently, Myles' text had pissed him off, too. Kenya took a deep breath, counted to ten then walked down the hall. Julius held Kenya's hand as they boarded the elevator. A few minutes later, they arrived on the ICU floor. Julius stepped off the elevator first, but Kenya hesitated.

"I'm right here with you," he assured.

She nodded as they walked to the waiting room. Mama Dorothy and a few of Jada's aunts, uncles and cousins were there. A few of them were crying while one of Jada's uncles was in a corner on his knees…praying.

"Mama Dorothy?"

Jada's mom turned to Kenya then hugged her tightly. "I'm so glad you're here, baby."

"This is my co-worker, Julius," Kenya introduced.

Hi, Julius. It's nice to meet you," Mama Dorothy responded.

"It's nice to meet you, too, ma'am. If there's anything that I can do, don't hesitate to ask."

"I really appreciate that, sweetie," Mama Dorothy replied then turned back to Kenya. "She asked about you."

"What's going on, Mama Dorothy? What surgery did Jada have?"

"Well, baby the cancer spread to her ovaries, uterus, liver and kidneys. She was here to have a hysterectomy done..." Mama Dorothy paused to get herself together. "I don't think she's gonna make it through the night, Kenya. She's dying."

"What do you mean *dying*? When did the cancer spread? Why didn't she tell me this?" Kenya was frantic. She reached inside her purse for her inhaler then took a long pull.

"Jada didn't want to upset you, so she's been putting up a

front. The doctors gave her less than a month when she found out that the cancer had spread. She tried to buy herself some time by having the surgery although they told her that it wouldn't help, but you know how stubborn she is."

"So, what can she do now? What's the next step? What about all the chemo and radiation?" Kenya wasn't able to internalize the news in her head.

"The cancer is just too aggressive, baby. Nothing is working, and Jada is tired of fighting."

"Less than a month? Why would she lie to me? I'm her best friend...her sister. Why didn't she tell me?"

When Kenya broke down crying, Julius held her closely before she hit the floor.

"She didn't want to bother you, Kenya. She wanted to come in and quietly have the surgery done, but there was a complication. She started hemorrhaging, so the surgeons couldn't even proceed. Luckily they were able to stop the bleeding, but now, that made things worse. Go in and see her, Kenya. She's the third door on the left," Mama Dorothy suggested.

Julius squeezed Kenya's shoulders. "Yes, go see her," he whispered then kissed Kenya on the cheek. "I'll be right here waiting for you."

Kenya walked slowly toward Jada's room. Her mind went into overdrive as she thought about what she would see after opening the door. She couldn't believe that Jada lied to her. She wanted answers. She needed answers. Kenya halfheartedly opened the door. Tears quickly flowed as she listened to the beeps from the blood pressure monitor and stared at all the tubes that Jada was connected to. Jada's body was frail, pale and small. Kenya wanted to run out of the room. She couldn't believe how quickly her body had deteriorated.

"I see you over...there staring...at me. Come on...over," Jada spoke through a vicious cough. "Let me...guess. My mother called...you."

Her voice was lower than usual. Kenya could tell that she struggled to speak. She walked over to Jada and gently grabbed her hand.

"I hate you."

"Now, what kind of shit…is that for you to…say…to a dying woman?"

"Why did you lie to me?"

"Technically, I didn't…lie. I'm still dying… just sooner."

"I should kill you right now for shutting me out of this. I should've been here with you and you know it!" Kenya cried.

"Stop that damn crying before I…have you removed…from the room."

"Do you need any water, Jada?"

"No, but I wouldn't mind a few…vodka shots."

"I'm serious, Jada."

"Shit...so am I."

Jada frowned when she tried to smile. Kenya could tell that Jada was in intense pain. Kenya spotted a small jar of Vaseline on the table next to her bed. She scooped a little out of it and spread it across Jada's chapped lips.

"Well, since you're making me pretty…grab that scarf over…there and…tie it around my head. I've gotta be pretty for my daddy."

"Will you stop talking like that?" Kenya said as she retrieved the colorful scarf. She gently lifted Jada's head and tied it around.

"Take my picture so that I can see how I…look."

Kenya's hand trembled as she snapped Jada's picture with her phone, then showed it to her.

"Damn! I'm too…sexy for my scarf," Jada attempted to sing. Kenya grinned.

"That's right, Kenya. Laugh. I'm not crying…so you…shouldn't be."

"Jada, what am I supposed to do now?"

"For starters, leave Myles' ass! You're…not happy with him, Kenya and you…know it. He's dangerous for your heart. He means you no…good."

Kenya couldn't believe Jada's selflessness. Jada was the one who was dying, but she worried about her well-being. "I don't want to talk about him right now," she cried and sniffled.

"Don't worry…about me. You still have Zoie," Jada said.

"But I want you! I need you! This isn't fair! Who's gonna

make me laugh now? Who's gonna stay on my ass and see that I do right now? Who am I gonna turn to when I need an ear to listen or a shoulder to cry on."

"Julius," Jada answered with a huge smile.

"You're crazy. You know that?" Kenya laughed. "He's just a co-worker."

"Yeah, but I see how he looks at you. Hell, you better...be glad I can't get 'em. I'm a bad bitch, so you wouldn't stand a chance...once I put on my Sunday's best."

They both burst out laughing. Jada's laugh turned into another vicious cough.

"I'm sorry," Kenya apologized.

"Sorry for what? I...needed that...laugh."

There was a brief silence as they stared at each other. Their eyes filled with tears.

"I'm really scared," Jada said, breaking down.

Kenya threw her body across Jada's, disregarding her pain. Jada moaned as she lifted her arm and wrapped it around Kenya's back.

"I know you're scared. I'm scared, too. Please fight this! You're strong! You're a fighter!"

"I'm tired," Jada whispered.

"I know, but you gotta fight this. I can't imagine you not being here for me and Zoie."

"I love you."

"I love you, too. Please don't give up."

"Kiss my Godbaby for me."

Kenya lifted her body when she heard a loud, long, solid beep a few seconds later. She wiped her hand across her eyes to clear her vision. She then glanced down at Jada. Her eyes were closed. Kenya glanced at the monitor. There was a flat line racing across the screen.

"Jada? Jada? Jada?" Kenya yelled out. No answer. "Jada? Jada?" Kenya shook her. No response. "Jadaaaaa! Noooooooooo! It's not time! It's not time! We weren't done talking!"

Seconds later, Julius, Mama Dorothy and two nurses burst through the doors.

"She's gone! She's gone!" Kenya yelled out.

Carla PENNINGTON

Chapter Nineteen

Myles vigorously tapped his foot on the floor of the elevator as he and Zoie rode it down. He was upset beyond belief that Kenya left without signing the papers.

Everything was in motion and going smoothly, he thought. *The pen was right there on the fucking paper.* "It would've taken less than ten seconds to sign that shit. Jada's ass wasn't going anywhere," he fussed as if Kenya were present.

The elevator doors opened once they reached the first floor.

"Move the hell out of the way," he barked at a few potential passengers as he forcefully rolled the stroller out.

Myles stomped out of the building and to the car where he secured Zoie in her car seat. She was asleep. Myles didn't bother to fold the stroller and store it in the trunk. He left it on the side of the car and hopped behind the wheel. He was that upset.

"Stupid! Stupid! Stupid!" he scolded his reflection. "You should've made her ass sign the damn papers! It's always about that Jada bitch! I hope her ass is dead because she's fucking shit up for me."

Before Myles started the car, he called the 1-800 number to the bank to check the balance. Even though Kenya had mentioned something about twenty-five hundred dollars a few days ago, he wanted to double check. Knowing he had to go back to New York soon, Myles had to figure out how that small amount of money would hold him over until Kenya sold the company.

"What the hell?"

Myles stared at the phone to see if he punched in the correct account number. He ended the call then repeated his previous actions.

"*I'm sorry. The account number you have entered is invalid,*" the automated voice informed again.

"What kind of shit is this? Did she close the damn account?" Myles questioned.

He repeated his actions again only to receive the same response.

"This has to be a damn mistake."

Myles pressed zero to speak to a live representative who quickly informed him that the account had been closed.

"This bitch has lost her damn mind. How in the hell am I supposed to survive without any money?" Myles yelled when he ended the call.

As Myles was about to call Candice from the bank, Kenya's name popped up on his screen.

"Did you close the bank account?" Myles screeched into the phone. He didn't even bother to say hello.

Kenya cried and sniffled on the other end.

"Myles?"

"What? Do you want me to run upstairs to see if the buyers have left? I can stop them if you're on your way back."

"No, Myles." Kenya sniffled again.

"Then why the hell are you calling me? There's nothing else for us to talk about."

"Myles…Myles, Jada is dead."

"So, you're on your way back?"

"What? No! Did you not hear me? Jada is dead!"

"I heard you loud and clear. Now, hear me loud and clear. Do you want me to stop the buyers from leaving? You need to be focusing on getting this money."

Kenya went ballistic. "Are you serious? I can't believe you! I just told you that my best friend is dead and all you're worried about is me selling the company!"

"Okay, she's dead! What can you do about that? You're wasting time, Kenya. Do you want me to stop them or not?"

"No!" Kenya screamed through cries. "As a matter of fact, I'm not selling the damn company now!"

Myles paused for a few seconds. "You're not what?"

"You heard me! I'm not selling the company!"

"Then I have no more use for you then."

This time, Kenya paused. "What do you mean by *you have no more use for me?*"

"You'll figure it out soon enough. And why the fuck did you close the damn bank account?"

"Is that what the hell this heartless attitude is all about? Money?"

"Look, what else do you want? I gotta go. I have an important phone call to make."

"You're twisted, Myles! Where's my baby? Where's Zoie?"

"Where else would she be? She's with her father."

"Myles, where are you? Bring my baby to the hospital."

"No. I don't think so."

"What the hell do you mean, you don't think so."

"It means I'm taking my daughter with me."

Kenya was hysterical. "Taking her with you...to where? What are you talking..."

Before she could finish, Myles hung up the phone then turned it off. He glanced to the back seat.

"Looks like it's just me and you kid," he said to a sleeping Zoie before pulling off.

Myles arrived home fifteen minutes later. Luckily for him, he caught all the green lights home and no cops were present to catch him speeding. Since Myles wasn't sure where Kenya might be, he had to move quickly.

He cracked the windows and left Zoie inside the car. He then raced inside of the house and hurried upstairs until he reached his destination. The safe. He could tell that Kenya had tried to open it since the keypad blinked continuously, which was a sure sign that she'd entered in several incorrect codes. This was the first time he'd looked at it since coming home three days ago.

"Stupid bitch," Myles huffed as he entered in 0404; the month and day his mother passed away, and a date that he never mentioned to anyone.

Once the safe was open, he grabbed his second cell phone and saw that Camilla had called a few times. He also grabbed what little cash he had left, his watches and two IDs. Next, he raced back into the bedroom and pulled a pillow from its case. He tossed the items from the safe inside then trotted to the dresser.

"You won't need these," he spoke sinisterly as he tossed Kenya's jewelry inside of the pillow case. He especially grabbed the cuff bracelet from Tiffany & Co. that he'd just gotten money from Camilla to buy her.

After grabbing a rolling suitcase, he raced back down the steps and placed the suitcase on top of the sofa. Myles paused when he heard Zoie's cries float inside the house from the garage.

"You'll just have to wait, lil' girl."

Myles placed the pillow case inside the suitcase and dashed inside the office where he snatched his laptop. He placed it inside the suitcase after returning to the living room. Once that was done, Myles glanced at the glass armoire that housed Kenya's Swarovski crystal sculptures that were blinking at him. He grabbed one of his *Sports Illustrated* magazines and one of Kenya's *O* magazines from the table. He ripped pages from them and gently yet quickly wrapped the crystals inside of each sheet. There were a few exotic birds and fish scattered about the room. Myles scooped those up as well.

"Swarovski, you may have just become a new friend," Myles said out loud as he estimated the cost of the crystals inside his head.

Lastly, Myles snatched the burnt orange throw from the back of the sofa and tucked it inside the suitcase. After zipping the suitcase, he bolted out of the door. He stopped abruptly when he saw the next door neighbor rocking Zoie and feeding her one of the bottles Kenya had prepared.

"What are you doing?" Myles asked with a stern look on his face.

"I went to check the mail and heard her over here crying. I came over to see if everything was okay," the thin, Caucasian woman answered.

"Well, thanks. I had to run in the house for something."

"You shouldn't leave her unattended like this. There are some crazy people out in the world."

Myles wasn't trying to hear the lecture. He needed to leave.

My *Counterfeit* Husband

"You're right. Her mom's friend just passed away and we were on our way to the hospital."

"Oh my! I'm so sorry to hear that."

"Yeah, so am I," Myles spat. "If you don't mind, can you change her diaper for me?"

The neighbor looked puzzled at first then complied. "No problem. My granddaughter is about her age. They are a joy, aren't they?" After patting Zoie on the back a few times, she laid her on the backseat.

Lady, just change the damn diaper. I don't have time for small talk," Myles thought. "If you say so," he answered. It seemed to take the woman forever as she continued to talk to Myles even though he would never respond. She finally stopped talking and focused her attention on Zoie.

"All done," the woman spoke before securing Zoie back in her seat.

"Thank you." Myles smiled then tossed the suitcase in the trunk.

"I hope everything will be okay. My condolences go out to you and your family," the neighbor spoke as Myles climbed behind the driver's seat.

"Yeah, yeah…whatever," Myles huffed causing the neighbor to give him a side eye.

She had to jump out of the way as he backed out of the garage, nearly running over her feet. As soon as Myles was down the street, he retrieved his private bat line phone and called Camilla. She answered on the first ring.

"Hey, darling."

"Hey, baby." Myles spoke in a low tone.

"You sound upset. Is everything okay?" Camilla asked with concern in her voice.

Myles knew it was time to put on his best performance. Things had gone in a completely different direction than he had expected. He needed to regain some control.

"No, everything isn't okay, Camilla," Myles said as he tried to squeeze tears from his eyes. He knew that once the tears fell then the sniffles would follow.

161

"What's going on? Are you crying? Talk to me, Maverick."

"Camilla, I can't keep going on like this. I'm ready to be your husband and I'm ready for you to be my wife."

"Honey, we'll be married soon. August is just around the corner."

"No, you're misunderstanding me, baby. I want to get married as soon as possible. We don't have to go all the way to Anguilla to express our love. We can go down to the courthouse and…"

"Courthouse?" Camilla nearly hollered at the idea. "That's beneath me, Maverick. I have higher standards than that, darling."

"I understand, baby, but I'm ready to marry you. My heart aches for you, Camilla. I don't wanna wait until August. I want to marry you now."

"Maverick, you're scaring me. What's the rush?" she questioned.

"I've thought about this a lot, Camilla. It's time, baby. Life is too short to wait."

Camilla was overjoyed from his words. Her heart smiled. She couldn't say no to him.

"We don't have to do Anguilla. I want to marry you, too. I can get something together at the hotel. One of my close friends was just ordained a few weeks ago. I'm sure he'd be happy to officiate over the wedding."

"That sounds good; something small. I don't want a slew of people. Just me and you."

"But Maverick, I want the world to know about our nuptials. Can you imagine the publicity the hotel would receive with our wedding photo in the *New York Times*? Can you imagine all of the people that will line up to have their wedding at the hotel? This is so exciting!"

He had to get Camilla under control before she invited all of New York's elite. "Camilla, slow your roll. This is our day. All we need is each other. No need to spend our money on extra people who are only going to be jealous of our love." Myles poured on his charm.

Camilla listened to his reasoning. Although she wanted a huge wedding with her friends, family and possibly foes witnessing it, he was all she needed. She convinced herself that her fiancé was right.

162

My Counterfeit Husband

They were the only two people that mattered.

"You're right, baby. We can make this happen," she happily agreed. "I'll call my secretary and get things going for tomorrow."

"No, make it happen tonight. I'll be in New York in a matter of hours."

Camilla was excited and concerned at the same time. "Tonight...but that's really pushing it."

"If anyone can make it happen, it's you."

Camilla appreciated his belief in her, but felt that she needed more time to make the wedding spectacular to her standards. Camilla's silence slightly worried him. However, there was no way he was giving up on his plan.

"Camilla, so much has happened that has made me see life in a totally different light. Life isn't promised to us. Baby, we may not see tomorrow and I wouldn't want to die knowing that you weren't my wife."

"Baby, you've got me worried. What's going on?"

"I'll tell you when I get there."

"Oh, Maverick! I'm so happy!"

"And baby, I'm coming to stay."

"What do you mean by *stay*?"

"You were right. I don't need this modeling job. I want to be with you, Camilla. I hate being away from you, so I finally quit my job."

"Are you serious? Oh Maverick, I love you so much! Thank you! You just made me the happiest woman in the world!" Camilla cheered.

"And that's not the only surprise that I have for you."

She beamed from ear to ear. "What else?"

"You'll see when I arrive. I'll call you with details later. I love you, Camilla."

"I love you, too, Maverick."

When they hung up, Myles glanced at Zoie's car seat.

"Daddy's little girl is about to seal this deal. You're good for something after all, Zoie."

My Counterfeit Husband

Chapter Twenty

Brooklyn pulled the final pair of Giuseppe heels from her closet. She'd talked about donating old clothes and shoes for a while, but rarely had the chance to do it. Now, she'd finally found the time since Camilla called earlier and canceled their scheduled meeting in SoHo. Even though she didn't give a reason, Brooklyn knew it probably had something to do with her man. The only time Camilla wasn't talking about business was when he came into town.

"Maverick, I really hope my aunt finds out that you're no good before it's too late," she huffed.

All of a sudden, Brooklyn felt ashamed for what she'd done to her aunt...sleeping with her fiancé. She was no better than the man Camilla was about to marry.

"If only you knew what you were getting yourself into, auntie," Brooklyn sighed as she thought back to his last words to her.

Now, we both have secrets.

Brooklyn knew that he'd cheated with Gabrielle, but there was nothing she could do about it without exposing her own fault in the web. In order to save herself, Camilla, was just gonna have to find out about her future husband on her own. That hurt Brooklyn, but it was the only way.

Before heading back down stairs, Brooklyn's phone buzzed for the hundredth time. She checked the text:

Baby, we need to talk. Pick up the phone or text me back.

Brooklyn took an angry, deep breath and tossed the phone back on the bed. She'd avoided calls and text messages from Leelia since the night she showed up at Camilla's penthouse. Leelia was upset that Brooklyn had ended things with her and couldn't understand why. Feeling the only way to deal with Leelia was to ignore her, Brooklyn carried the rest of the shoe boxes downstairs and placed them next to the items she'd carried down earlier.

"Some lucky women are gonna have a wonderful day when they come across this stuff," she said while eying the numerous designer boxes.

Brooklyn turned to go back upstairs when suddenly the doorbell rung.

"Damn, I didn't expect the Salvation Army so quickly. They probably want first pickings after learning that they were picking up in an upscale neighborhood." Brooklyn laughed as she opened the door. However, the laughing quickly subsided.

"Leelia, what are you doing here?"

"I needed to see you, Brooklyn since you won't answer my calls or texts."

"And you know why I'm not answering."

"Can I at least come in so that we can talk?"

"You can come in, but there's nothing else for us to talk about."

"Well, I beg to differ."

After Leeila walked inside, Brooklyn closed the door.

"I see you finally got around to cleaning out your closet," Leelia said, looking at all the items on the floor.

Brooklyn wasn't in the mood for small talk. "So, what do you want?"

"You know what I want Brooklyn. I want you, baby,"

Leelia walked up to Brooklyn and gently grabbed her face. Brooklyn stepped back.

"Stop it! I told you the other night that I can't do this."

"You didn't mean that, baby."

"Yes, I did! You followed me to my aunt's penthouse! That's crazy, Leelia!"

"I just couldn't take the fact of you possibly cheating on me."

"Well, you don't have to deal with it anymore. I told you that we're done. You can stop calling and texting me because I'm not an-

166

swering or replying."

"You don't mean that, Brooklyn."

"Why do you keep saying that? Yes, I do and let me show you just how much I meant it."

Brooklyn picked up a box that sat next to the sofa.

"What's this?" Leelia asked when Brooklyn handed it to her.

"Your shit! Your toothbrush that I specifically told you not to leave. A pair of thongs, a bra that I found under my bed, your sequin Converse sneakers, and that ghetto ass t-shirt that you had made for me with your picture on it."

"But these things need to stay here for when I spend the night."

Is she serious, Brooklyn thought. They pushed the box back and forth to each other until Leelia finally knocked it out of Brooklyn's hands.

"You can't end this!" Leelia shouted. "We're good together and you know it!" Leelia stepped to Brooklyn and grabbed her face again. "If you want to sleep with men that's fine. Just don't leave me, baby. I love you."

Brooklyn turned her head when Leelia tried to kiss her. "You need to leave. You're way out of line."

Leelia continued her attempts to kiss Brooklyn as she continued to fight her off.

"I bought you something," Leelia spoke as if Brooklyn wasn't trying to get rid of her. She pulled out a folded envelope from her pocket. "I booked us a seven day cruise."

Brooklyn shook her head in disbelief. "You're fucking insane!"

"That's not all, baby," Leelia continued. "I made us reservations at the spa this week. We're getting the works; the seaweed wrap and..."

"Leelia, we're over! We're done! There is no more us!" She pushed the envelope away.

"You don't mean that," Leelia said once again.

"Yes, I do! I can't deal with your jealousy and clinginess."

"Who is she, Brooklyn or better yet, who is *he*? Is it the guy that claimed to be your aunt's fiancé? Is he the reason you don't want me anymore?"

Brooklyn was prepared to take that night to her grave, and now it was being brought up once again.

"Oh my gosh! I told you who he was! He's my aunt's fiancé! There's no one! I just don't want you! You're too much! You need help."

"No, all I need is you, baby. Let me take you upstairs and change your mind about wanting to be done with me."

"Please leave."

"I can't. I love you," Leelia cried louder and harder.

At that moment, Brooklyn realized why Leelia's prior relationships always went sour. She was psycho.

"Leelia, I'm not trying to hurt you. I just can't do this anymore. This isn't normal. I need to live a normal life."

"With a man? I told you that I…"

"No! Stop! You need to leave."

"I'm sorry for whatever I've done, baby. We can work this out."

Brooklyn walked over to the box that Leelia knocked out of her hand and picked it up. She then shoved it in her ex-girlfriend's chest.

"Leave! Now! I've been nice to you about this, but if you don't leave, I'll be forced to call the police."

"After all we've been through, you'd call the cops on me?"

"What have we been through, Leelia? Nothing! I want out...plain and simple. You've proven to be more than I can handle or willing to deal with."

"Oh okay…well in that case let's see what your dad thinks when he finds out about you."

Brooklyn didn't appreciate the sinister look in Leelia's eyes.

"So, because I don't want you, you're going to expose me to my dad?"

"I'll do whatever it takes to keep you. I've even looked into sperm donors for us start a family together."

Brooklyn stepped back. "You did what?"

"I have four potential donors lined up. All we need to do now is figure out which one of us will carry the baby."

Brooklyn was way past stunned. "It really is official. You've seriously lost your damn mind! Get the hell out of my house, Leelia!"

Brooklyn shoved Leelia out the door along with her box of belongings. Moments later, Brooklyn slammed the door in her face when she opened her mouth to speak.

"I might have to get a restraining order against her crazy ass." Brooklyn sighed when she leaned against the door. "I need a damn drink after that."

She walked to the kitchen and grabbed a bottle of Patron tequila, along with some triple sec, lime juice, and sour mix. After grabbing some ice from the freezer, Brooklyn poured a measurable amount of each liquid into the blender, placed the top on, then hit the mix button. When the contents were mixed and crushed to her liking, she turned the blender off.

"What the hell?"

Brooklyn hurried to the front door of her brownstone and swung it open after hearing her car alarm blaring. She gasped once she saw her car. All four of the tires were flattened and two windows had been broken.

"You'll be mine again!" Leelia yelled out of her car window after speeding off and blasting Mariah Carey's song, *We Belong Together.*

"What the fuck have I gotten myself into?"

Camilla stood at the airport terminal gate and anxiously waited for her man to walk through. She couldn't believe that he was finally coming to stay for good. Her heart raced while her stomach twisted in knots. She was a nervous wreck. Camilla held her breath when the door opened to allow the passengers to disembark. She locked her fingers together to stop them from trembling. She'd picked him up from the airport several times before, but this time was different. He was coming *home.* The smile that painted Camilla's face turned to a confused lip curl when she saw him step out with a baby in his arms.

When Myles spotted Camilla, he hurried over to her. "Hey gorgeous," he said with an enormous smile.

"What's going on, Maverick?" she mumbled. Camilla turned her head when he tried to kiss her.

"What's wrong, Camilla? Aren't you happy to see me?" he questioned.

"Of course I am, but the last time I saw you, you didn't have this *type* of luggage." Camilla pointed at Zoie.

"Well, this is the other surprise I told you about over the phone."

"I don't understand."

All of a sudden, Myles conjured up a few fake tears. To add effect to his act, he lowered his head inside his hand. He fought to keep himself from laughing.

"Baby, what's going on?" Camilla asked with a worried expression.

"My sister…my sister Jada, died a few days ago. That's why I told you that I didn't want to talk this morning over the text. That's what I meant when I told you I was dealing with some important issues."

Camilla covered her mouth for a second. "Oh my God, Maverick! I didn't even know you had a sister. I know that your mom and dad are deceased. I figured you were the only child."

"My sister was all I had left of my family. We fell out a few years ago. That's why I never talked about her."

"I'm so sorry to hear about this, baby. I won't pretend to know what you're going through and how you're feeling right now." She rubbed his back in a circular motion.

"I really appreciate that. I'm all my sister had left in this world, Camilla and I owe it to her to make sure that her daughter is safe and taken care of."

Camilla stared at Zoie.

"This is Z…Chloe. I'm gonna take care of her. *We're* gonna take care of her. Chloe is the child that you prayed about. She's our child now, baby."

The tears that filled Camilla's eyes slowly trickled down her cheeks.

"Camilla, this is why I wanted to get married now. Life is too short. Nothing is promised to us."

"Can I hold her?" Camilla asked as she reached out for Zoie.

"Of course," Myles said, handing the baby to her. "Baby, it's still early. We can head on over to the courthouse and knock this wedding thing out," he suggested.

Camilla ignored him as she rocked Zoie in her arms. "Is she really ours?"

He smiled. "Yes, baby, she's ours."

"Your family must have strong genes because she looks exactly like you." Camilla giggled.

"What about her father? Why isn't he taking care of her? Was he there when your sister died?"

"Trust me, we don't have to worry about her father," Myles responded with a slight grin.

"So, shall we have Isaac drive us to the courthouse? Our family is coming together piece by piece. Let's make you and I official, Camilla."

"Baby, I told you a woman of my caliber will not be caught dead in a courthouse. My secretary is getting everything together for tonight like we agreed on the phone."

"Well that's good enough. I'm sorry, it seems like I'm rushing, but I'm just anxious to make you my wife."

"I'm anxious, too. Now, let's get your things and go back to the penthouse. We have a lot to discuss and tons to do before tonight."

"Actually, baby, I was in such a hurry to get to you that I only packed a small carry on," he said, pointing to the rolling suitcase.

"That's okay. You know I don't mind shopping and looks like we have to shop for nursery items as well." Camilla kissed Zoie's chubby cheeks. "What kind of formula does she drink?"

Shit, Myles freaked as he thought back to Kenya breastfeeding Zoie. "Ummm. I have no idea."

"Well, I have a friend who's a pediatrician. She'll be able to tell me what formula is best for her. Now, let's get the two of you home."

"I like the sound of that." Myles smirked as he walked behind his new soon to be wife.

Carla PENNINGTON

Chapter Twenty One

Myles stood in the mirror and smiled at the black tuxedo that draped his chiseled body. Camilla was determined to have *her* wedding one way or the other. He couldn't believe all that she'd done in such an extremely short period of time. Myles glanced around the penthouse that was filled with dozens of flowers and candles along with a four tier wedding cake on a nearby table. Myles wondered why Camilla chose such a huge cake when there were only four people in attendance; him, her, Isaac and the officiator. But he didn't question anything that she'd done. It was her money to throw away. He was just happy that he would soon have access to it.

"Oh my, Maverick, you look so handsome." Camilla gleamed when she stepped out of the bedroom with the baby in her arms.

Myles' eyes locked on Camilla in the mirror. He stared her up and down from head to toe. He was shocked at how stunning she looked in her white, spaghetti strap, mermaid fitting dress. She could've given any twenty-one-year-old woman a run for her money.

"Baby, you look amazing," Myles countered with a huge smile as he walked up to his bride. When he tried to kiss her, she quickly pulled away. "What's wrong?"

"Nothing. We have to save that until we're announced as husband and wife."

"Well, we need to hurry because I can't stand not being able to kiss you."

"We will get everything going as soon as Chloe is done eating. She was a little fussy at first, but finally calmed down. I guess she's used to her mother's milk and not this powdered stuff." Myles glanced at Zoie and prayed that she'd hurry up and fall asleep. "I think she misses her mom, too. She fought me a little when I was trying to dress her and would wiggle around and whine when I would hold her. I don't think she likes me."

"She's a baby, Camilla. She'll come around once she realizes that you love her. Just keep showing her affection. You're gonna be a great mom."

"I hope you're right."

"I know I am. You've always wanted kids, Camilla and now you have a daughter of your own. You'll feel better after adopting her."

"A-A-Adopt?" Camilla stuttered through a smile.

"Yes. We'll be a family; husband, wife and child. She can call you mom, Camilla. Isn't that what you've always wanted?" When a tear rolled down Camilla's cheek, Myles stopped it from hitting her dress. "Baby, don't cry. You're gonna mess up your make-up."

Camilla fanned her face. "You're right. I don't want to have raccoon eyes on the photos." She giggled.

"What photos?"

"Our wedding photos, Maverick. The photographer should be here any second."

He frowned. "I thought we agreed to no photos, Camilla."

"Maverick, we've gotta have a few photos. What will we show Chloe or our grandkids?"

Damn! She's thinking way too far ahead, he thought.

"You act like you have something to hide. You take pictures for money so why can't you take any with me...your soon to be wife."

"I have nothing to hide, baby. It's just that photographers are sleazy and can sell our photos to tabloids. I don't want anyone profiting from our happiness and stress us out in the process. Let's just get married and be happy."

Camilla stared at Myles with a somewhat vulnerable look on her face. As much as she wanted wedding photos, his happiness meant more to her. She took a deep breath and nodded in agreement.

"Look, baby." Myles nodded his head toward Zoie. "She's fallen asleep. You see, she's warming up to you already. Now, are you ready to become my wife?"

"Yes, more than anything!"

"Then go lay the baby down and get back here so we can say our, *I do's.*"

As Camilla walked to the bedroom, Myles slapped her on the ass.

"You're a piece of work." Isaac said, walking up to Myles. "Where'd you get that baby from?"

"You need to mind your own business and stay in your place as *the help* before I have you replaced."

"Replaced?" Isaac laughed. "I was here before you and I'll be here after Camilla finds out you're an asshole. Brooklyn has been telling me things about you."

"Well, you shouldn't believe everything you hear. Besides, I have Camilla wrapped around my finger and when I become her husband, I become your boss. Remember that."

Myles cockily patted Isaac on the back and walked off to pour himself a shot of vodka at the bar.

Moments later, Camilla returned.

"I'm ready, Maverick." She beamed after reentering the room.

"Let's get this party started," he cheered before finishing off the shot.

Once Camilla locked her arm inside of her fiancé's, they walked into the front of the living room where the officiator waited.

"Baby, you did say that he had the marriage license, right?" Myles whispered in Camilla's ear.

"Yep. Everything is all taken care of."

"Okay, great," Myles said, thinking about the fake driver's license he pulled from the safe.

The two of them stepped in front of the fireplace.

"Are we ready to begin?" the officiator asked in his deep, Barry White voice.

Myles and Camilla smiled at each other then nodded at the officiator who quickly began the proceedings. After his opening words, the officiator asked if Myles and Camilla wanted to exchange vows. Myles opted out of doing so, but Camilla didn't. Once again, Myles was upset with her. He wanted to get through the procedure as quick as possible.

"Maverick, you have brought so much joy and happiness to my life. I was on the verge of giving up on love until you showed me that it was still possible. I was afraid at first because of our age difference, but learned that the saying was true. Age ain't nothing but a number. Love has no age. I love you, Maverick Lewis." Her eyes quickly filled up with tears.

"Do you have any vows, Maverick?" the officiator asked.

"No, I don't. She took the words right out of my mouth," he replied.

"Hmph," Isaac voiced from the sideline.

Myles glared at him. As the officiator continued with the ceremony, Myles was ecstatic when he reached the final lines.

"I now pronounce you man and wife. You may kiss your bride."

Within seconds, Myles planted a huge kiss on Camilla's lips that sent her world spiraling.

"I hate to interrupt this moment because I know the two of you want to celebrate, but I really need to get going. My granddaughter is coming into town from Texas, and I wanna be home when she arrives."

"I'm sorry for interrupting your day, Thurmond," Camilla apologized.

"It's okay, Camilla. After all you've done for me and my family over the years, this is the least I can do. I just need for the two of you to fill out this marriage license and I'll file it at the county records department tomorrow. "

"I really appreciate you, Thurmond."

When Camilla threw her arms around his neck, Myles realized that marrying Camilla was a wonderful idea. She knew a lot of people. After everyone signed the document, Thurmond quickly said his goodbyes and left.

Camilla walked over to the cake table. "I got your favorite flavor, baby. Red Velvet," she said, picking up the triangle shaped knife. "Let's cut the first slice together."

Myles joined Camilla at the table. After cutting a huge piece, Myles fed Camilla some while she did the same.

"And you better not smash it in my face, either," she warned.

"I wouldn't do that," Myles replied with a large grin. "So, what time are we going to the bank tomorrow to put my name on the accounts, Mrs. Ellington-Lewis?" he asked slyly.

"As soon as they open, baby."

"Sounds good. Now, let me show you another way I can eat this cake."

Myles smeared a slice of cake across Camilla's breasts and buried his face into it. Camilla was tickled pink.

"Maverick, you're so bad!"

"That's only the beginning, baby." Myles scooped Camilla up in his arms.

"Baby, Chloe is asleep."

"Well, you may want to keep your screams low so that she won't wake up." Myles turned to Isaac who was leaning against the wall with an angry look on his face. "You can let yourself out, *help*. Your services will no longer be needed tonight."

"Ms. Ellington, do you…"

"Mrs. Ellington-Lewis!" Myles corrected.

"It's okay, Isaac. I'll see you tomorrow," Camilla intervened before fireworks lit up the room.

Isaac slammed the door on his way out.

"We will have to deal with him, Camilla, but until then, let's go consummate this marriage."

Kenya paced her living room floor as she listened to the two officer's converse. She couldn't stop her tears from falling. When she arrived home a few hours earlier and Myles wasn't there, she immediately wanted to call the police. Julius convinced her not to and to give Myles a little time to blow off some steam. Kenya agreed even after learning that Myles had left his white phone. However, after a few hours of waiting, she couldn't wait any longer. She couldn't believe that Myles had taken Zoie. Of all the shady things he could've done to show his anger, it never crossed her mind that taking their daughter would be one of them. *Is this God's way of punishing me for what I've done,* Kenya asked herself. *If so, I need to come clean.*

"Ma'am, I apologize, but there's nothing more we can do at this point, but file an incident report once we get back to the station," the thin, Caucasian, male investigating officer spoke. "Like I told you before, since your daughter hasn't been gone very long, we can't call it an abduction right now. Also, we have to factor in that she's with her father."

"And like I told you before, *officer*, her father doesn't give a shit about her!" Kenya barked. "He doesn't take care of her! I do!"

Kenya was beyond annoyed and upset. The cops had been in her home for a little over an hour and had offered her no hope.

Julius stepped in. "Kenya, calm down."

"I'm not calming down until I get Zoie back! They can at least issue a damn Amber alert! It's eleven o'clock. They should be home by now!"

"We can't do that unless there's confirmed evidence of the child being abducted. In addition, the child has to be at risk for serious bodily harm or death," the black, female officer informed.

"She is at risk of serious bodily harm! I breast feed her! How in the hell do you expect her to eat?"

"That's not enough, to go on ma'am," the female officer replied.

"Are you not hearing me? My husband doesn't take care of her!"

"How many times did you call him?" the male officer questioned.

"I told you…only once and that's because he left his phone. When I heard it ring, I knew something was wrong." Kenya snatched Myles' white iPhone off of the table and shook it in the male officer's face. "I'm sure he left it on purpose so that I couldn't contact him. Don't you think that's suspicious?"

"People unintentionally leave things, too, ma'am," the male officer stated.

Kenya was nearly at her wits end. "Okay then what about the money? I told you that he's been stealing my money."

"It was a joint account, right?" the female officer confirmed.

"So what? It was still *my* money! He didn't add anything to it."

The male officer scratched his pointy nose. "It was still a joint account, ma'am and he is legally your husband. Just give him a few more hours. He may be giving you time to grieve since your friend just passed away."

"He didn't give a damn about her!" Kenya screamed.

"Ma'am, I need you to calm down. I see this happen all the time. You did say he was upset about something. He may be intentionally making you worry because of that. I see married couples play tit for tat all the time," the male officer continued.

"Tit for tat? What about him lying about his job? Isn't that considered fraud or something?"

"No, it's not. Besides, you're his wife. How could you not know that he didn't have a job?"

Kenya was a few seconds from clawing the male officer's eyes out. "A marriage is supposed to be based on trust. I trusted him."

"Then maybe you should trust that he'll do the right thing in regards to your daughter."

At this point, Kenya was far from livid.

"Don't you think that was a bit inappropriate to say?" Julius asked.

"I was just saying," the white officer attempted to explain.

"Are you defending him? Would you do something like this to your wife?" Kenya questioned.

"I'm not married, ma'am," the male officer replied.

"Then you should shut the hell up!"

"Let's all just calm down here." The female officer stepped in after realizing the situation was getting heated.

"She's right. Calm down." Julius tried to comfort Kenya by massaging her shoulders. "You know Myles is just doing this shit out of spite. He'll be back soon. I'm sure of it."

Kenya jerked away from him. "I want my daughter home now, Julius," she said. "She doesn't have anything to eat. Why would he do something like this?"

Julius shrugged his shoulders. "I really don't know."

Kenya couldn't hold it together any longer. She fell into

Julius' arms and cried uncontrollably. The female officer walked up to Julius and handed him two cards.

"If anything changes, give either one of us a call," she spoke.

"You mean like if my child is dead?" Kenya snapped through sniffles against Julius' chest.

Julius accepted the cards and waved the officers away. Moments later, they were out the door.

"Kenya, they're really here to help you," Julius addressed Kenya as he walked her over to the sofa and sat her down.

"Julius, they're not helping. I know there is more they can do. What if my baby is somewhere hurt?"

"We've called all the hospitals, Kenya. Myles is just pissed and wants to make you sweat, that's all."

"Well, it's working." Kenya snatched the remote from the sofa, clicked on the television and turned to the local news.

"Have you eaten today?"

"No, I haven't." She sighed through a few more tears.

"Would you like for me to fix you something?"

Kenya ignored Julius' question. Her eyes were fixated on the television.

"Kenya, did you hear me?"

"Julius, hand me my purse off the table," Kenya panicked as she waved her hand wildly.

"What's going on?" he asked after handing Kenya her purse.

Again, Kenya ignored him as she retrieved an item from her purse. Kenya gasped after looking back at the television screen.

"Oh my God! She was in my house! She was in my house!" Kenya freaked out.

"What are you talking about, Kenya? Who was here?"

"That missing girl, Krystal Turner! She's on the news!" Kenya quickly went through the small wallet, then pulled out the driver's license. "See, it's her!"

After grabbing the license and looking back toward the T.V. all Julius could do was say one word, "Damn."

Chapter Twenty Two

"How may I help you, ma'am?" an officer asked when Kenya walked up to the desk at the police station on Westinghouse Boulevard.

After hearing about Krystal's disappearance and having proof that she was in her home, Kenya was on a mission to make the police listen to her. This time they had no choice.

"I need to see Officer Brandt," Kenya said, referring to the name on one of the cards. "Is he still on duty?"

"Yes. Is he expecting you?"

"Yes," Kenya responded. "He just left my house about an hour ago. He told me to contact him if I had proof about my daughter being kidnapped."

"Kenya, don't jump the gun just yet. You're here about the Krystal girl," Julius whispered in her ear.

"If Myles is crazy enough to take my daughter, he's crazy enough to do something to that girl."

Julius didn't want to make her anymore upset then she already was, so he left the situation alone. When Kenya gave the desk officer her name, he told her to wait a minute, then walked in the back.

"He has to hear me out now," Kenya said to Julius regarding the officer.

"Don't you think there may be another explanation for this?"

"What other explanation is there? Myles already admitted to her being in my house and now I have proof. I have a gut feeling that he had something to do with her disappearance."

"Or maybe what Myles said is the truth. She left her wallet."

Kenya glared at him. "Whose side are you on, Julius?"

"You know I'm on your side. I just don't want us to find out later on that Myles was telling the truth."

"Then act like it," Kenya snapped.

Julius felt like a child being chastised for tracking dirt on his mother's freshly mopped kitchen floor.

"Mrs. Whitaker, how may I help you?" Officer Brandt asked when he approached her. Kenya handed the wallet to him. "What's this?"

"I just saw the missing girl, Krystal Turner on the news. That's her wallet. I found it in my house."

"Do you know her?" Officer Brandt inspected the wallet on one side, then flipped it over.

"No, I don't. My husband told me that he interviewed her for a nanny position. I don't know when that actually took place, but he said she must've mistakenly dropped it since I found it under my sofa."

"Did you know anything about this interview?"

"Not at all. We never discussed hiring a nanny. As you can see, Officer Brandt, my husband is a liar, and he's definitely hiding something…I know he is."

"Actually, a patrol officer found Ms. Turner's car in a shopping center near your home. They just radioed that in minutes before you arrived, actually."

"See…he must've done something to her." Kenya turned around and gave Julius a, 'I told you so' look.

"But the fact that the wallet was in your home and you're the one who found it, seems a bit odd."

Kenya's eyes widened as she quickly wondered if the officer was insinuating that she was a suspect.

"So, what are you trying to say? I've never seen this girl a day in my life! I couldn't have possibly done anything to her!" Kenya yelled hysterically.

Julius wrapped his arm around Kenya's shoulders to stop her from trembling. "Kenya, calm down. I'm sure he's not saying that you're a suspect."

"Yes, he is! That's what he's implying!"

"Mrs. Whitaker, I'm not implying anything," Officer Brandt added. "I've just been trained to analyze every possible avenue and to not rule anything out."

"Well, don't analyze me because I didn't do shit!" All heads turned when Kenya exploded. "I don't know this damn girl! If you find her then you might be able to find my daughter! I know my husband had something to do with both of their disappearances. He kidnapped my child! He stole from me! He wasn't the man that I thought he was! You have to believe that I had nothing to do with this."

Julius squeezed Kenya tighter as the officer stared at her helpless state. The tears poured from Kenya's eyes profusely as she thought about Zoie. "It's gonna be okay," he comforted.

Kenya cried harder after hearing Julius' words. The only way that Zoie would be okay is when she was back at home, safe and sound. She turned to Officer Brandt and pleaded to him once again.

"He took my daughter. He took my only child away from me."

After seeing Kenya's demeanor, the officer finally put himself in her shoes.

"Mrs. Whitaker, I'll notify my captain right away, so we can get the ball rolling on your case. We'll also alert the media so they can spread the word to the community. As soon as I enter your husband and daughter's name into the database, that information will go out to all patrolling officers. We'll need to search your home for evidence."

"That's fine. Do whatever you need to do. I just want my daughter back."

"Don't worry. We're gonna bring her home."

Kenya and Officer Brandt spoke for a few more minutes before she and Julius left the station.

"Kenya, I've got a surprise for you tomorrow," Julius spoke while helping her into the passenger's seat.

"Julius, no. I can't do any surprises right now," she rejected while shaking her head. "I just want to go home and crawl under my covers until Zoie is found. This entire ordeal has me emotionally drained."

"That's why you *need* this surprise and I'm not taking no for an answer.

"Julius, I really appreciate everything you've done. You've

been here for me when I needed it most."

All of a sudden, Kenya burst into another round of tears. "I'm sorry for being so emotional," she spoke through a sniffle.

"No need to apologize," Julius replied before glancing at his watch. "It's past midnight. Let me get you home so that you can rest." He walked around to the driver's seat and climbed inside. "Before I take you home, did you want something to eat?"

"Julius, the only thing that I want to do is sleep until I get the call that Zoie is okay," Kenya responded solemnly before facing the window.

She didn't have an ounce of strength left in her to hold a conversation with him. He cranked the car and drove Kenya home. The thirty minute ride was silent.

"Do you want me to fix you some tea or something?" Julius asked after helping Kenya into bed.

"I appreciate that, but I just want to lay here until I fall asleep."

"Okay. Get some rest. Don't forget though tomorrow you're going to the spa for a little relaxation."

"Julius…"

"I'm not taking no for an answer and I don't want to hear any excuses. You need this."

Kenya didn't care what Julius said. Her entire focus was on finding Zoie. A spa day was out of the question.

"We'll talk about it in the morning," she said.

"Okay. I'll be downstairs if you need me."

Kenya smiled before turning onto her side and closing her eyes. After shutting the bedroom door behind him, Julius quickly walked downstairs. Once in the kitchen, he slipped inside the walk-in pantry, pulled out his phone and dialed a number. He desperately wanted to go outside to make the call, but Kenya had secured the alarm. He didn't want it to go off.

"Hello?" the person answered.

"So, you had to take shit to another level this time, huh?" Julius barked.

"What are you talking about?"

"You took the damn baby. Have you lost your mind?"

Myles laughed. "That baby is gonna help me with Camilla. I
know that wasn't a part of the original plan, but it's working out.
She's already talking about adopting Chloe."

"Umm…do you mean Zoie?"

Myles laughed again. "It's Chloe now."

"Man, this shit is foul. You shouldn't have taken Zoie from
Kenya. She's devastated, Trey," Julius said calling Myles by his true
government name.

"I don't give a shit, *Darren*. She should've signed the damn
papers." Myles put emphasis on Julius' real name.

"Man. you need to give that baby back and figure out another
way to secure shit with Camilla."

"I did. We just got married. I've moved on to bigger and better
things."

Julius' eyes were wide open. "Already?"

"Look cuz, I had to do what the fuck I had to do. Do you know
how much time I spent waiting on that bitch to sell her company? I've
already blown all of her money so I could've been gone." He laughed
again. "That bitch thinks she's slick, too. She had a separate account
with over a million dollars in it. But little does she know, I got to that
shit, too. I was fucking the broad, Candice from the bank and she's
the one who told me about it. She also put my name on the account so
I could get access to the money. Kenya's dumb ass never goes into the
account, so I knew by the time she found out, I would be long gone."

As Julius listened to his cousin, he thought back to what he did
prior to moving to Charlotte. As a career criminal himself, Julius was
heavily involved in check and credit card fraud, along with getting
fake ID's, passports and social security numbers, which is how Myles
was able to start marrying his victims. He'd made a good living off of
that business and normally didn't get directly involved with Myles
and his women. But when Myles presented him with an opportunity
to help with Kenya and the Creative Minds get rich scheme, Julius
knew he'd make a lot more; half of what Myles took from the company actually. The only thing he hated was acting like a highly edu-
cated accountant. After Myles persuaded Kenya to fire her old
controller and hire Julius, he quickly stepped into the role. His job
was to consistently tell Kenya that the company was doing bad, and

try to convince her to sell. But Julius hated when she came to him asking about budgets and quarterly forecasts. If it wasn't for the assistant controller that he forced himself to have sex with from time to time, Julius' cover would've been blown months ago.

Julius peeked out the small crack in the pantry door to make sure Kenya hadn't come downstairs. "But what about the kidnapping shit? I didn't sign up for that."

"Once you agreed to come on board and help me with this shit your ass signed up for whatever went down. Nigga, if you'd done your job and pushed Kenya to sign those papers we'd both be paid right now and she would have her baby!" Myles yelled.

Julius huffed into the phone as he listened to his cousin blame him for not getting the deal done. "Look, this shit is not my fault. Maybe if you would've spent more time with Kenya, she might've sealed the deal months ago," Julius retaliated. "You need to give the baby back."

"Are you falling for that bitch or something?"

"No. It's just that you're too impatient and impulsive," Julius spoke in a low tone.

"Well, you sit back and wait on her ass to sell. But I'm not…I'm done. Kenya's baby is about to make me some real money."

"Zoie is your child, too," Julius reminded.

"She's gonna belong to Camilla as soon as I take what I can from her and roll the fuck out." Myles laughed.

"This shit ain't funny. In all the years you've been doing this shit, you've never kidnapped someone. Ever since you got rid of Porsha, you've been tripping. This is not how we're supposed to be getting this money."

"We get this money however we can get it."

"So, what was the purpose of you getting rid of Krystal? She didn't have any fucking money."

Myles wished he could wring Julius' neck through the phone for being so weak. He couldn't believe that they came from the same family.

"You gonna bring that shit up after you didn't help me get rid of her body?"

"I told you, I was tied up and I couldn't get away when you

called me that night."

"Nigga that's some bullshit. Since when does eating pussy come before helping me do something as important as that? Your weak ass just didn't want to be involved," Myles taunted.

"Whatever," Julius fumed. "I'm not going down for murder or kidnapping and that's fucking final."

"Cuz, you're an accessory to this shit! If I go down, you go down."

"No, I'm not." Julius stood his ground.

"You've always been weak. I brought you in this shit to make some fucking money and this is the thanks I get? I made you into the muthafucka that you could never become on your own! Did you forget that I was the one who first got you into that credit card shit in the first place? Yeah, you branched off into the fake ID shit on your own…I'll give you that. But I had Kenya thinking that you graduated from Georgetown when I'm the one who actually helped you graduate from the streets."

"Don't fucking go there. I earned my spot. I'm the one who had to fuck that ugly ass albino bitch at the office to do my damn work."

"Of course, because your ass can barely add and subtract. You don't know shit about accounting."

"Look, just bring Zoie back and I'll help you come up with another plan," Julius said, ignoring his cousin's insult.

"Ah shit! So you have fallen in love with Kenya. See, that's your fucking problem right there. You fall in love with bitches and not the money. You're too weak, cuz. By the way, were you gonna fuck her when I walked in on the two of you that night?"

"Would it have mattered?"

"Nah. I just wanted to know 'cause it looked like you wanted to."

"I was just trying to play my part."

"I should've played mine, too and knocked your ass out like any normal husband would've done after seeing his wife in another man's arms."

Julius stared at the phone and wondered if Myles was serious and a tad jealous. Julius knew that his next words would piss Myles off even more.

"This shit is serious. Kenya isn't playing. I just left the police station with her."

"What?"

"Yeah, I thought that would get your attention. That Krystal chic was reported missing and Kenya turned in the wallet that was left at your house."

"Nigga, that should've been the first thing you said when I answered the phone. Why didn't you stop her?"

"Are you serious? How in the hell was I supposed to stop her without looking suspicious?"

In the midst of what he'd just learned, Myles kept his cool. "They're not gonna find her body."

"I hope the hell not. The cops are planning to investigate that and about Zoie's disappearance."

"You need to *handle* Kenya, man. She's fucked things up for me enough as it is."

"What in the hell do you mean by *handle*?"

"The same way I handled that Krystal bitch and Porsha back in Connecticut."

Julius had to bite his tongue to keep from screaming. "Hell no."

"Look, like I said earlier, if I go down then you go down."

Julius was thrown back by Myles' words. "So, you'd sell me out for some shit that *you* did?"

"We're in this together, cuz."

"*You* killed them…not me. *You* kidnapped Zoie!"

"So what...you're still an accomplice."

"Look, if you want Kenya out of the picture then you need to come back and do it yourself." Julius put his foot down. "Oh, by the way, I need you to send me some money soon. I'm damn near broke. Since I've been in Charlotte with your ass, I haven't had much time to focus on my other business."

"Whatever nigga. Since you still wanna stay down there and play house with that bitch, you need to figure out how to get some money. You also need to get a handle on this shit before it gets out of hand. I'm not going to jail."

"Neither am I."

"Look, I've gotta go. I think my new wife just called my name."

"We need to connect real soon and discuss this," Julius said before Myles hung up.

Julius jumped and accidentally dropped his phone when he heard the pantry door open. When he looked up, Kenya was standing directly in front of him. She looked pissed.

Damn, how much of my conversation did she hear, he thought nervously.

"Was that Alexia?" Kenya asked.

Julius was relieved. She obviously hadn't heard much. "Yeah," he replied. "She's not taking the break up too well and keeps calling me."

"Why are you hiding in the pantry? I don't mind you talking to her, Julius. You don't have to hide that from me."

"I wasn't hiding. I actually came in here to look for some chips, and got distracted by our conversation," he responded. "What are you doing down here anyway? I thought you were tired?"

"I can't sleep. I just keep thinking about how Myles has a safe in his closet that I need to get into. Maybe there's something in there that can help me find my child."

Julius was worried since Myles had never mentioned having a safe to him before. He hoped his cousin wasn't stupid enough to leave a paper trail of all the mischief they'd done. *I really need to get the fuck out of this business*, he thought.

Carla PENNINGTON

Chapter Twenty Three

The next day, Myles rolled over in the bed and reached for Camilla, but she wasn't there. His eyes fought to open due to the bright sun shining in his face. He hated that Camilla found it necessary to open the curtains each morning. Since he didn't hear the shower going, Myles assumed she was in the kitchen or downstairs in the gym. Stepping out of the bed, he walked into the living room to find Camilla gushing over the new clothes that she'd bought for Zoie.

"Hey, sleepy head," Camilla addressed him enthusiastically.

"Hey, baby." He walked over and kissed her cheek "I thought you might've been exercising."

"I did that earlier. I've been up since six a.m. I'm so excited that I could barely sleep. I've already been out."

"What's this?" Myles asked as he nonchalantly thumbed through the clothes.

"I told you last night that I needed to go shopping for Chloe."

"Well, did you get me anything?" He displayed an innocent smile.

"No, but I'll take care of that tomorrow. You've got a few things in the bedroom to hold you over until then in case we have to go out. I've got a few things to do this evening in regards to the hotel."

"Can't you do that another time? You promised me that we were going to the bank today."

Myles wasn't taking any chances with Camilla as he'd done with Kenya. He needed to get the ball rolling as soon as possible.

"Something came up that needs my attention."

"Well, we can go to the bank before or after." Myles was determined.

Camilla looked up at him. "Why are you in such a rush? I told you that I'm gonna take care of it."

Myles could hear the concern in her voice. At that point, he decided to tone his anxiousness down a notch.

"There's no rush, baby. I know you're a busy woman. It's just that I used the majority of my money to renovate my townhouse back in Florida so it would sell easily. I'm a little low on cash and don't wanna be walking around like that. It's cool though. I can always go back to modeling until my house sells. It's probably..."

"No," Camilla quickly interrupted. "I don't want you away from me for weeks at a time anymore. We'll get it done, baby. Chloe and I need you here."

I'm good at what I do, Myles thought as Camilla fell right into his web. He glanced around the room. "Speaking of Z...Chloe, where is she?"

"I left her in the bassinette in our room. Didn't you check on her when you got up?"

"Actually I didn't. I had no idea she was even in there," Myles responded. "As you can see, I don't do well with babies."

"How would you do well when this is your first time having to deal with one?" She chuckled.

"You need to contact some of your rich friends about nannies."

"It's too soon for a nanny, Maverick. We need to bond with Chloe."

"White folks get nannies as soon as they spit their babies out. I don't see why rich black folks can't do the same. We're getting a nanny as soon as possible."

"Wow...someone is very cranky. Do you need to be *relieved?*"

Camilla stepped up to Myles and eased her hand inside of his boxer briefs. He stepped back.

"I'm not cranky. I'm just tired. Chloe kept me up all last night with all that fucking crying."

"Well, from what I saw, you slept better than she did," Camilla replied. "Chloe probably just misses her mom, Maverick. Plus, she didn't eat that well, so she might've been hungry. It's gonna take her a while to get used to a different routine, that's all."

"Well, what are we gonna do because I can't go through that shit every night?"

"I talked to my pediatrician friend early this morning and she said that Chloe is gonna have to get used to the milk and that she may spit up and poop a lot until she does."

"Well, I don't do shit and vomit, so you need to get in touch with some kind of nanny today. I didn't quit my modeling job to become a stay at home dad."

Camilla ignored Myles as she smiled at Zoie's new garments. "I can't wait until Chloe wakes up so she can try on this cute little sundress." Camilla lifted the dress so that Myles could see. "Isn't this adorable?"

"Yeah."

Myles could care less about the dress especially since there was nothing in the bags for him.

"Oh by the way, Maverick, when is your sister's funeral? I'd like to pay my respects and meet more of your family. I'm sure they'd like to meet the woman who is going to be taking care of Jada's child." Camilla's words nearly sucked the life out of him. They were unexpected. "Oh...and we're gonna need Jada's death certificate, Chloe's birth certificate and social security card when we start the adoption process. I'll contact my attorney to find out what else we'll need."

Myles had to think quick on his feet because he wasn't prepared for the conversation.

"I'll get all that stuff, but I'm not attending the funeral. I don't wanna see my sister laying up in some casket."

Camilla dropped the clothes that were in her hand and gave him a disbelieving look. "What do you mean you're not going? She's your sister."

"I'm not going to the funeral, Camilla. I don't do well at them. Besides, I told you she was all I had left in regards to my family. So, the only people that will probably be there are folks that I don't even know."

"That can't possibly be true, Maverick. I'm sure you have a few uncles, aunts or distant cousins somewhere."

He shook his head. "Nope."

"I can't fathom why you wouldn't want to attend your own sister's funeral, but if that's your decision, I'll respect that. I can go alone. I just want to pay my respects to her."

"Why? You didn't even know her."

"Because I owe her that much for the gift she has given me. She's part of you, Maverick and Chloe is her daughter. I'd like to see the woman whose child I'm about to raise as my own."

"Again, why?"

"Because it's the right thing to do, Maverick."

"If I'm not going then you're not going either!" he yelled.

His sudden attitude startled Camilla and it showed all over her face. Camilla couldn't understand the anger and was shocked because he'd never yelled at her before. Seeing her expression, Myles knew he had to quickly correct his mistake. He walked up to Camilla and pulled her into his arms.

"Baby, I'm so sorry. I didn't mean to yell at you like that. Please forgive me."

"Then tell me why you're so adamant about not attending your sister's funeral."

"Camilla, you just don't understand. Even though my sister and I had a huge falling out some time ago, she was still the only family I had. I loved her. I just don't wanna see her like that. I don't wanna remember her like that. All I wanna remember is the two of us running up to the ice cream truck as kids or me sizing her boyfriend up when she went to the prom." Myles desperately tried to force a few tears to come out, but nothing happened.

Camilla felt sorry for her husband and could tell that he was extremely hurt. "Baby, I totally understand and I apologize for pressuring you. Can you at least tell me her last name?"

"Richardson. Why?"

"I'd like to send flowers."

Shit! Myles cursed himself after realizing he'd given Camilla Jada's real last name.

"Do you know what kind of flowers your sister liked? Oh, and tell what's the name of the church in Jacksonville, too," Camilla continued.

Myles had enough. He quickly had to take Camilla's mind off of Jada, and knew just how to make that happen...sex.

"Baby, we're newlyweds. Let's act like it," Myles said before sliding his tongue between Camilla's lips.

"But Chloe may wake up any minute," Camilla playfully resisted.

"That's exactly why we're getting a nanny. I want you whenever I want you." Myles lifted Camilla off the floor and carried her over to the wall.

"We can't do this now."

"You asked earlier if I needed to be *relieved*. I do now. Besides, you're already ready for me," he said while sliding Camilla's thong to the side. "And I'm ready for you." Within seconds, he'd pulled out his dick and forcefully entered her.

"Maverick! Oh my! Oh my!"

Myles carried Camilla to the gray, chaise lounge and laid her down while still inside of her. He hungrily removed her ombre maxi dress and tossed it on the floor. He then tore the thong from her body. Camilla enjoyed the roughness.

"Chloe may wake up, baby," Camilla moaned through labored breaths.

"Then I'd better hurry up."

At that point, Myles lifted Camilla's legs and pushed her feet until she was nearly folded.

"Maaaaav! Maaaaaaaav!"

He looked down and smiled at the shine that Camilla's juices had released onto his hardness. Camilla freed one of her legs from his hold. Myles stared into her eyes then released her other foot. As he worked her middle, he covered her nose and mouth with his hand as loud moans escaped her lips. Camilla didn't resist. Instead, she rolled her pussy on his shaft as he widened and extended her insides. A minute later, Camilla attempted to turn her head so that she could breathe, but Myles pressed down so that she couldn't move.

"Not yet, baby. Not yet. You can take it," Myles coached.

Myles watched Camilla's eyes. He secretly hoped that she'd shed tears like Krystal had done when he squeezed the life out of her. To his surprise, a single tear rolled out of the corner of Camilla's eye as she started to move widely about trying to break free.

"Cum with me, Camilla. I'm gonna give you my babies this time."

Myles' last words slightly calmed Camilla. She's wanted his seeds in her for the longest. Moments later, he felt his love bursting through as he felt Camilla's body start to twitch. Her eyes rolled to the back of her head. She could no longer take it. She clawed at Myles' hand, but he pressed harder.

"We're almost there, baby!"

Camilla kicked and swung wildly, but couldn't deny the orgasm that followed seconds later. Myles joined her. He removed his hand and fell onto the floor to catch his breath.

"Have you decided which car you're getting me as my wedding gift?" Myles asked through deep breaths. "I've had my eye on the Bentley or the Aston Martin."

"I thought I told you to stop doing that rough sex stuff, Maverick."

Instead of entertaining her concerns, he continued with his own selfish conversation.

"I really like the Aston Martin Vanquish."

"You really don't need a car in New York, Maverick especially when we have a driver that will take us wherever we want to go."

"I'm my own man, Camilla. I need my own car," he replied. There was no way Isaac would know about his every move.

"Guess I understand that," Camilla responded. She paused for a moment. "Now that I think about it, it would be nice to have my *husband* drive me around for a change." Camilla winked at him when she turned around. "I'll surprise you."

"Well, you won't know how that feels until the car gets here."

"Oh! Speaking of surprises," Camilla said after hopping up. She walked over to her Louis Vuitton briefcase and pulled out a copy of *In Touch Weekly* magazine. "Look at what my secretary found today." Camilla flipped through the pages while walking back over to Myles who was now sitting in a chair. She handed the magazine to him. "Do you remember that photo we took at dinner with my brother? We all look so nice." Camilla smiled from ear to ear.

Myles nearly blew a head gasket. In a fit of fury, he threw the magazine across the room. A few of the sheets ejected from the staples.

"Maverick, what's wrong? Why are you so upset?"

"I told you that I didn't want to take that fucking picture, Camilla!"

"I still can't get my head wrapped around the fact that you don't like taking pictures when you're a model. What's the problem?"

"That's why I don't like taking pictures!" he yelled while pointing at the magazine. "There's no telling what they're saying about us in there!"

"Who cares what people say? Are you ashamed to be with me?"

"No, I'm not. I just don't want my fucking picture taken. Is that so hard to understand?"

"Look, you woke the baby up," Camilla said when she heard Zoie's cries.

"I don't give a damn! How do you expect me to trust you in this marriage if you can't respect my wishes?"

"Maverick?" Camilla gasped. "Baby, I'm sorry."

Myles pushed her away when she tried to hug him. "Go tend to your damn baby," he said before stomping toward the bathroom and slamming the door.

My Counterfeit Husband

Chapter Twenty Four

Brooklyn sat behind her desk and kicked off her five inch Brian Atwood t-strap sandals. She'd only been at work for an hour and her feet were already screaming for attention. After reaching down to massage the ball of her left foot for a few seconds, she eased the ballerina slippers on that were hidden under the desk.

"Those damn shoes looked uncomfortable when I ordered them online. I should've followed my first instinct and deleted them from the cart," Brooklyn reprimanded herself.

Once the foot and shoe battle was dealt with, Brooklyn continued onto her normal tasks. She hadn't checked her voice messages or email in days. She needed to respond to vital ones and delete unimportant ones that took up unnecessary space in her inbox. She'd intended to take care of them from home the day Leelia showed up unexpectedly with her drama and threats, but never got around to it. If vandalizing her car wasn't enough, there was one particular threat that worried Brooklyn and caused her to lose all focus; the threat that Leelia would tell Brooklyn's father about her lifestyle.

Brooklyn glanced at the box that was on her desk. She smiled after opening it for the fifth time. She knew her dad would love the black diamond, David Yurman cufflinks that she'd purchased for his Father's Day gift. He was a sucker for cufflinks.

Brooklyn thought back to the numerous calls her dad had made to her over the last few days, and couldn't help but wonder if Leelia had made good on her warning. Of course, Brooklyn ignored all the calls. Just in case he knew her secret, she wasn't ready for that conversation. She could never be prepared for the wrath he would unleash onto her if and when he found out.

"Crazy bitch," Brooklyn said to herself after thinking about the calls she'd ignored from Leelia as well.

Leelia's threat wasn't the only reason that Brooklyn was unable to focus at work. She hadn't seen or heard from her aunt Camilla since she told Brooklyn to cancel their meeting. The guilty part of her wondered if Camilla was distant because Maverick had told her about their encounter in the penthouse. Although it would've been a stupid move on his part, she didn't trust Myles and had no idea what he could've possibly had up his sleeve. The stress of not knowing in either situation had her completely on edge.

Brooklyn glanced at her response to one of the emails she was replying to and noticed dozens of typos and errors. "I need to take a damn break."

At that moment, she deleted the error filled email and minimized that screen before clicking on the Internet Explorer icon.

"Let's see what these fools are talking about on Facebook since I haven't logged on in a while. Hopefully someone will make me laugh with their status," she said, logging on.

Brooklyn spent a few minutes scrolling through her newsfeed. Her emotions went from laughing to being upset as she read some of the posts.

"Now, I see why I haven't been on here. People have too much time on their hands for some of this foolish nonsense." After reading a few more posts, Brooklyn finally clicked on her personal wall.

"What the hell?" she shouted after seeing a post on her page.

Why are you ignoring me? You need to stop hiding, Brooklyn. It's time to show the world who you really are. It's time to come clean.

She quickly clicked on Leelia's page to find the same post along with a photo of herself she took while in London. Brooklyn scrolled through a few of the comments.

What did she do?
What do you mean by that?
She's fly as hell, Leelia. Is that your new boo?
Isn't she the niece of that rich lady Camilla Ellington?

"You've gone too damn far this time, Leelia," Brooklyn said

200

as if she was in the room.

Brooklyn read a few more replies. Her anger intensified at the speculations and rumors that were now being spread. When a knock on her door came a few seconds later, Brooklyn never bothered to look up. She figured it was her secretary, Aubrey since everyone else was announced. Brooklyn also knew it wasn't Camilla because she would've walked directly inside.

"Come in, Aubrey," Brooklyn said while looking at the screen.

"So, I guess you're fucking your personal trainer now, huh?"

Brooklyn finally looked up to find Leelia standing there with a frenzied look on her face.

"What in the hell are you doing here, Leelia? You need to leave! Aubrey! Aubrey!" Brooklyn yelled out for her secretary. She wanted her to call security.

"Aubrey isn't at her desk," Leelia spoke then walked up to Brooklyn.

Brooklyn quickly tensed when Leelia neared her. She didn't know what to expect. When Leelia tossed a photo on her desk, Brooklyn glanced at it in disbelief. It was a picture of her at the gym the day before. She'd decided to go back after a long hiatus to try and relieve some of the stress.

"Oh my God! Why the hell have you been following me, Leelia?"

"Is she the reason why you're leaving me? Are you fucking that Jillian Micheals looking bitch?"

"You're crazy! Get out of my office!" Brooklyn yelled.

"Just be honest with me!"

"No, I'm not sleeping with her. She's just my trainer at the gym!" Brooklyn fired back. "First you fuck up my car, and now you've got people on your Facebook page making accusations about me! If you don't leave me alone, Leelia I'm gonna have you arrested for stalking, harassment and now trespassing!"

"The accusations are true, Brooklyn. Once you face the fact, you'll feel a lot better. There's no need to keep it in the closet anymore."

"Leelia, it's not up to you when and if I come out. You don't dictate my life."

"I'm not trying to dictate your life. I'm just trying to help you."

"By broadcasting the shit on Facebook? How is that supposed to help me? If anything, I'm pissed! Have your read these comments?" Brooklyn turned the screen.

Leelia didn't bother to look. "I know what people are saying."

"Why would you expose me like that on a social site? My business isn't everyone else's business."

"I didn't come out and say that you were a lesbian, Brooklyn."

"You may as well have! You're a lesbian and everyone knows it so they automatically assume that I'm one, too!"

"Baby, this would be so much easier if you just come out and own who are. Besides, I already called and told your aunt, Camilla."

Brooklyn was in complete disbelief. "You did what? How could you do that to me?"

"Well technically, I didn't come out and tell her *everything*. I didn't even say your name, or my name for that matter, but I did tell her that she would find out who I was once secrets were revealed."

"How the hell did you get her number?"

"From the contact list in your phone. I copied each number down once we started dating."

"I can't believe this! Did you call my father, too?"

Leelia grinned. "Maybe…maybe not."

Brooklyn jumped up from her chair and pointed to the door. "You need to leave! I'm officially and completely done with you! This was the last straw!" she belted.

Leelia stepped up to Brooklyn again, disregarding her anger and words. Grabbing her arms, she forced a kiss on Brooklyn's lips.

Brooklyn pulled away. "I've had enough!" She reached for the phone, but Leelia stopped her.

"I don't know why you keep fighting me, Brooklyn. You know you want this."

Leelia forced another kiss onto Brooklyn that included the tongue this time.

"No, I don't want this," Brooklyn resisted softly. "You need to leave."

Brooklyn hated herself for getting slightly aroused while she attempted to fight Leelia off.

"Stop fighting this, baby."

"Leelia, stop. Please!" Brooklyn begged as she turned her head wildly to avoid anymore of her kisses.

Leelia grabbed Brooklyn's face to stop her from moving. Brooklyn's breaths were labored as Leelia stared into her eyes. Brooklyn was only kidding herself. Leelia was irresistible. She leaned in to kiss Brooklyn again.

"What the hell is going on in here?"

Brooklyn quickly turned toward the door to find her father and Aubrey standing there. Her father displayed a furious expression on his face while Audrey covered her mouth in shock. In an attempt to save face, Brooklyn pushed Leelia away.

"A-A-Aubrey, call security," she stuttered.

Leelia stared at Brooklyn in disbelief and total awe. "Don't bother calling. I was just leaving." Leelia proceeded to walk out the door but stopped when she reached Brooklyn's father. Brooklyn's heart pounded. "You'll feel much better once you come clean," she said just before walking out.

Brooklyn stared at the frown lines on her father's forehead as he furiously paced the floor.

"Uhm, Aubrey, can you give my dad and I some privacy?"

Aubrey quickly nodded then closed the door behind her.

"So, do you care to tell me what that was all about, Brooklyn? What's going on? I had to come all the way down here to talk to you since you wouldn't answer my calls and this is the shit I walk in on?"

Brooklyn's nerves started to get the best of her. Her hands and legs began to tremble. "Dad, I really don't want to talk about it."

"You have no other choice! I was calling you to discuss where we were going to dinner for Father's Day, and this is what I run into."

"Dad, it's difficult."

"Look, I've got all day and neither of us is leaving until you tell me what's going on."

Brooklyn grinned. "*All day*...now, we both know that's a lie. I'm sure within the next few minutes you'll have to get back to Gabrielle," she attempted to flip the script and take some of the heat off of her.

"For your information, Gabrielle and I are done."

"What do you mean you're done?" Brooklyn questioned curiously.

"It means we're over. She said that I wasn't fulfilling her needs sexually, and that she'd met somebody else, so she left. Look, I don't wanna talk about that. I wanna talk about you," he replied sternly as if he knew that Brooklyn was trying to change the subject.

I wonder if that person is Maverick, Brooklyn thought.

"Well, are you gonna talk?" Pierce questioned.

"Dad, I told you it's complicated. I don't want to talk about it. Not now anyway."

"I don't have time for your childish games, Brooklyn. Tell me or I will draw my own conclusions."

Brooklyn stared at her father. His facial expression told her that his conclusion had already been drawn.

"Are you gay?" Pierce asked.

Brooklyn lowered her head. It was at that moment that she realized Leelia hadn't spilled the beans to her father. And for some strange reason and at that very moment, she wished Leelia had actually told her father. It would've been a lot easier if he'd already known. So many scenarios raced through Brooklyn's head as to how she would answer her father's question. Each scenario pointed to telling a lie. But she knew that one lie would lead to another…then another. She was desperate to live a normal life and lies would only complicate things even more. Thoughts continued to boggle her mind. Something told her that she couldn't continue with a life of lies and that Leelia was right. It would be easier to just get it all out. Brooklyn took a deep breath.

"Daddy, yes, I'm gay." A huge weight had been lifted off her shoulders.

"You're kidding me, right? Is this some kind of damn prank? If it is, it's not funny," Pierce replied with a nervous laugh.

"It's no prank, daddy. I'm gay."

As Pierce laughed demonically, Brooklyn didn't know what to think or say at that point.

"Your mother was right all along."

"What? Mom knew?" Brooklyn questioned curiously.

"She had her suspicions, but I told her that there was no way you would disappoint me like that."

"Dad, this is not something you can turn on and off."

"No, it's actually a disgrace to my fucking family, that's what it is. I will not condone this type of behavior and until you change back to *normal*, you're out of my will!"

Brooklyn's eyes filled with tears. "Daddy, this is normal. It's normal to me," she defended.

"There's nothing normal about you licking another woman's..." Pierce stopped. "I can't even say it! The thought is sickening."

"Daddy, don't be like this! Please! I'm still your daughter!"

"You're no daughter of mine! I may as well be dead to you now!" Pierce stormed towards the door then stopped and turned back around. "Thanks for the fucking Father's Day gift, you damn dike!" He stomped out.

As soon as the door slammed shut, Brooklyn fell to her knees and cried like a baby.

Carla PENNINGTON

Chapter Twenty Five

Julius walked the locksmith to the door once while Kenya stood in the middle of the living room floor staring at both the safe and file cabinet. After having trouble getting a locksmith to come to her home the night before, she was happy the task was finally done. Not a single locksmith in the area agreed to help since she couldn't provide proof of ownership. She even tried contacting the company that manufactured the safe. They couldn't offer any help for the same reason although she had the serial number.

Kenya spent a huge part of the night trying to figure out possible combinations, but none of them worked. With tons of anger and frustration, she ended up crying herself to sleep. However, she woke up in better spirits when Julius told her he'd found a locksmith who was willing to open the safe for a fee higher than usual. His shady methods required drilling into the face of the lock in order to reach the lever. It was like watching a character from the *Ocean's Eleven* movie as the man used tool after tool in order to reach the safe's bolt.

After paying the locksmith, Julius hurried back into the living room. To his surprise, Kenya hadn't opened it yet.

"What are you waiting for?"

"I'm just afraid of what I may find in there."

"Then don't open it."

"I have to. There may be something in there to help me find Zoie."

"Do you want me to open it?" Julius offered.

"No, I can do it." Kenya's right hand trembled as she placed it on the safe's door that was slightly ajar. "Here goes nothing," she said while slowly opening the door.

Julius was just as eager as Kenya to know the contents of the safe and prayed to God there was no incriminating evidence inside. He even called Myles while Kenya was asleep to see what they were about to find, but he didn't answer.

Suddenly, Kenya gasped.

"What…what is it?" Julius questioned curiously.

"It's empty," she informed.

Kenya was disappointed while Julius was thrilled, but he couldn't show his emotions. Instead, he hugged Kenya after seeing the frustrated look on her face.

"Maybe he took everything or maybe there was never any-thing inside," Julius attempted to console.

"There was money in the safe, Julius. I know because he would go into it to get money for me when I needed it."

Damn. He had her on a really tight leash, Julius thought.

"I was so sure that something would be in there to help me find Zoie or learn more about Myles and why he did this shit to me. I wanna know why he took my baby," she continued.

He's impulsive and impatient. That's why, Julius thought.

"This is a small stepping stone, Kenya. The police are looking for Zoie now. We just have to be patient. They'll find her."

"Patient is not a word in my vocabulary right now, Julius. Maybe there's something in the file cabinet."

Julius crossed his fingers hoping that would be empty, too. "I'm sure there's nothing in there."

"If there was nothing to hide then he wouldn't have locked it."

Kenya pulled away from Julius' gentle hold and stepped to-wards the file cabinet. She pulled the top drawer open. Julius tensed when she began pulling papers from it.

"That dumb ass nigga," Julius mumbled.

"What did you say?"

"Looks like he left something," Julius answered before step-ping behind her. "What did you find?" He wanted to make sure that there was nothing that incriminated him in the stack of papers that Kenya thumbed through.

"Fucking parking tickets," she said after handing the stacks of pink paper to Julius. "There are over twenty of them and they all seem to be unpaid."

"Maybe he paid them online or something," Julius tried to defend his cousin.

Kenya didn't pay too much attention to the cell phone bills because her eyes quickly zoomed in on the credit card bills that were in the mix. Myles had over ten credit cards and they were all maxed out and overdue.

"Oh my, God!"

"What is it?"

"All of these credit cards are in my name!"

"Are you sure?" Julius tried to play dumb.

"He's run up over eighty thousand dollars worth of credit card debt in my damn name!"

Julius couldn't offer a defense for Myles with that proof. "Let me see those." He wanted them to make sure he wasn't in that pot of boiling water with Myles.

Kenya handed the papers to him and continued going through the stacks."Bank statements showing all of his withdrawals," she added. "I know my dad is turning over in his fucking grave at how stupid I've been."

"You're not stupid. You're just a married woman who trusted her husband. I don't see any harm in that."

"You've gotta be fucking kidding me! I can't believe this shit! Look at this, Julius! My car note is two months behind! What the hell has he been doing?"

"Maybe there's an explanation, Kenya."

"When the mortgage company called about this, I should've investigated more! How could he do this to me?"

Kenya continued to flip through the stack while Julius looked over her shoulder. Luckily for him, there was nothing that could link him to anything.

"Everything is addressed to a P.O. Box, Julius. I married a fraud...a liar...a cheat!" Kenya was appalled and ashamed. Instantly, she burst into tears. "He's been stealing my money and not paying any bills! I can't believe how naïve I've been. What am I gonna do about this?"

Julius hugged Kenya tightly when she fell into his arms.

"Everything is gonna be alright."

"The bank has probably started the foreclosure process on my house! What was he gonna say when they came to evict us and throw all of our belongings out on the lawn? Did he even give a damn that our daughter would probably be out on the streets?" Tears continued to stream down her face. "Julius, who did I marry? I'm such an idiot. I can't believe I allowed him to do this to me."

"Don't say that Kenya."

Suddenly, she looked up at him. "I bet you he was preparing to take my money once I sold the company? That's why he was pushing the sale. Has he ever mentioned anything crazy to you about Creative Minds…you know financially. Did you ever see him snooping around the accounting department?"

Julius shook his head. "No, not at all."

"Oh my, God! I'm such a fool."

"No, you're not. Stop saying that."

"I should've known something was wrong when I told him that Jada was dead and all he could talk about was me selling the company. You must think I'm stupid for giving him control of my finances, don't you?"

"I don't think that, Kenya. Married couples are supposed to trust each other."

"But I was too trusting. I should've waited to marry him like Jada told me to." Kenya was in complete disbelief. "Actually, I shouldn't have married him at all."

All of a sudden and out of nowhere, Kenya kissed Julius. He gently pushed her away. "What are you doing?"

"Julius, please just take me away from this nightmare."

She attempted to kiss him again, but he pushed her away for the second time.

"This isn't right, Kenya. You're emotional and vulnerable right now. You don't know what you're doing."

"You don't understand how much I need this right now."

"And then what? Your pain will still be there once we're done."

"I don't care, Julius. Just take me away right now." Kenya removed her shirt and dropped it on the floor. She then reached behind her and unhinged her bra dropping that on the floor as well. Kenya stepped to Julius again and pressed her breasts against his chest. "Please, Julius," she begged. "Please. Take me out of my misery." She unbuckled his pants. "Let me help you make up your mind." Kenya dropped to her knees taking Julius jeans and boxers with her.

"Kenya, you don't have to do…" Julius' words were lodged in his throat when her mouth covered his erectness. "Oh, shit!"

Kenya was stunned when Julius yanked his dick from her mouth then joined her on the floor.

"Did I do something wrong?" she questioned in a childlike voice. "Is it my weight?" Kenya embarrassingly placed her arms across her chest.

"Nothing's wrong with your weight, Kenya. You're beautiful," Julius said as he slowly removed her arms from her chest. "I just want to do this right."

He caressed Kenya's face in his hands then kissed her slowly. Julius knew that what they were about to do could possibly do more harm than good, but he justified it. It was Kenya's idea not his. Kenya maneuvered out of her camouflage leggings.

"I want you, Julius."

Kenya pulled Julius on top of her as she laid her body on the floor. Julius stared at her as she waited for him to enter her nest. He could see the desperation in her eyes.

"It's okay, Julius," Kenya assured.

Sensing his hesitation, Kenya slowly used her hand to play with her goodies so he would get the hint that she was ready for him.

"I want you too, Kenya." Julius kissed her again.

At that moment, he slid his arm under Kenya's back and assisted her over onto her hands and knees. There was no way Julius could look at her knowing he was responsible for part of her pain. He slowly entered her after gliding on the condom he retrieved from his wallet. He wasn't taking any chances knowing Myles' track record.

"Julius!" Kenya bellowed and balled her fingers into fists.

Kenya was ecstatic to have Julius dancing around inside of her. He wanted her and she could tel, which made her willing to give herself to him. She stretched across the floor when Julius pushed her back down.

"Yeah! Just like that!" Julius smiled naughtily as he watched his eleven inches of dark chocolate dip and dive inside of Kenya's pussy.

The glisten on Julius' dick turned him on. He squeezed Kenya's love handles as she backed into him matching his strokes. Kenya was amazed that her body responded more to Julius than it did to Myles. Her juices secreted freely and in abundance. She could hear the juices filling up inside of her. Not once did she feel ashamed about her weight. Julius' actions proved that he wasn't bothered by the extra pounds. That excited her even more. With her left cheek planted on the floor, Kenya reached under her thigh and spread the bottom of her ass so that Julius could drive all the way inside of her.

"Oh shit!" Julius exclaimed.

"That's right, baby! Get all up in it!" Kenya moaned.

Julius's sweat dripped onto Kenya's back while Kenya's sweat doused the floor. Kenya released her butt and lifted her body.

"Go deeper, Julius! Deeper!"

Julius's slapped his thighs against Kenya's vagina as hard as he could. He swiped the back of his hand across his forehead to wipe away the sweat that started to drip into his eyes.

"Yes! Go deeper! Go harder!"

Julius pounded even harder causing Kenya to scoot across the floor. She ended up in front of the wall with nowhere to go. A few more hard pumps, her head would be a new decoration. Kenya pressed her hands against the wall to keep from being drilled into it. The move only helped him bang her even harder.

As he listened to Kenya purr and coo, Julius thought back to Myles' suggestion of getting rid of Kenya. Julius realized how easy it would be at that particular moment when he grabbed a wad of her hair and pulled her head back. He could've easily strangled her. He envisioned his arm wrapped around her throat then her body collapsing to the floor after he squeezed the life from it.

"Oooooo, Julius!" Kenya moaned.

Julius quickly shook the murderous thoughts from his mind. He realized that he genuinely cared for Kenya. Unlike Myles, he had a heart.

Chapter Twenty Six

Brooklyn was still distraught about Pierce's reaction to her news. She expected him to be upset, but not to the point of calling her names. Over the past two days, he'd ignored all of her calls and didn't respond to any messages she left whether voice or text. Despite how her father acted and how he abruptly found out, Brooklyn silently thanked Leelia for helping her come to terms about who she really was as a person. It was long overdue.

Too bad her ass started acting crazy. We could've possibly worked things out, Brooklyn thought. She still refused to answer any of Leelia's attempts to contact her.

As Brooklyn continued to think about the situation, her phone began to vibrate against the nightstand. Hoping her father had found a change of heart, she grabbed the phone and quickly looked at the screen. She was disappointed when Pierce's name didn't appear, but decided to answer anyway since the person calling was equally important.

"Hey, Auntie Camilla."

"Hey, honey. I haven't heard from you in a while."

"I could say the same about you." Brooklyn tried to force a laugh that turned into an ugly cry, but she held it together.

"I guess you have a point there. How have things been in the office?"

Brooklyn had no idea what was going on because she hadn't been there. Whenever she tried to step foot out of the house, her tears would force her back into bed. Instead of Kleenex tissues, she walked around the house with a hand towel to soak up her tears.

"I'm not gonna lie to you, Auntie Camilla. I haven't been in. I needed some time off."

"You haven't been in? Why didn't you tell me? Are you ill? What's wrong?"

Brooklyn couldn't hold it together any longer. She immediately started crying.

"Brooklyn, what's the matter? Talk to me!"

"H-Have you talked to my dad?"

"No, I haven't. Why? Is everything okay with him? What's going on?"

Brooklyn hesitated before telling Camilla what happened. "My dad and I fell out. He's upset with me."

"You and your dad fall out all the time, Brooklyn. Give him a few days, he'll come around."

"You don't understand. It's different this time."

Camilla could hear the pain in Brooklyn's voice and realized something drastic must've happened.

"Why? What did you do?"

"H-H-He's upset because I told him that I was... I was gay." Another weight had been lifted off her shoulders. Brooklyn didn't bother waiting for a reaction before she continued. She wanted to get everything off her chest. "I know you're disappointed in me, but please don't be mad." She didn't know what to say or think when Camilla started laughing. "Why are you laughing?"

"Because this is funny."

"Funny? You're not mad?" Brooklyn questioned.

"Why would I be? This is your life. Besides, I've known for a while."

Brooklyn was almost speechless. "Are you serious?" She couldn't help but wonder if Leelia had called her again.

"Of course. Your mom and I used to talk about it all the time."

"My dad said the same thing. If my mom knew, why didn't she confront me about it?"

"Just like me, she figured you'd come out when you felt comfortable. It's about time you found the strength to tell me and your

214

dad. I'm actually proud of you."

Brooklyn was shocked. Never in a million years would she have expected the conversation to go in the direction it was going in.

"I still don't understand. How did you know?"

"Because I always notice how excited you get when a beautiful woman walks into the room. I mean, we've been around some fine ass, Denzel Washington, Blair Underwood, type of men and you could care less. Also, I picked up on the chemistry between you and Aubrey. You have a thing for her. You have to because I would've fired her ass a long time ago. She is a horrible secretary."

Brooklyn giggled. "Yes, she is."

"You're like a daughter to me, Brooklyn. I'm supposed to know these things. I would never turn my back on you because of your sexual preference. I love you no matter what. Besides, your mother would want me to be here for you."

Brooklyn wished that her father felt the same way. "What about my dad? He called me a dike and said that I was a disgrace to the family."

"What? Oh, I need to have a few words with him. But you know your dad is stubborn and old school. If they still made eight tracks, he'd be using those instead of CDs."

"Actually, Auntie Camilla, we're downloading music now."

"You get what I'm trying to say."

They both laughed.

"Believe me, sweetie, your dad will come around. He has to, you're his only child."

Brooklyn sighed. "I hope you're right."

"Pierce tries to be a hard ass but he really isn't. Hell, he might even be upset about Gabrielle leaving him and he's taking it out on you. Trust me, you'll always have his heart, Brooklyn. He's just upset at the initial shock. Give him some time. I know my brother."

Brooklyn found comfort in Camilla's words.

"Well, since we're coming clean, I need to tell you something about me now." Camilla paused for a few seconds. "Maverick and I got married and I'm a new mom."

"What?" Brooklyn gasped. "Married? A new mom? How? When?"

215

"Catch your breath, child. It's a long story, but that's the reason why I haven't been in the office. Maverick and our new daughter, Chloe, have been keeping me occupied. I can't wait for you to meet her, Brooklyn. She's so beautiful. You're gonna spoil her rotten."

"I don't know what to say," Brooklyn spoke through shock and shame. She felt bad about what she'd done to her aunt. She desperately wanted to tell Camilla about her and Maverick, but since she sounded so happy, Brooklyn didn't want to be the one to destroy that. "Give me all the juicy details, Auntie. A new man and a new baby. I'm listening."

Just as Camilla was about to tell her story, her phone beeped.

"Hold that thought, honey. This is my new husband calling now. I promise…we'll talk later." Camilla didn't wait for a goodbye before she clicked over. "Is this my sexy, new husband?" she asked playfully.

"Oh my, God, baby! I love you to the ends of the earth!" Myles cheered into the phone. "They just delivered the Aston Martin to me! I was hoping you would chose that one!"

"I knew you'd like that over the Bentley. The Aston Martin fits you perfectly. Did you see the papers for the thirty thousand that I put in an account for you?"

"Yes, I saw them! Thank you so much, baby!"

Myles had to pretend that he was happy about the bank account part although he really wasn't. He wanted access to the big money. He could easily spend thirty thousand dollars in a few hours. He wondered if this was Camilla's way of keeping tabs on him and his spending habits before she added him to the bigger accounts.

"I left my black card on the nightstand so that you can pick up some clothes, too."

"Where are you? You left out before I woke up. I wanna celebrate. I wanna take you out in my new car."

"I had to run to Delaware for a quick business meeting, but I'll be back later tonight."

"Well, when you come home, I'm gonna lick you like you're melted ice cream."

Camilla smiled. "I look forward to it and I'm gonna lick you like you're the cone."

216

"Mmmmmmmmmm, I look forward to that, too. I don't hear the baby in the background. Is she asleep?"

"Chloe was really cranky before I left and might be coming down with a cold so I left her with Isaac."

"Isaac? Do you think you should have left her with him? Does he know anything about babies?" Myles pretended to care.

"Isaac has been with me for years and he's practically family. I trust him. Besides, he has three children and five grandchildren so I'm sure he knows a thing or two about kids."

"If you say so." Myles had talked long enough. He was ready to test out his new car and put some wear and tear on Camilla's card. "Well, baby, I hope the meeting goes well. Call me as soon as you're done or on your way home."

"I definitely will, baby. I love you."

"I love you, too."

"Ma'am, we're here," Camilla's towncar driver said as soon as she hung up.

Camilla looked out the window and watched a few people climb the steps of the church. She felt bad for lying to Myles and having her secretary Google Jada Richardson's name. When the information for Jada's funeral popped up from a newspaper announcement in Charlotte and not Jacksonville where Myles told her his family was from, Camilla grew a bit suspicious. She knew Myles would be pissed after learning that she attended the funeral, but didn't care. She needed Chloe's family to know who would be taking care of her. Camilla didn't understand why Maverick couldn't see her reasoning. But she'd face that storm when it blew her way.

"When Jesus is my portion. A constant friend is he. His eye is on the sparrow. And I know he watches over me," a woman with a beautiful voice sang.

Staring at Jada's pearl white casket, Kenya couldn't believe that her best friend was laying inside. At that moment, she was happy that Mama Dorothy decided not to open the casket during the ceremony. Kenya couldn't bear seeing her friend like that. Dealing with her passing was already painful enough, so seeing her body would only be a reminder. Kenya felt bad that she hadn't been much help to Mama Dorothy during the planning process, but most times she didn't want to face reality. Kenya desperately wanted Jada to call her phone with a funny story or to simply curse her out. All the little things that were routine in Kenya's life were now gone, and she was having a difficult time letting that sink in. Everything seemed so surreal.

She wished Julius was there to hold her hand and lie to her by saying everything would be okay. He'd been a great support system during all of this, and Kenya hated that he couldn't attend due to an emergency at Creative Minds. Kenya didn't even notice when the woman stopped singing. Everything was such a blur. Between Jada dying, Zoie's disappearance and finding out that Myles was a fraud, Kenya couldn't get herself together, and it showed in her appearance. Along with her wrinkled dress, messy ponytail and makeup that was horribly done, Kenya was a complete wreck.

The police calling that morning didn't help the situation either. The detective in the Missing Persons unit working her case informed her that Myles' car was found at the Greensboro airport. He also informed her that they would go through the airport surveillance to try and determine where Myles went since he didn't use the name, Myles Whitaker, which only added more confusion. Knowing that Myles used a false name sent Kenya over the edge. She really had no clue who she was married to. The first thing Kenya planned to do the following Monday was file for a divorce.

I can't wait to start using my maiden name again, she thought. Every time someone called her Mrs. Whitaker, Kenya cringed.

"She's with her Father in Heaven now."

The pastor's final words interrupted Kenya's thoughts. She couldn't believe that she'd disappeared inside her head during the entire eulogy. Once Jada's casket was carried out by several pall bearers, and her family was escorted out, the remaining congregation stood up and made their way outside. Kenya stood next to the family limo in her dark Gucci sunglasses and waited for Mama Dorothy to join her.

"Excuse me."

Everyone turned to the voice that belonged to Camilla.

218

"I'm so sorry for your loss," Camilla said as she walked up and hugged Mama Dorothy. She hugged Jada's two uncles along with her three aunts as well. When she reached Kenya, Camilla extended her arm and displayed a warm smile. "I'm so sorry to hear about your loss, sweetie."

"Thank you," Kenya replied.

"Are you Jada's sister?"

"No, I'm her best friend."

"Oh, well you're a beautiful best friend."

"Thanks," Kenya said, hoping Camilla would go away. She wasn't in the mood for small talk, and certainly not with someone she didn't know. "Thanks again for the kind words." Kenya turned to Jada's mother who was being bombarded by other people saying their condolences. "Mama Dorothy, please get in the limo. We have to get to the burial."

Camilla instantly looked surprised. "Her mother?" *I thought Maverick said their parents were dead.* "That's Jada's mom?" She looked at Mama Dorothy as she made her way into the car.

Kenya nodded her head. "Yeah."

"That's interesting. I thought her mother passed away. Hey, you wouldn't happen to know a guy named Maverick Lewis would you? I'm trying to see who his family is."

"No, I don't. Who are you by the way?"

"Oh, hi, my name is Camilla Ellington-Lewis." She extended her hand.

"Nice to meet you, Camilla. I'm Kenya."

"I know Jada's brother, Maverick."

"Brother?" Kenya frowned. "Jada doesn't have a brother. She's an only child."

Camilla scratched her forehead. "Wait...so this is Jada Richardon's funeral, right?"

"Yes, it is."

"Well, that's odd that you're saying she didn't have a brother. Did Jada have any children?"

"No she didn't. What's this all about?"

Camilla was extremely concerned. "Wait...none of this makes sense. So, her mother is alive and well, she doesn't have a brother named Maverick and she didn't have a daughter around four months old."

"No, she doesn't have a daughter. She doesn't have any kids." Kenya's insides twisted as she suddenly grew nervous. "What's the daughter's name?" she asked.

"Her name is Chloe."

"Chloe?" Kenya mumbled. "Would you possibly have a picture of Maverick? Now, that I think of it, Jada did tell me about a half brother a while ago. She showed me a picture of him so I would know if it's him or not," she lied.

"Actually I do. I took a picture of him last night while he was asleep. He hates taking pictures."

Kenya's stomach dropped after hearing those words because it was the same excuse that Myles often told her. Camilla pulled out her phone and went directly to the picture.

"This is him," she said, handing Kenya the phone. "Oh, and if you go to the next photo, you'll see Chloe. Actually, I have a few pictures of her. She's so cute."

Kenya could barely hold herself together after seeing Myles asleep on a sofa. While it looked like he didn't have a care in the world, she was worried sick.

"H-How do you know him?" Kenya asked. It felt like she was about to have an asthma attack. She could barely breathe.

"I'm his wife. I came to the funeral to introduce myself to his family and let everyone know that I'll take good care of Chloe, but I'm so confused."

At that moment, Kenya took her index finger and swiped it across the phone screen. When the picture of Zoie popped up, she immediately covered her mouth to keep from screaming.

"You're not the only one confused because I'm his wife, too," Kenya finally said.

Chapter Twenty Seven

Julius sat on Kenya's sofa and flipped through the television channels. Since returning from the funeral, Kenya was extremely distant and didn't want to be bothered. She even declined Julius' offer of Chinese food that he'd picked up on his way over. Julius wondered if she was upset that he wasn't at the funeral. If so, he understood because he'd promised to be right by her side. Since she wouldn't talk to him, Julius had no exact way of knowing what was going on. In his mind, Kenya's standoffish manner could've been contributed to her going through the motions of burying her best friend and missing Zoie. He really didn't know what to think when she locked herself in the office and only came out when she needed to run upstairs to retrieve something. He wanted to ask what she was doing, but couldn't afford her snapping on him again. The two times he tapped on the door to see if she was okay, she'd yell, so he left her alone.

Julius felt bad about lying to Kenya earlier. There was no emergency at the office. If Kenya had known that he secretly met with the buyers at a restaurant near Northlake Mall, she'd kill him for sure. He'd set up the secretive meeting with hopes of proving to Myles that he could indeed take care of business. During the meeting, Julius presented the buyers with a forged document of Kenya's signature stating that she'd given him full power of attorney to represent her for the deal. Obviously, Julius thought that was all he needed to move forward, but he was wrong. As Julius thought back to the conversation he had between him and the buyer's lawyer, all he could do was shake his head in disappointment.

"I don't understand. I have a signed legal document here stat-

ing that Mrs. Whitaker gave me permission to represent her during this sale," Julius said.

"Yes, we understand that, but since this deal is so large, Mrs. Whitaker still needs to be here to confirm everything," the lawyer stated. "We actually thought she would be in attendance today. We were ready to move forward."

"I told you that she sent me down here to take care of everything because she's attending her best friend's funeral. She has a lot of other things going on right now. So what...you all don't trust me?"

"No, it's not that at all. We're aware that you've been handling a lot of Mrs. Whitaker's affairs, but I just want to look out for the best interest of my client. With that being said, I would be more comfortable if Mrs. Whitaker were present."

"I promised her that this would be taken care of today. I'm the one who brokered this deal, remember? Her signature should be all that you need to put me in charge."

"Contact us when Mrs. Whitaker is available. Until then, we can't go through with this."

"Assholes," Julius mumbled after breaking his thoughts. "I could've been halfway to New York by now with the six hundred thousand upfront cash."

If the sale had been complete, Kenya was due to receive 2.5 million dollars once all her employees moved out of the building, but there was no way Julius could've stayed around to swindle the rest.

Although his feelings for Kenya were strong, Julius' feelings towards money were stronger. He felt sorry for what she was going through, but he had to look out for himself first. Unlike Myles, Julius didn't spend his money wildly and that was why he was never hard up as Myles often was. Julius knew that one day their scheme would end and he wanted to have a nest to fall back on when it did. Julius was all about survival and lived for tomorrow while Myles lived for the current day. By Kenya not talking to him, it gave Julius time to think about his next move. He could've easily left town once the plan with the buyers didn't work. But Julius was determined to figure out another way for Kenya to sell the company before she found out he was involved in any wrongdoing.

All of a sudden, his phone rang. He looked at the screen. After seeing that the number was blocked, Julius assumed it was Myles. He was the only one who called that way sometimes. Julius glanced back at the office door to make sure Kenya was still inside before turning up the volume on the television.

"Your ass better be calling to tell me that you're bringing Zoie back," Julius whispered. He paused for a moment so Myles could respond, but there was dead silence. "Hello? Hello…Trey…can you hear me?"

"So, you're a fucking liar, too, huh?"

Julius swung his head around like the girl in *The Exorcist* movie when he heard Kenya's voice. After noticing the phone up to Kenya's ear and a few papers in her hand, he quickly hung up his phone.

"What are you talking about?" Julius questioned. His heartrate began to increase.

Kenya walked up to Julius and threw several papers at him. He quickly tried to figure out the best plan of action as he glanced down at the cell phone bill, especially when he saw his number highlighted numerous times.

That dumb muthafucka left a paper trail, Julius thought as visions of the file cabinet popped in his head.

"Looks like you've known my husband for a long time," Kenya said smugly.

"Of course I know your husband, Kenya," Julius tried to weasel out of the mess he was in.

"Don't fucking patronize me, Julius! You all never cared for each other. There was no way you should've had his number."

"But he gave me his number one day. Once you got pregnant, he wanted me to call him in the event of an emergency."

Kenya shook her head. "And you keep lying, too. See what you don't understand is that, I had the number to this phone." She held up Myles' white iPhone. "But the cell phone bill that's in your hand belongs to another number. A number that I knew nothing about which means my husband had two phones."

"Kenya I…"

Suddenly, she threw the phone at him, aiming for his head. Luckily, Julius ducked just in time.

"Shut the fuck up! I looked at all the bills, Julius. You and Myles talked several times a day from that number, even at three or four o'clock in the morning sometimes. I heard you, Julius. I heard you mention Zoie's name when you first answered the phone. You thought it was him who was calling you!"

Julius didn't respond. He didn't know how to.

"So, is Trey his real name?"

Once again, he didn't answer.

"I can't believe this. I can't believe he married another woman named Camilla. I can't believe that I allowed him to do this to me...I can't believe I allowed *both* of you to do this to me."

Julius' eyes grew larger than a half dollar.

"Oh yeah, I know about Camilla. I met her earlier. She came to Maverick's sister's funeral."

Julius gave Kenya an odd look.

"Don't play dumb! I know that Myles is Maverick; I know that he told Camilla that Jada was his sister and that he was taking care of Jada's baby, Chloe. She showed me a picture of *Maverick* and *Chloe*. Sounds like a fucking soap opera, doesn't it?"

Julius felt the walls closing in on him and it was all because of Myles' greed.

"Kenya, let me explain."

"Explain what? Explain how you knew Myles had my daughter when you were here consoling me about her being kidnapped? Explain how you knew he was gonna allow another woman to raise her? Is that what you want to explain to me, Julius? Is your fucking name even Julius? You know what, I don't give a damn if it is or not."

"Kenya, I swear to you. I didn't have anything to do with him kidnapping Zoie. That was never part of the deal. As you can see, I told him to bring Zoie back to you."

"Is that supposed to make me feel better?"

"Kenya, I'm truly sorry."

"Was having sex with me part of the deal that you just mentioned?"

"You wanted that. I didn't. I tried to stop you."

She jerked her head back. "This is fucking unreal!"

"Kenya, trust me, we can work this out. I promise."

"Are you serious right now? See, that's the problem. I did trust you, and look what you did to me."

"Kenya, I never meant to hurt you. I swear. It wasn't supposed to go this far."

"That's another fucking lie. You're still trying to hurt me."

"W-What are you talking about?" Julius worried.

"Well, for one you told me that something came up at Creative Minds that you had to take care of today. You never mentioned an emergency meeting with the buyers," Kenya informed. "So…how did that go?"

Julius became even more nervous. "Umm…it went okay. I'm sorry. I thought that I'd mentioned that meeting to you."

"No, you didn't. I guess you also weren't gonna tell me how you tried to sell the company without my permission." Kenya shook her head. "Imagine my surprise when their lawyer called and told me what happened today. Imagine my surprise when I learned that you were there on my behalf…without my knowledge. You set the meeting up behind my back. Did you not think I would find out? You know when I drove home from the funeral, at first I was excited to tell you what I'd found out about that deceitful asshole. But when I got the phone call from the lawyer, I was livid. That's when I decided to come home and look through my lying ass husband's file cabinet once again to try and find some proof before I approached you." She displayed a dissatisfied and hurtful expression. "You should've seen my face when I looked on that phone bill and saw your number. I couldn't believe it. I didn't want to believe it. But once I heard your voice on the other end of the phone, everything was confirmed for me."

"Kenya, I figured you were still going to sell so I tried to handle it for you because of all the things you had going on."

"By forging my signature on a fake ass Power of Attorney document? You were going to rob me blind like Myles tried to do. You're just trying to justify your reasoning for trying to steal my money? I guess you figured that today was a perfect opportunity since I was at the funeral. I guess you figured that since I was grieving I wouldn't realize what was going on. You had that 'kick a bitch while she's down' mentality, huh?"

"But it wasn't like that."

"Fuck the money, Julius! You knew that asshole had my daughter, she's worth any amount of money that I have."

"Kenya..."

At that moment, she ran up to him and slapped his face. "Shut up! I don't wanna hear anymore of your lies! Everything you did for me was all a lie! At the hospital with Jada...a lie! Being by my side when I was about to sell the company...a lie! Allowing me to cry on your shoulder when Myles took Zoie...a lie! All of the sweet things you've said to me and done for me were all lies! I wonder how many other women have fell victim to your scheme."

"Kenya, just let me call and talk to him. I'll get Zoie back."

"No need. Besides, I don't need you to warn him that you've been caught."

Julius didn't reply. He could only stand there and allow Kenya to berate him. He tensed when someone knocked on the door moments later.

"Right on time. That may be your ride," Kenya said with a sly smile on her face.

"What ride?"

When Kenya opened the door, Julius nearly pissed on himself when he saw the lawyer from the meeting, Officer Brandt and the detective from the Missing Person's unit.

"Kenya, what's this?" Julius asked.

"What does it look like? You fuck me, you get fucked back," she responded with another devious grin.

Chapter Twenty Eight

Late for her morning jog, Brooklyn raced downstairs to her living room. Trying to do a quick five minute warm up, she proceeded with a few light aerobic exercises to loosen up your muscles before doing several stretches. Once that was done, she tightened the laces on her Nike Air Max running shoes, then bounced outside. Brooklyn hadn't jogged in over a week since she was still upset that her father continued to ignore her calls and texts. When he returned the cuff links that she had delivered to him for Father's Day, she nearly had a break down. Camilla continued to assure her that Pierce would come around, but Brooklyn was unsure. All of her efforts as well of those from Camilla had been shot down. Brooklyn had seen her dad upset before and he'd given her the silent treatment on multiple occasions, but this time was different. It was going to take an act from God for her dad to come around.

With the stress of her father's reaction, Brooklyn had been under the weather for the past few days, so she decided to go for daily runs in order to feel better. So far, the exercising hadn't helped her sickness, but it did take her mind off things. Brooklyn was happy that Camilla allowed her to take a small vacation to get herself together. Because of all her drama, Brooklyn hadn't even been around to see her aunt's new baby. In a strange way, Brooklyn still wasn't ready to be in the same room with Camilla and her husband, so until that time came, she was going to keep her distance.

Brooklyn turned to lock the deadbolt on her door then smiled when she saw a rose petal at the top of the stoop. It was from a single rose she'd received the night before when on a date with her personal trainer, Taylor. That night was the only thing Brooklyn felt good about. Brooklyn was resistant when the trainer asked her out earlier that day while at the gym. She felt weird about going out with someone new so soon after her crazy break up with Leelia, but agreed to the date since Taylor wasn't aggressive. Brooklyn also agreed to it because she wanted to forget about her troubles for a few hours.

The two of them met at a jazz club that night. They talked, laughed, ate, drank and even danced until the club closed. Brooklyn was amazed that no one stared or judged them when it was evident that she and Taylor were *together*. Brooklyn didn't have to hide who she was and it was a wonderful, exhilarating feeling.

Brooklyn couldn't believe that they'd spent over five hours in the club. Taylor seemed to be a great person, but Leelia was glued to the back of Brooklyn's head the entire time. Brooklyn had to get Leelia out of her system before she jumped into a new relationship. Although she informed Taylor that she wanted to take things super slow, Brooklyn looked forward to their second date. Brooklyn even went as far as to tell Taylor a little about her relationship with Leelia. Brooklyn thought Taylor would run off afterwards, but she didn't. Taylor was mature and understanding about the situation. *"Let me know when you're ready. I'm on your time."* Those were the last words that Taylor said to Brooklyn before kissing her on the cheek.

After traveling down memory lane, Brooklyn set the timer on her watch. The start of her jog was awkward because she was too busy smiling and replaying her date with Taylor in her head. Brooklyn was also happy that she hadn't heard from Leelia in the past few days. Brooklyn figured that she'd finally got the hint and moved on.

When Brooklyn reached the corner and was about to turn left, she nearly tripped over her feet when Leelia suddenly jumped out from behind a car.

"Are you fucking crazy?" Brooklyn shouted after catching her balance.

Brooklyn wanted to take her words back after seeing the state that Leelia was in. It looked like she hadn't taken a bath or brushed her hair in days. The fact that she wore a t-shirt with the words, *I love Brooklyn* on it also didn't help the crazy persona.

"So, you think you're just gonna move on from me like that?" Leelia spoke eerily. "Do you think it's that easy?"

Brooklyn grew nervous as she tried to run past Leelia, but she quickly blocked her path. "Leelia, you need to move out of my way. What's wrong with you?"

"There's nothing wrong with me, Brooklyn. I love you. What's wrong with me loving you?"

Brooklyn tried to be as calm as possible. "Leelia, I told you that we don't work. I'm sure there's someone out there that's good for you. You may…"

"You're the one who's good for me!" Leelia interrupted loudly. "I want you! I told myself that no one will ever leave me again."

"Please calm down."

"No, I'm not gonna fucking calm down."

Brooklyn's heart raced when she looked down at Leelia's hand and noticed a gun.

"W-W-Why do you have the gun, Leelia?" Brooklyn panicked.

"To make you love me," Leelia replied as if she believed her own words.

"With a gun? If you love me then why do you need the gun?"

"Because you need a little help."

"Leelia, this is not the way to make someone love you."

Leelia raised the gun and pointed it at Brooklyn. "We'll see."

"What are you doing? Put that gun down!" Brooklyn freaked out as tears spilled from her eyes.

"Let's go back to your place and make up."

Brooklyn slowly raised her hands in the air and walked backwards as Leelia walked toward her. "We can talk about this without the gun."

"Yeah, let's talk. By the way…you have some nice dance moves."

"What are you talking about?"

"Did your trainer teach you those dance moves?"

Brooklyn wondered for a few seconds before she realized what Leelia was referring to.

"You followed me last night?"

"Turn around!"

Brooklyn did as she was ordered.

"You said you two were just friends. You lied to me!"

"We are friends, Leelia. I swear!"

"She kissed you, Brooklyn!"

"It was just on the cheek!"

"You two were grinding on the dance floor like you were ready to jump each other's bones! Friends don't do that!" Leelia pushed Brooklyn so that she would speed up her walk. "How could you do that me? How could you cheat on me with that weight lifting bitch? We're gonna talk about this, and you're gonna call her ass over so that I can talk to her, too."

"I'm not doing that, Leelia."

"You'll do as I say!" Leelia grabbed Brooklyn then placed the tip of the gun against her back. "Now, let's get inside the house and make that call," she growled in Brooklyn's ear.

Brooklyn knew that if she went inside the house that she would be leaving out on a gurney or inside a body bag, so she had to do something.

"Somebody help! Help me! Please!" Brooklyn suddenly screamed as loud as she could. "Somebody help! She's got a gun!"

A few people that were a small distance away turned when they heard Brooklyn's cries. "Help...please help me!"

"That was stupid!" Leelia barked before firing a single shot.

Brooklyn stood in shock for a few seconds before dropping to the ground. The pain was excruciating and unbearable. She desperately wanted to call out her father's name, but couldn't seem to make her mouth move. She could only hear the sounds of several foot steps running along with a woman screaming before closing her eyes to complete darkness.

"Camilla?" Myles called out after entering their penthouse.

He tossed his keys and aviator styled Prada sunglasses on the table. He'd just returned home from having his white Aston Martin washed after his road trip to Philly; a trip where he met a new victim...an attorney. He'd left out early that morning to test out the car's capabilities on the highway. Once he got back, Myles didn't want a pinch of dirt or dust on his new toy so he got it cleaned once again. In the short time he owned the car, Myles had it washed at least six times.

"Camilla? Baby, are you here?"

After receiving no response, he figured she was gone.

"Good! I've had a relaxing day and don't feel like listening to Zoie's crying ass."

At that moment, Myles pulled out his cell phone to call his cousin. After realizing he'd missed Julius calls a few times, Myles tried to call him back over the last day or so, but each call went directly to voicemail. As he was about to dial Julius' number, a knock on the door stopped him. He figured it must've been Camilla and that she'd left her key card because the average hotel guest didn't access to their floor.

"Baby, did you leave your..." Myles paused in total shock after opening the door.

"Hello, Mason."

It looked as if Myles had seen a ghost from the way he stood there.

"Aren't you gonna invite me in?"

He was paralyzed with fear and completely astonished.

"Aren't you gonna invite me in, Mason?" the woman asked again.

"P...Porsha, what are you doing here?" Myles asked after she removed her sunglasses. He stared at the five foot six woman that stood before him. No longer having an hourglass figure, Myles could tell that her health had declined.

"Guess you thought I was dead, huh?"

Myles quickly thought back to the night he strangled his wife Porsha in Connecticut. Just like Krystal, he did think she was dead, so seeing her now was exactly like talking to her spirit.

"Maybe we can discuss this over a drink," Porsha suggested as she tried to walk past him. He blocked her.

"How in the hell did you find me?" Worry festered through his bones.

When Porsha tossed a magazine at him, Myles caught it before it hit the floor.

"I thought you said you didn't like to take pictures? You look good in that one, but at least you could've smiled."

Myles fumed as he stared at the picture of him and Camilla at Pierce's dinner. While he was distracted, Porsha slipped inside the penthouse. But Myles snatched her arm before she made it too far inside.

"You need to get the hell out of here, Porsha! You have no business being here!"

"You're joking, right?" she asked sarcastically then chuckled. "I'm your damn wife! I have every right to be here!" She pulled away from him. "I actually thought you would be glad to see me after you left me for dead that night." All Myles could do was stand there. For once, he couldn't find the right words. "All I can say is thank God for my neighbors. They saved my life."

Once again, Myles thought back to that dreadful night in Connecticut when Porsha found out he'd spent all her money. He remembered getting into a heated argument with her, then seeing red when she threatened to call the police. He also remembered the neighbors knocking on the door after obviously hearing her high-pitched screams. Since Myles didn't see any movement from her body, he thought she was dead. However, instead of answering the door, he quickly escaped out the back of their townhome and into the darkness; never looking back.

"I'm thankful my neighbors got me to the hospital just in time so there was no permanent damage. Even though I lost my memory for a few months, I could've been in a coma for the rest of my damn life after what you did to me."

For once, Myles was backed into a corner. He needed to get Porsha out of the house before Camilla showed up.

"Look Porsha, things didn't work out for us back in Connecticut so…"

"You're damn right things didn't work out for us!"

"You need to leave before I call the police."

"Call them!" Porsha taunted. "I want to hear you explain to them how you tried to kill me. I want to hear you explain how you're married to me and to her!" She snatched the magazine back and pointed to Camilla's picture.

"You have no proof that I'm married to her."

Porsha smiled wickedly. "Oh, but I do!"

Both Myles and Porsha turned to Isaac's voice. Camilla was right beside him holding Zoie.

"Where did you come from, baby?" Myles asked.

"We were in the back waiting for you," Camilla replied smugly.

"Waiting for me?" Myles questioned.

"Yes, when the guard downstairs alerted me that someone was trying to get up here because her husband was here, I was intrigued. Imagine the conversation we had while you were out gallivanting around in *my* damn car."

"But baby, you bought that car for me," Myles whined.

"Is he serious?" Camilla asked Isaac sarcastically.

Isaac laughed.

"So, is this what you do, marry and steal from vulnerable women, Mason?" Porsha asked.

"No, it's Maverick," Camilla corrected with a smirk.

"I thought it was Myles."

Everyone turned to the door to find Kenya standing there.

Once again, Myles was in complete shock. *Where the fuck is Julius*, he thought.

"You've been a busy man," Kenya said to him. "Three wives? That's against the law you know…that's bigamy."

"There's probably more," Porsha added.

Suddenly Myles got a bit of courage. "Good luck on getting proof that I married any of you bitches. Hell, none of you even have a picture of me in a tuxedo," he snapped back.

"Actually I have video of the two of you saying *I do*," Isaac added as he held up his phone. "I thought it might come in handy one day."

Myles was just about to lose it on Issac when two NYPD officers suddenly walked into the penthouse. At that point, he knew things were headed downhill.

"I think she belongs to you," Camilla said to Kenya after

233

walking over and handing her Zoie.

Kenya hugged Zoie tightly and cried uncontrollably. Moments later, she looked up and eyed Myles with an evil scowl. "Oh, by the way, you're not the only one who can keep secrets."

He tried to play it off, then smiled. "I don't keep secrets, Kenya."

She smiled back. "But I do. Remember the day you met me, and I was crying my eyes out. Well, I told you that I was crying because of Jada, but that was a lie. I was actually crying because I'd just found out that I was one month pregnant." Kenya paused as everyone in the room hung onto her every word. "Zoie is not your daughter, *Trey*. Her dad's name is Lance; you know the guy you wanted me to fire from my company."

It looked like he wanted to attack her as Myles made his way over toward Kenya. However, before he could take three steps, the officers blocked his path.

"Trey Donovan Watts, you're under arrest."

Myles couldn't help shake his head at the mention of his real birth name. He also thought about the woman he'd just met in Philadelphia who he planned to call as soon as he got to the precinct. *I'll be out in a few hours bitches.*

𝒠pilogue
One Year Later

Brooklyn laid across her bed and clicked on the order status box of the baby jogger stroller that she'd ordered a week ago.

"Look, lil' fella, it will be here in two days," Brooklyn said to her three month old son, Chase who lay next to her.

After being shot in the shoulder and rushed to the hospital, Brooklyn soon learned that she was pregnant. After learning the news, she wished Leelia had killed her because it didn't take long to realize who the father was. Brooklyn knew Myles was the only candidate since she hadn't been with another man in years, so she cried herself to sleep during her entire hospital stay. Brooklyn even thought of aborting the baby, but couldn't convince herself to do it after dreaming about how excited her mother was. What she dreaded most was telling Camilla. She even hid the pregnancy for as long as she could. Camilla eventually called her on it and was a little hurt that Brooklyn didn't tell her that she was expecting. Since she never informed her who the father was, Camilla just assumed her niece visited a sperm donor since she was a lesbian. In the beginning, Brooklyn was okay with her aunt thinking that way, until she could no longer live with the lie. After much hesitation, she finally sat Camilla down and told her everything that happened. As expected, Camilla didn't speak to her until she came to Brooklyn's baby shower eight months into the pregnancy. Brooklyn was overjoyed when Camilla eventually forgave her. She was also excited about the newfound relationship with her father.

After Pierce learned of the pregnancy, he immediately dove back into his daughter's life. He didn't even act concerned after learning who the father was, and about their one night stand. Pierce was just happy to have a relationship with his daughter, and even more elated about having a grandson. Not only did he set up a trust fund for his first grandchild, but over time he learned to accept the crazy dynamics of his daughter's lifestyle. Although she'd had a baby, Brooklyn was still gay, and that was something he eventually came to terms with.

Brooklyn's relationship with Taylor took a turn in a positive direction as well. Brooklyn assumed Taylor wouldn't want to deal with her after learning about the pregnancy, but she was wrong. Not only was Taylor supportive throughout her shooting recovery and pregnancy, but she never left Brooklyn's side during Leelia's entire first degree attempted murder trial. Brooklyn was ecstatic and relived after the judge handed Leelia a ten year sentence. She was also grateful for the many witnesses who came forward to help get Leelia convicted. At that moment, she knew the constant nightmares of Leelia coming to finish the job would cease and that she could finally move on with her new family. Even if there were a lot of challenges along the way, after all that she'd been through, she was up for the challenge.

Kenya stood in front of her new restaurant and watched the contractors secure the sign on the front of the building. She couldn't wait for the grand opening of her dream restaurant called *Jada's*. After all that happened in Charlotte, and once the sell for Creative Minds was finally complete, Kenya decided to move and make a fresh start for her and Zoie in Norfolk, Virginia.

After moving to Virginia, Kenya secured a nice home for her and Zoie that she paid cash for along with new furniture and a brand new car. Having to pay all the credit cards balances that were in her name and any other bills that were once behind, the last thing Kenya wanted was anything that reminded her of her dysfunctional marriage. She got rid of everything she owned including all the clothes he'd picked out and started fresh.

My Counterfeit Husband

She was also excited about her marriage being annulled. Because he'd used a fraudulent name on each of their licenses, the marriage was considered invalid for her, Camilla and Porsha. She couldn't speak for the other women, but Kenya was happy that she didn't have to go through a long, drawn out process. The faster she got rid of Myles, the faster she could get on with her life. She was thrilled to know that he would be locked up for what he'd done. Kenya was furious once she tried to transfer her parent's life insurance money from PNC to a smaller, local bank in Virginia only to find out that her ex-husband had gotten access to her money and all of it was gone. Kenya didn't waste time getting down to the bottom of the situation and soon learned that the woman, Candice had been his partner in the crime. Instead of withdrawing the cash like Myles, she was transferring the money into her own account. Just like Myles, Candice was found guilty of theft, and was sentenced to three years in prison. However, Kenya was beyond disappointed when Julius only received probation for his fraud and forgery charges due to lack of evidence.

Both Myles and Julius had definitely left a wound on Kenya's heart and made it hard for the next man who entered her life. Although she finally allowed Zoie's real father, Lance to come and see his daughter, she made it clear that she wasn't interested in a relationship with him. In fact, Kenya had gone on a few dates with Lance, but didn't want things to get too serious. She even brought Zoie along on each date, so he wouldn't get any ideas about having sex afterwards. Even though Kenya was in a new place, she wasn't ready to trust anyone, so if Lance or anyone else wanted to be in her life, they would just have to accept her rules. The once naïve Kenya was long gone.

Camilla sat at the table and waited for Myles to enter the room at the Lewisburg Federal Correctional Center. She knew if anyone found out that she was visiting him after all he'd done to her, she'd be laughed at and certainly talked about. Although she had a reason for continuing to keep in touch, Camilla knew her decision would only be stupid to everyone else, so she kept her monthly visits a secret. This visit was different though.

Camilla looked up when the buzzer went off and the guard escorted her ex-husband inside. It was always odd to see him in his oversized blue scrubs and bald head.

"Hey, baby," Myles greeted with a huge smile. He reached across the table for Camilla's hand and kissed it.

She quickly pulled her hand back. "Don't start, Maverick. Or do you wanna be called Myles." She could never get used to Trey.

"No touching!" one male guard yelled.

"Camilla, I'm happy to see you again," Myles said, ignoring the male guards as usual. "Seems like forever since you were here before."

She rolled her eyes at him. "Well, you'd better take a mental picture because this is the last time."

"Don't say that, Camilla, baby. I enjoy your visits. And you still look good. Actually you look damn good, even better than before." He eyed her black Marc Jacobs cropped pants and white high-low tunic. "I miss wearing that designer shit."

"Look, I didn't come to talk about clothes. I came because I wanted to say this to you face to face."

"Did you put any money on my books?" he asked.

"Not this time."

"Why not? I'm running low."

"That's part of the reason I'm here."

"Before you go into that, is Brooklyn ever gonna send me a picture of my son? What's his name again? Chad?"

"His name is Chase," Camilla corrected with a frown.

"Is she gonna send me a picture? I'd like to see him."

"No, she's not. Besides, Brooklyn knows you don't care about him. You obviously didn't care about Zoie, so why would she bother?"

"I did care. I brought her to you when you wanted a child, didn't I?"

Camilla frowned again. "You're a real asshole. Anyway, once again I came here to tell you that this will be my last visit. I'm done. This is my last time coming to Pennsylvania. You'll have to find someone else to put money on your books from now on."

"But all I have left is you. There is no one else. Do you know how hard it's gonna be to do time without having any money? I got thirty years up in here."

Camilla thought back his first degree attempted murder, fraud, theft and forgery charges. He ended up having his trial in Connecticut since what he'd done to Porsha took priority over his deceit for her and Kenya and was eventually convicted on majority of the counts.

"Honestly, I should've never helped you in the first place, but for some strange reason I felt sorry for you. I felt sorry for my nephew's father," Camilla chuckled. "That shit sounds so crazy, but it's true. I slept better at night once I decided to forgive you."

He was quiet.

"Do you even care what you did to me?"

"Yeah, I care and you know that. Just please don't shut me out," he begged.

"I'm sorry, but this is it. It's time for me to move on and I've found a wonderful man to help."

"I'm happy for you, but what does that have to do with me?"

"Everything. He treats me like a queen."

"He doesn't have to know what you do for me, Camilla. I need that money, baby."

Camilla stood up. "You'll have to find another way to get it. I have to go. I'm taking my man to Brazil tomorrow." She turned to the guard. "I'm ready to leave now."

"Camilla, don't do this to me. I still have a few feelings for you." He hoped his charm still worked.

Camilla ignored his comment and walked out.

"Hey man," the guard addressed Myles when he stood up with a defeated stance "Your attorney is on her way up so stay here."

As Myles sat back down, Camilla walked out of the prison with her head held high.

"Is everything okay?" her man asked when she got inside the car.

"Better than ever."

"I'm happy to hear that."

"I've finally closed that chapter in my life, Dylan. Now, you and I can start a new one."

239

Julius smiled slyly while pouring Camilla a glass of champagne. "I can't wait." When their driver pulled off, Julius glanced back at the prison one last time and displayed a deceitful grin. *Who's weak now, cuz,* he thought.

Myles turned to the door when he heard the buzzer and his female attorney walked in. When the guard wasn't looking, he copped a feel of her curvy butt. She smiled.

"You'd better stop that," she whispered to him.

"Well, there's more where that came from when I get out of here." He winked at her. Even as a convicted criminal, Myles was still able to turn on the charm. The fact that his attorney moved from Philadelphia to Connecticut just to represent him proved how good he was. "So, what's my new release date? You told me that the D.A. was contemplating about giving me a lesser sentence if I gave up the name of the person who makes my ID's and all the other shit." Since Myles hadn't heard from his cousin in over a year, he had no problem snitching on him at this point. "Wish I'd done this at the damn trial."

"About that," the attorney spoke dryly and without confidence.

Myles gave her a worried look. "What's wrong?"

"Things don't look too good."

"What do you mean?"

"You might be brought up on murder charges."

He froze. "You're joking, right?"

"I wish I was. Apparently, the authorities in South Carolina found the missing girl, Krystal Turner's remains a few months ago. They didn't inform anyone until they got the DNA results back confirming that it was her." She paused. "There was also a fetus. The D.A. is requesting that you take a test. If the results come back positive, you know what means, don't you?"

For the first time in his life, Myles was at a loss for words. "Damn, I guess payback really is a bitch."

LCB BOOK TITLES

See More Titles At
www.lifechangingbooks.net

ORDER FORM

MAIL TO:
PO Box 423
Brandywine, MD 20613
301-362-6508

Ship to:	
Address:	
City & State:	Zip:

Date: _____ Phone: _____

Email: _____

Make all money orders and cashiers checks payable to: **Life Changing Books**

Qty.	ISBN	Title	Release Date	Price
	0-9741394-2-4	Bruised by Azarel	Jul-05	$ 15.00
	0-9741394-7-5	Bruised 2: The Ultimate Revenge by Azarel	Oct-06	$ 15.00
	0-9741394-3-2	Secrets of a Housewife by J. Tremble	Feb-06	$ 15.00
	0-9741394-6-7	The Millionaire Mistress by Tiphani	Nov-06	$ 15.00
	1-934230-99-5	More Secrets More Lies by J. Tremble	Feb-07	$ 15.00
	1-934230-95-2	A Private Affair by Mike Warren	May-07	$ 15.00
	1-934230-96-0	Flexin & Sexin Volume 1	Jun-07	$ 15.00
	1-934230-89-8	Still a Mistress by Tiphani	Nov-07	$ 15.00
	1-934230-91-X	Daddy's House by Azarel	Nov-07	$ 15.00
	1-934230-88-X	Naughty Little Angel by J. Tremble	Feb-08	$ 15.00
	1-934230820	Rich Girls by Kendall Banks	Oct-08	$ 15.00
	1-934230839	Expensive Taste by Tiphani	Nov-08	$ 15.00
	1-934230782	Brooklyn Brothel by C. Stecko	Jan-09	$ 15.00
	1-934230669	Good Girl Gone bad by Danette Majette	Mar-09	$ 15.00
	1-934230804	From Hood to Hollywood by Sasha Raye	Mar-09	$ 15.00
	1-934230707	Sweet Swagger by Mike Warren	Jun-09	$ 15.00
	1-934230677	Carbon Copy by Azarel	Jul-09	$ 15.00
	1-934230723	Millionaire Mistress 3 by Tiphani	Nov-09	$ 15.00
	1-934230715	A Woman Scorned by Ericka Williams	Nov-09	$ 15.00
	1-934230685	My Man Her Son by J. Tremble	Feb-10	$ 15.00
	1-924230731	Love Heist by Jackie D.	Mar-10	$ 15.00
	1-934230812	Flexin & Sexin Volume 2	Apr-10	$ 15.00
	1-934230748	The Dirty Divorce by Miss KP	May-10	$ 15.00
	1-934230758	Chedda Boyz by CJ Hudson	Jul-10	$ 15.00
	1-934230766	Snitch by VegasClarke	Oct-10	$ 15.00
	1-934230693	Money Maker by Tonya Ridley	Oct-10	$ 15.00
	1-934230774	The Dirty Divorce Part 2 by Miss KP	Nov-10	$ 15.00
	1-934230170	The Available Wife by Carla Pennington	Jan-11	$ 15.00
	1-934230774	One Night Stand by Kendall Banks	Feb-11	$ 15.00
	1-934230278	Bitter by Danette Majette	Feb-11	$ 15.00
	1-934230299	Married to a Balla by Jackie D.	May-11	$ 15.00
	1-934230308	The Dirty Divorce Part 3 by Miss KP	Jun-11	$ 15.00
	1-934230316	Next Door Nympho By CJ Hudson	Jun-11	$ 15.00
	1-934230286	Bedroom Gangsta by J. Tremble	Sep-11	$ 15.00
	1-934230340	Another One Night Stand by Kendall Banks	Oct-11	$ 15.00
	1-934230359	The Available Wife Part 2 by Carla Pennington	Nov-11	$ 15.00
	1-934230332	Wealthy & Wicked by Chris Renee	Jan-12	$ 15.00
	1-934230375	Life After a Balla by Jackie D.	Mar-12	$ 15.00
	1-934230251	V.I.P. by Azarel	Apr-12	$ 15.00
	1-934230383	Welfare Grind by Kendall Banks	May-12	$ 15.00
	1-934230413	Still Grindin' by Kendall Banks	Sep-12	$ 15.00
	1-934230391	Paparazzi by Miss KP	Oct-13	$ 15.00
	1-93423043X	Cashin' Out by Jai Nicole	Nov-12	$ 15.00
	1-934230634	Welfare Grind Part 3 by Kendall Banks	Mar-13	$15.00
	1-934230642	Game Over by Winter Ramos	Apr-13	$15.99

			Total for Books	$

* Prison Orders- Please allow up to three (3) weeks for delivery.

Please Note: We are not held responsible for returned prison orders. Make sure the facility will receive books before ordering.

Shipping Charges (add $4.95 for 1-4 books*) $ _____

Total Enclosed (add lines) $ _____

*Shipping and Handling of 5-10 books is $6.95, please contact us if your order is more than 10 books.
(301)362-6508

CPSIA information can be obtained at www.ICGtesting.com
Printed in the USA
LVOW06s2345110314

377027LV00010B/202/P